DEATH AND THE DANCING GIRL

Jenny Harrison

Published by Lamplighter Press

Cover design and formatting

Bev Robitai

www.thebookcoach.weebly.com

KDP edition

ISBN: 978-0-473-72623-2

:

Dedicated to all lost children.
May they find their way home

Other Midnight Hero titles

London, May 1957
Eight displaced Polish friends gather for a party having survived the worst of World War II in Europe.
But, before dawn, one will die.
Detective Andrew Perry has his work cut out as he probes unhealed trauma, lies, and well-hidden secrets to solve what appears to be a senseless murder.

Young Matthew Flint is a man on a mission – revenge. After escaping from a POW camp, he joins the Polish Underground and becomes one of their most relentless agents.

A taut gripping story of the damage war can do to one man's heart and the power of love to heal.

Chapter 1

On a bleak and snowy Christmas Eve, the first since the war in Europe had ended, Tom Blake found out he had a child who was lost somewhere in France.

*****

Southern England had been blanketed in heavy snow for more than a week. The small village in Kent lay under a white shroud and leaden skies. He listened to the sound of Sunday bells muffled as through a dark scarf, and the occasional crack of a broken branch crashing from a nearby tree, and then silence again. Nearing midnight and the wintry weather still howled around him in isolated gusts and shrieks.

Tom Blake sat alone in front of a small fading fire with an untouched glass of whisky on a table beside him. This would be his first Christmas alone.

Last Christmas his mother had been here, fragile but still the vivid, cheeky old bird he loved. The Christmas before? Tom tried to remember. It was a blur, those war years. At least one festive season had been spent with mates in a canteen somewhere in the bleak Scottish Highlands where they were being trained. He remembered coloured paper chains hanging in swathes across the room, a 'lucky dip' so that each man got some small thing. Most received a pack of cigarettes and soon the air was a thick fug of smoke. A couple of

Christmases in France, in a forest somewhere and one in a musty damp basement with the *maquis* and very little festivity other than a drag at a bottle of wine shared between the men.

And only that once with his mother. She had seemed a little older and a little frailer. She'd kissed him goodbye, and her tender hug had been a little longer than usual. He was told later, not long after he'd gone back to France, she had slipped away in her sleep. She never did like making a fuss, Tom thought ruefully. He hadn't been there, and it pained him to think she had died alone.

Tom knew too well death came in many forms. He had seen it in France during the war. And in the end, wasn't it always just the dying person and The Shadow caught in a lover's embrace of death? There could be loved ones around but in that ultimate infinite moment it was one person and death. Still, he wished he had been there at his mother's bedside, for his own sake as well as hers. A comfort in these increasingly bleak and lonely days.

He poked at the fire, it flared briefly, then sat back and picked up his whisky glass.

Tom stared at the straggly orphan of a Christmas tree he'd bought. What had he been thinking? Too small and crooked to be of any interest to families, he'd felt sorry for it and wanted to give it a home, even though there was no one with him to enjoy it. He brought it back to the cottage on the roof of his aging Austin and set it up in the corner in a large copper pot with plenty of soil to anchor it down. He'd found a few old Christmas decorations in a box in the attic and placed them carefully on the thin branches. Despite his care, it still bent over like a weary sentry. Tom remembered decorating more splendid trees with his father, his mother bossing in the background. Now this small dreary specimen stood in his living room with more memories clinging to its branches than decorations.

Under the tree, Tom had placed a parcel wrapped in brown paper and addressed to himself. It contained a pair of woollen socks he'd bought in London a month ago. Hard to get when everything was still rationed, he'd made a celebration of it. Even added a small card, 'To Tom, from Tom.' A Christmas tree needed a few presents under its branches. Tom's meagre assortment gave the small fir tree an authority it lacked.

There was also a smaller package containing a gold filigree bracelet. Tom had wrapped it in silver paper he'd found in the box of Christmas decorations. Tied with a red ribbon and addressed to his wife, Madeleine Aubert, No, 13 Somewhere, France, Europe. With all my love always.

He suddenly felt dreadfully alone.

On that wintry night in 1945, when Tom Blake and his forlorn little Christmas tree were keeping each other company, a loud banging on his front door broke through the haze of whisky and despair.

Alarmed, Tom left the warmth of the fireside and went to stand beside the front door. Nearly midnight, his pulse was racing. Who the…?

He peeped through the curtain of the front window, saw only a dark shadow. The door handle rattled. Regretting he had no weapon other than his mother's favourite crystal vase; Tom grabbed it and held it. Fight, flight? No question. He was ready to kill.

He released the lock, and slowly allowed the door to swing open.

A dark silhouette filled the doorway. A large man in a woollen overcoat, with a worn scarf pulled up to his ears, stamped his feet in the cold. Snowflakes had settled on his shoulders and in his hair. He held his hands under his armpits and shivered.

"Thomas," he called. "*Salut,* greetings from France."

As soon as the man spoke, Tom knew who it was, Lucien Aubert, Madeleine's brother. He was suddenly filled with desolation. He's come with bad news, he thought. What else?

He put the vase down. "Lucien? What in God's name are you doing here?"

The man shot out a gloved fist and Tom grasped the outstretched hand.

"Come in, come in," he said. "You must be freezing. How on earth did you get here? You must have walked for miles."

Tom stood aside as the tall man scraped his shoes on the outside scraper, shook the snow off his head and came in breathing out a wraith of frigid air.

The visit of his brother-in-law was unexpected and not entirely welcome. It could only mean the stirring up of memories Tom had tried to bury. Since Madeleine disappeared in France, Tom had needed to put all thoughts of her aside. It was essential if he was to continue living. Existing, really. It was the only way he could survive, by forgetting his wife. By letting go.

Lonely? Yes, but he could handle that. What he couldn't handle was being dragged back into the past.

All the pain, despair, and misery, all the mystery, wondering where Madeleine was, whether she was alive or dead. He was sure Lucien Aubert was about to force him to feel something when he would much rather stay in his blind cocoon of oblivion.

But Tom knew what Lucien had come to tell him. Finally and irrevocably. Madeleine was dead, and he couldn't bear the thought.

He threw another log onto the fire, and it flared up. "Hang your coat up there in the hallway, Lucien, and come and sit down. Let me pour you a drink."

"This is a pleasant room," Lucien said as he shed his overcoat and scarf and settled into an armchair. Tom looked around at the ageing wallpaper, the sofa sagging under the weight of years, the bookcase along one wall filled with his parents' old leather-bound books and his own hard-cover novels. And the skeletal little Christmas tree in the corner. Yes, he supposed it was pleasant. At least it was warm.

Lucien stretched out his hands to the fire and then rubbed them back into circulation. He looked exhausted, thin, almost emaciated, with dark smudges under his bloodshot eyes. His clothes, like Tom's, were shiny with wear.

"I had difficulty in finding you, *mon ami*. Your particulars are still secret." Lucien took the proffered whisky glass and lifted it. "*Santé*. Your health, Thomas."

"And yours, Lucien." Tom sipped his whisky. "Where are you staying?"

He wasn't sure he wanted to know. It was merely conversation. The sort you had when bumping into an acquaintance at the club. Let Lucien state his business and leave.

Leave? Tom glanced out at the snow building up until it was a wall between him and the world. Where would Lucien go?

The Frenchman shrugged. "I'm throwing myself on your mercy. I was unable to arrange something, so I ask permission to sleep on your sofa, just for tonight? I won't be a burden, Tom. But I'm tired. I need to rest. The train from Lyon was stop-start all the way. I got to Paris and had to wait a day for a seat on the train to Calais. Then I had to wait for a place on the ferry. And then on your train from Dover to Ashford, a long journey. It feels like I have been travelling since last Christmas. Is there any decent accommodation in your town?"

"Nothing like that, I'm afraid. Closest would be Ashford, where you got off the train. We're only a handful of houses, a church, and a pub. I don't even think the pub has rooms to rent. Anyway, I wouldn't dream of turfing you out," Tom said heartily, hiding his reluctance. Someone in his space, having to keep his back to the wall and his eyes open. It made him wary. "You can stay here. There is room. Have you eaten? I'll make us some tea."

"It would be most welcome, but I would prefer something stronger." Lucien pointed to his empty whisky glass.

"My apologies." Tom poured the whisky for Lucien and placed it by his chair. "I don't have wine that would pass muster with a *vigneron* like yourself. And

I'm afraid you'll think this whisky is a poor substitute. I'll put together something for us to eat, shall I?"

He went to the kitchen, opened a cupboard, pulled out bread, margarine, pickles and cheese. There was also some sliced cold ham.

He called out as he arranged the food on a large platter. "Did you say you came from Paris or from your vineyards?"

"From the farm. I had to go through Paris and the railway is still disrupted. Several times we were shunted to a side rail and had to wait while a goods train rolled by. Sometimes for hours. Very tedious. Finding you has been, as you would say, a mission. You have chosen to live in a secret place, out of the way. Such a small village, not even on any map. Have you deliberately hidden or don't your Masters want you traced?"

Tom noticed they had both fallen into speaking in French. "A bit of both, I expect. I am still officially part of the British war machine, and I may be sent overseas again. I'm on compassionate at the moment. After VE Day I came down here to my parents' home. My mother had died, you see and there were things to sort out. So, I've been here a while."

"My condolences, Tom. Madeleine told me your father had passed over when you were still a very young child. You and your mother must have been close."

"Yes, we were. I was in France when she died. I got the news through a *maquisard* who got a message from someone else telling me she'd passed away. I wasn't even here for her funeral. We were too busy sabotaging trains in southern France."

7

"Ah, yes, I read about it. Carrying wolfram or something from Spain."

"Yes, we were quite successful. Managed to put a dent in the German war-machine by limiting the amount they eventually got. Anyway, when I came back after it had all ended in Europe there was a lot to do, settling the estate, clearing the house, making it liveable. It's a nice little place, peaceful. But I'll have to go back to London sooner or later."

"How do you see your future?"

Tom shrugged. "Get a job at one of the universities, I expect, if any would have me. I'd love to just bury myself down here. Stay huddled up with no one to worry about, but one must eat, of course."

Tom realised he was still holding the platter of food. He placed it on a small table close to Lucien, together with linen napkins and side plates.

"Here you are," he said. "Not much, I'm afraid. I'll share and we can call it a midnight feast."

Lucien ate as if he hadn't had food for a long while. He drank his whisky in gulps then put the glass down as Tom sat staring into the fire, a sandwich forgotten in his hand. Eventually he stirred, handed the whisky bottle to Lucien.

"You are here for a reason," Tom said. Not a question. Lucien would not have tried so hard to find him on a mere whim. "Do you have news?"

Lucien poured more whisky for himself and offered the bottle back to Tom. "Thank you, Tom. This was most enjoyable. To answer your question, no, I have no news of Madeleine. And you?"

"I had a Red Cross postcard in 1943. A postcard with only the words *je t'aime*. And her name. Nothing since. And you?"

Lucien patted his pocket. "I have a letter here, from Madeleine."

Hope flared. "She's alive?"

Lucien shrugged. "I'm still trying to find out. But I do not know where this letter came from. So it's hard to trace where she was when she wrote it."

"Who brought it to you?"

"A stranger."

"What did the letter say?"

"I haven't opened it."

"Good God, man. Why?"

"Because it's addressed to you. That's why I've come to England, to deliver Madeleine's letter." Lucien pulled out an envelope from an inner pocket, crumpled as if it had travelled a long way and been through many hands.

Tom drew back. He couldn't take it. Not yet. To touch something Madeleine had touched was a step too far. He needed to take a breath, prepare himself. Lucien seemed to understand for he placed the letter on the table.

"Other than this letter, when did you last see Madeleine or hear from her?" Tom asked. His lips were stiff and words difficult.

"I saw her in 1942. She came to the *domaine*. We were harvesting, *les vendanges*. That would have been October 1942. She came to help. As for the child…"

"Child? What child?"

Lucien looked startled. "Did you not know? Your child, Tom. You have a daughter."

Chapter 2

"A daughter?" Tom sat up. "Are you sure?"

"Of course I am."

"Madeleine with a daughter? Our child? Oh God. I didn't know. Where are they?"

And why didn't she tell me?

Lucien shrugged. "I have no idea. When Madeleine came to the chateau that time, she was silent, thin and white. I thought something was wrong, but she wouldn't say. The child wasn't with her and Madeleine said nothing, so I wondered. Had something happened?"

Tom picked up his glass and took a sip, his hands were shaking. They'd spoken of children, of course. What newly married couple didn't? But Madeleine had wisely said it was too early. There were so many reasons for delaying a family, all of them sound. They'd only been married a few years; they'd left France to settle in England and were struggling to find their place in a new world. Tom needed to establish himself at the bank, get a promotion or two. The money for lowly bank employees wasn't good, and as a foreigner in London, Madeleine's opportunities for employment were constrained. Not too many jobs for French art historians out there and she was reluctant to go for a second-best job.

For all that, life had been carefree. He'd been the same frivolous Tom Blake he'd always been and had continued to sweep his beloved Madeleine into his crazy world, wild with fantasies and big dreams. One day they'd be rich, super-wealthy with a holiday home in the Caribbean and a mansion in London. 'Oh, you want a home in France too? No problem.'

And then he'd made the biggest mistake of his life and Madeleine had left him. He had assumed at the time she'd gone back to France, to her family. Or perhaps to the apartment in Paris where they'd lived as students, enjoying carefree years before real life took over.

But he knew.

The moment Lucien spoke of a child, he knew. He and Madeleine had had only one weekend together after war was declared. It must have been then the child was conceived.

Sitting in his shabby living room on that bitterly cold December night, he knew it was his child as if some ancient imprint had suddenly opened out in front of him. He didn't even have to count the months. This was his daughter.

Coldness settled around his heart. No, I can't, he thought. I can't. Not another one to mourn. He spent his waking hours grieving for Madeleine. Longing for her. And now he could not bear the thought of another person to add to the graveyard of his mind. Wasn't it enough he was crushed without Madeleine? Now there was a child as well.

"My child? Are you sure?" His question was unnecessary.

"I asked Madeleine, and she was sure," Lucien said. "She said you'd come over in 1940 and you'd been together for a weekend. Is it true?"

Tom nodded. He was in Paris in the spring of 1940, undercover, with money to purchase a small printing press for the forgery of documents and to recruit a team. He'd called on a few of his fellow Sorbonne students still in Paris. Found two he could trust. It was early days. War had been declared but, because Hitler was busy in other parts of Europe and had not yet invaded France, everyone was calling it a 'joke' war. Parisians took it light-heartedly, still filled the cafes and restaurants, walked along the Seine and picnicked in the parks, not fearing an invasion by the Germans or desperately pretending it would never happen. The waiting game of war or, as the French called it, *le drôle de guerre* was making people complacent, at least on the surface. It wouldn't stay a joke for long.

His employers, Special Organisations Executive or SOE, were not yet organised enough to be effective, but his old colleagues, Emile and Michel, were enthusiastic and already bubbling with plans. An underground newspaper, ID documents, food rationing cards, storage of arms, small groups that could attack trains. It all sounded so exciting. It would be an adventure with loads of fun.

He'd set up the two in a small suburban house on the outskirts of Paris with a printing press in the cellar, then he had gone rogue for a week, and had gone looking for Madeleine. After she had left him and disappeared, he'd had no contact. She was somewhere in France, and he had to find her.

He went first to the one person who would know, her brother, Lucien Aubert. But Lucien's business office was closed up, a sign on the door directing visitors to the family vineyard near Lyon. Tom had then gone to the Louvre, seeking out a close friend of theirs, Phillipe Moreau. He'd been a young tutor when Tom and Madeleine were at university, always on the outside of their group, always the loner longing to be in. They'd treated him as a bit of a joke, He was too old for their childish escapades. But he had kept on trying. A nuisance in the end.

No luck. Phillipe didn't know or didn't want to tell him. Then to the apartment which they had shared with other students on the off chance someone from their past would still be there and might know something.

And there she was. Shocked and then hesitant until he explained why he was in Paris. He had been with her for a weekend of love and forgiveness. It was at the start of a war, the like of which they could never have imagined. But Madeleine still loved him despite his many failings, and suddenly everything seemed possible. He'd left with a promise to return. If he could. She understood his life was now no longer his own. He was under orders, in service to the British war machine. They had kissed passionately when he left, making promises they could never keep.

It was the last time he'd seen her.

Was the child conceived then? It must have happened. Just when he thought his emotions had been numbed enough for him to exist, Tom felt a surge of anger. She hadn't told him, never written, hadn't asked Lucien to contact him. Didn't she want him to know?

He reluctantly acknowledged it was hard getting messages through after the May 1940 invasion into France and the Germans' casual stroll into Paris on 14th

June of that year. After that, the occupiers had controlled everything. He had not been sent to Paris again. Someone else had taken over the burgeoning resistance in the city and his work had taken him south into Vichy territory. After each mission he'd come home to this cottage, hoping for a letter. Each time his mother, knowing what he wanted more than anything, shook her head sadly. There had been nothing from his wife.

*****

In the living room of his small cottage the fire flickered.

"A child, Lucien?" He tried to keep the tremor out of his voice.

"Yes. Her name is Sophie and she'd be about five years old now, if she's still alive."

Tom picked up the letter, noticed his hand was shaking. There was a seal holding it closed, with just his name and then Lucien's.

"And you heard nothing?"

"A letter at the end of 1942. From the Foreign Office," Tom said. "They told me Madeleine Blake had been arrested by the Gestapo. They promised to write again when they had further news. I thought perhaps she might have been involved in some Resistance work although I never heard anything along the grapevine. But that would have been quite normal. We were all confined within our own little groups, we heard nothing about anyone else."

"Did you hear from the Foreign Office again?"

Tom shook his head. "No. I wrote asking them, but they replied they'd heard nothing more and I mustn't

15

hope. But, of course, one always does. Had you heard anything about her? Or from her?"

Lucien shook his head. "Everything was so difficult during those years. I know Madeleine stayed in the apartment. She had to work as she was supporting herself and her two friends, the Jewish couple. You might remember them. I feel a great sense of guilt, Tom. Madeleine asked me to persuade our parents to release her inheritance from our grandparents and I refused. She needed the money to live. It meant she had to find a job and I fear she may have found one with people who were in the Resistance."

"They weren't paying jobs, Lucien."

"I think perhaps they had become involved in some sort of secret activity."

"That would be why the Gestapo arrested her.?"

Lucien shrugged. "I didn't know that. Now, I fear the worst."

Tom gazed at Lucien who was struggling to keep his eyes open, almost asleep in the saggy armchair. "Where were you when this letter came? In your Paris office or at the vineyard"

Lucien stretched and yawned. "I was at the vineyard. I'd closed my business when the Germans arrived and had gone home. We, my father and I, assumed the Germans would want to keep the vineyards and farms going. We were right. They wanted our wine and our produce, milk, meat, eggs. And of course, our wine. We were left alone as long as we produced what they wanted. Until almost the end of the war."

Tom missed the bitterness in Lucien's voice. His thoughts were only for Madeleine and the child.

"You worked for the Resistance?" Tom asked.

"No, I didn't. I was conscripted into the French Army. But that is another story."

Tom wanted to ask more but he could see Lucien was exhausted.

"After I went into the Army, Adam Janssen, my master winemaker, was there so the grapes were looked after as well as one man could. He has a deformed left foot, and he played it up so they left him alone. My father's health continued to wane. His lung problems were worse in the winter. Adam said there were sometimes people hiding in the cottages next to the stables. He made sure there were always escape routes. Later I did a bit helping the Resistance. That is also another story."

"But you weren't caught?"

"Yes, once." Then Lucien grew silent, his face eroded by the flickering of flames emphasising deep lines of grief. "But my parents…"

"What happened, Lucien?" His voice gentle.

Lucien was silent. The dying light from the embers played over the lines on his face.

"You see it was like this," he said. "They came when I was away, but Adam told me. His mother was our housekeeper, you may remember her."

*****

They came to the farm. Not orderly as one expects from the Germans, but a rogue group of looters. It was 1943 and the Germans had become brutal and lawless. After their defeat in Russia they knew the end was near

17

and it turned them into brutes. More so than they had been at the start of the war.

The first thing Adam Janssen had seen was plumes of dust on the road. Two truckloads of German soldiers, their rifles gleaming in the winter sun. An officer got out. Fat, bald, loud. A *Felgendarm*, or '*kettenhund*' as the steel gorget round his ample neck made him look like a chained dog. His rifle across his shoulder.

"*Schnell! Schnell!*" He shouted, and the men ran, some into the house, some towards the sheds.

"Check everything. There must be wine stored somewhere. You! Go inside. Feel along the walls of the kitchen. Look for a hidden door. These bastards hide it from us."

Adam asked, "What is this? What do you want?"

"We have information you are hiding your best wines. Where are they? It is against the law to hide your best wines from us."

"You need to speak to the *négociant* for this district. He is the man who buys our wine."

"I'm not talking about *négociants, dummkopf.* I know what they do. I want your wine, your best wine. Now."

"There is no wine."

"And where is the owner?"

"He is away."

The *Felgendarm* raised his rifle. "Where is he?"

"He is taking the last of our stock to Lyon. For sale. If you want our wine, why don't you go to Lyon and buy it."

The German struck Adam across the face. As he lay on the dirt, his lip torn open, the German raised his rifle and aimed. Shot. The bullet went into the ground beside Adam's head.

"The next bullet is yours," the man said. "Now tell me. Where is the wine."

At the noise old man Aubert, Lucien's father, walked out of the front door. He leaned heavily on his walking stick. It was in his nature to be polite, even to the enemy. He invited the officer in for a glass of wine.

"You may like to sample our best, sir."

"Exactly what I'm here for, *M'sieur*. Your best wine. Stand here," the officer ordered, and Monsieur Aubert, ever the gentleman, obeyed and stood by the fountain, one hand gripping his walking stick and the other clutching the stone of the fountain.

Group by group the Germans returned, all shaking their heads. Adam sighed with relief. He and the old man had done a good job in hiding it. Now they could get back to work. But the *Feldgendarm* had not finished.

"Who else is here? Your wife?" He shouted at Monsieur Aubert. But Madame Aubert had heard the furore and came rushing down the steps shouting and waving her arms.

"Go away. Go away. You are not welcome here."

Monsieur Aubert held up his hand. "My dear, be still."

"Janssen," Madame Aubert called to her housekeeper. "Come here. Tell these dogs to leave. At once."

"No." Adam shouted. "No!"

His mother walked down the steps. Slow and stately. She knew. Adam could see the look of resignation, her eyes downcast until she saw him. And she smiled, a look of love like a blessing. Adam's mother recognised the signs of death just as he did. She had seen it in Belgium during the Great War, the sadism and power of the German Army. And yet she came out. And stood with quiet dignity as the German soldiers lined them up.

They were made to kneel. It was a slow process as they were old.

They finally got to their knees, facing the stone walls of the chateau. Monsieur Aubert in the middle, he stretched out his hands and each woman held on.

"So, the French aristocracy, lined up like cattle," the *Feldgendarm* sneered. "Is your blood blue? We'll soon find out."

Then he shot them.

Chapter 3

Tom had heard such stories. But this was close to home. They were Madeleine's parents.

"This is dreadful news. I'm so sorry, Lucien." He tried to be compassionate, but all the while a picture of a small lost girl kept intruding. Lucien went on, almost unaware of Tom. "Adam said they lay there, lined up beside the water fountain. Each with a bullet to the back of the head. Execution-style. He buried my mother and father next to their ancestors in the family graveyard. Janssen too for she deserved to lie in peace with the people she had served so faithfully."

"They were betrayed?"

"Without a doubt. I have a score to settle when I get back."

"You know who it was?"

"Yes." Lucien stirred. "I will deal with her in my own time."

"A woman?"

Tom felt a shiver of apprehension. Lucien's face was carved stone as he sat up from his slouch in the armchair. "Never mind. The less you know..."

Tom stuffed the letter into his pocket. "I expect you're tired," he said. "Let me get the guest bedroom ready for you."

Lucien got to his feet. "Aren't you going to open the letter?"

"Later," Tom said.

Lucien looked disappointed. "Yes, I am tired. I apologise for intruding. I'm hoping the letter will give us a clue to where Madeleine is."

Tom said nothing. Instead, he went about settling Lucien in the spare room, with extra blankets and a hot water bottle.

Bidding Lucien goodnight, he tamped down the living room fire, placed the fire guard around it and left a few embers still glowing in the dark. Then he went to his bedroom, closed the door and sat on the side of the bed.

Madeleine had never been in this house, yet she was everywhere, even if her fragrance was only imagined. Roses. Autumn roses when their perfume was strongest. Her footsteps as light as her laughter. She was there, in every corner, in every space of this house, in every molecule of his body. She sat beside him in the living room as he watched the fire. She stood beside him when he made his evening meal. She lay beside him as he tried to sleep. She soothed him when nightmares shook him awake. He had placed her there, in every nook and cranny of his home and his heart.

And now there was another figure. Lucien said the child would be about five years old. Probably like Madeleine, blonde with blue eyes. Would the child be serene like her mother or risk-addicted and excitable like her father? He could imagine her skipping down the path to the front door of this cottage. Lavender bushes on either side, her small hands stripping the leaves, inhaling the perfume and handing them to her mother. Madeleine would smile, receiving the scraps of lavender, and he would lift the child up and swing her around, laughing.

He'd build a swing in the back yard hanging from the oak tree his great-grandfather had planted. And then she would sleep in the bed that had been his as a child with Peter Rabbit and Flopsy, Mopsy and Cotton-Tail stencilled on the wall above her head.

He stood suddenly. Looked around the shabby room. Looking for an escape from the pictures in his mind.

He could not bear the thought of his child lost somewhere in a devastated Europe, alone and motherless.

Where could she be? Who was she with? Was she with Madeleine?

If so, why hadn't Lucien heard anything? Why hadn't he?

*****

The small bedroom where he slept was cold, with a sneaky draught edging in through an ill-fitting window frame. Tom pulled the thick curtains closed and instantly the room felt cosier, warmer, closing in on him like a well-worn cardigan. He lain here as a child, in the narrow bed pushed against the wall, watching his model aeroplanes twirling in the cool night breeze, dreaming of adventures. Then, when the adventures came, when he'd been picked by the Special Operations Executive, the ones who were instructed by Churchill to 'set Europe ablaze', and trained as a special agent, he had dreamed of other adventures. All heroic, of course, but most had not ended that way. There was nothing heroic about garrotting men or sabotaging trains. He suddenly remembered late in the war, the *maquis* fighting against

23

teenaged German soldiers, when Hitler was scraping the barrel and putting retirees and children in the field. They'd come across a group of them, their grey-green fatigues soiled and stained, their eyes filled with terror, so young he doubted they'd started shaving. The *maquis* came at them with bayonets and the boys cried for their mothers. It had stopped the war-maddened men, and they had walked away. Some of the German teenagers then picked up their weapons and shot two men in the back. The *maquis* returned and then it was over. They'd carried their two wounded men away and cared for them until they died. The German teenagers had been left to the crows.

Tom shook his head, trying to shed the memories crowding in. Pray God there will never be another war like the last one. And pray God he would sleep well tonight.

In the bedroom fireplace he stacked up some kindling from the coal scuttle, shoved a wad of newspaper into the grate and lit it. Soon there was a small spiral of flames twisting upwards. He shivered and crouched on the small carpet close to the fire.

When he began to feel warm, Tom slipped his finger along the edge of the envelope and took out Madeleine's letter.

Beloved,

I write to tell you we have a child. Our little girl came on the eve of Christmas, 1940. Our own gift to each other. Her name is Sophie and she is beautiful, blonde with eyes the colour of the sky.

She is an angel sent to us, Tom. I know this because she has a small birthmark on her back that looks like angel's wings. I talk to her all the time and tell her about you. I say, 'Papa Tom' is coming soon.

Papa Tom is coming. Always I say to her you will come and take us home.

I sent postcards, but they were sent back to me. Where are you?

I am still in the apartment with my friends. They helped with the birth, which was hard. If you get this letter, please come.

Be brave. Stay safe. We need you.

Je t'aime

Maddie

Dated February 1941 when their child had been only two months old. And he hadn't been there to hold her.

He wondered why it had taken her so long to write this letter if the child had been born at Christmas. Alright, only a few months and life could not have been easy. It sounded as if she'd been unwell after the birth. He smoothed the letter with his fingers, imagining it was Madeleine's cheeks he was touching. *Je t'aime*. I love you, he whispered.

Tom re-read it, put it down, then picked it up and read it again, his sense of anguish growing. What was making him feel so terrible? There was something...

And then it hit him.

He let out a groan. Today was Christmas Eve and it was Sophie's birthday. She was somewhere in France. Alone and lost. On her birthday. And he couldn't bear to think of it.

Sophie. He said it out loud. Sophie. Again. It was like hearing the ocean for the first time, the rumble and crash of waves.

Sophie.

He tried not to imagine her. It would do no good. After all, he would never meet her.

But it was diamond-clear from the letter, Madeleine had wanted to come home. To be with him.

But why wasn't she with her family? What had happened that she was in Paris with Emily and Aaron when she had the child? She should have been at the chateau with family around her.

Surely Lucien would know where she was. He had to know. He said there was more to reveal. Tom jumped up and went to the door of his room.

Then stopped.

It was midnight and Lucien would be asleep. He'd have to wait until morning.

Tom lay down on his bed clutching the letter to his chest. He was exhausted, not physically but mentally. His mind whirled with unanswered questions, with unmitigated pain. He went over the events of the past, seeing where it had all begun. Outside the snow fell like full stops onto the blank page of the garden, and sleep was a long time coming.

And with sleep came nightmares. Always the same ones. Tom lay sweating, wondered if he could go down to the living room and pour himself another whisky. But, fearful of waking Lucien, he lay in bed rigid until sleep crept over him again.

*****

Tom had been a scholarship boy at school, doing well enough to gain a place at Oxford. In 1932, he had graduated with honours, a rare occurrence for the son of a lowly vicar. He was a 'bright fellow' his tutors claimed, but he needed 'rounding off'. And so, as suggested by more than one professor, he sent an application to the Sorbonne in Paris to do post-graduate work. As Tom was not yet ready to forsake the heady and irresponsible life of a student, he eagerly left England for France with a sort of joyous abandon. Lucky me, he thought, when he found digs in a very posh apartment owned by an architect called Lucien Aubert. Luckier still was meeting Lucien's little sister, Madeleine, also ensconced in the apartment.

She too was an art historian. He'd been impressed by her courage, asking hard questions, expecting honest answers, not accepting mealy-mouthed replies from dandified and arrogant lecturers. Digging, digging. No one else in the class stood up to a lecturer spouting nonsense as Madeleine had, not even Tom Blake. They had fallen in love over Tom's expertise in restoring medieval manuscripts and Madeleine's interest in the Knights Templar. They sat in cafes, arguing good naturedly about the Middle Ages; how cruel those in power were. How so many innocent lives had been lost in the Inquisition and later. Such things would never happen today, Madeleine had said stoutly. We are

27

civilised now. But Tom argued, people don't change. Men who grab power will do anything to hang onto it – even to killing innocents.

Madeleine was adamant; she and her generation would never let it happen, and he loved her for her idealism and innocence.

After the rigour of Tom's graduate course at Oxford, the post-graduate degree in France was meant to be one long party. He had promised himself he would not set foot in any library ever again, but that was where Madeleine spent her time and so, eventually, did Tom.

Then she had taken him to the vineyard close to Lyon, to meet her parents.

He remembered how nervous Madeleine was, begging him not to call her Maddie in front of her mother.

"She hates it, and she'll grab onto it as an excuse to deny us our romance. You are going to marry me, aren't you?"

"In a heartbeat," he'd said stoutly and unwisely. "As for your folks, they'll love me, so don't worry."

"I know them, Tom. It won't be easy."

He hadn't believed her and had made a right cock-up of the meeting. He remembered it all too well.

*****

On the day they had been 'invited' – ordered to – summoned to present themselves at the chateau, they'd travelled from Paris by train, then on a side railway to a small station, the one closest to the vineyard. From there they'd walked.

The old home had appeared slowly out of the heat haze. Set on a hill surrounded by the vines, it rose like a stately stone box, with a steep sloping grey roof and round turrets at either end. Madeleine said her Papa called it a chateau and the family copied him although it was nowhere near as large or as splendid as some other chateaux in the area. To the side were the sheds where the large vats and presses laboured. Beyond were the stables, partly converted into storage and accommodation for pickers who came for *les vendanges*, the annual harvesting and the harvest festival that followed. The driveway curled around a row of rhododendrons dried out by the summer heat, and led to a small, gravelled courtyard with a fountain set dead centre. As children, she and Lucien had played in the water as it gently curved out of a dolphin's mouth. Now the fountain was dry, and the basin filled with leaves. Tom tried to imagine Madeleine as a small child frolicking in the water. Cute, no doubt, with those large blue eyes and blonde hair so fine it looked like gold thread.

Madeleine was chattering. Tom could tell she was nervous. One generation ago, she said, the area had been hard-hit by Phylloxera, a grape disease which had decimated most wineries. She said that forty percent of vineyards in France were devastated, including this one, Chateau d'Aubert. It had been a struggle to re-plant and nurture new vines, especially since the remedy was grafting with resilient rootstock from overseas. But slowly year by year, things improved. Papa had been making a success of the business when the Great War changed everything. He had served in the French Army and had not come back the same man who had left. They weren't the only ones to have been hard-hit by the war. Nearly every family in France had lost a son, a brother, a husband, an uncle or had him come home a living, shambling wreck. Papa was one of the four and a half million soldiers injured, although Papa's wounds were not as visible as most others. In the years after the Great War, the grapes did not fare well under his trembling hands and his gas-damaged lungs. He was really too broken and too fragile to hold the place together. No wonder he had wanted Madeleine to marry well. It would have solved many of their problems.

"What about your brother? Is he no help?"

"Lucien has a thriving architectural business in Paris. I don't think he wants to be isolated down here on the farm. You will be kind to them, won't you, Tom?"

"Of course, my dearest. Of course."

But he hadn't.

Looking back, he wondered if, in the beginning, it had been a bit of a game. Tom, the conqueror, versus her parents, the old *vigneron* with his walking stick and his ruined lungs and the dragoness. Madame Aubert had planned Madeleine's life. There was an older man in the district, also a *vigneron* or winemaker. What was his name? René something. Oh yes, René Guillard. For Madeleine to marry him would mean the combining of two local vineyards into one strong business. Financially, the merger was a no-brainer, until their daughter came home trailing a drink-sodden disrespectful Englishman.

Her parents had been deplorable towards him. He should have expected it, behaving the way he had, joking and fart-arsing around like a bloody teenager. No wonder he'd made such a bad impression. Now, his older more mature self burned with embarrassment. To do that to Madeleine, after he'd professed to love her, was shameful.

No excuse, but it was the first time he'd heard an Englishman's favourite Sunday lunch used as a pejorative. 'Rosbif'. He hadn't known whether to laugh or cry. He had never met anyone who so actively disliked him, and he'd tried to be as likeable and as charming as possible. But here in the grey stone walls of the chateau, his charm and likeability were of no earthly use. Perhaps Madeleine's parents had seen through him and seen the naughty irresponsible little boy underneath. Or perhaps they were too attached to the idea of the local man as husband. Whatever, he was not a success.

Had he married Madeleine out of revenge? It no longer mattered why they had slipped into a small church in a Parisian side-street and pledged the happy-ever-after thing. It had started out as a flamboyant almost lustful adoration of the beautiful French girl. His love, a real love, for her had been a slow growing plant. By the time Madeleine left him, he knew she was the centre of his universe. There would never be anyone else.

And he had blown it. He had lost everything.

Madeleine Aubert had returned to France and, at the time, he assumed she was ensconced in the welcoming arms of her family, all agreeing the English were a bunch of scoundrels and she'd got off lightly.

When the war started, it took a while before the Germans entered Paris. In May 1941, eight months after they'd declared war, they crashed over the border between Belgium and France. The Germans had ignored the Maginot Line, the beloved status symbol of French defence, the concrete bunker system the French people had relied on to keep them safe. An illusion, of course. The Germans had driven their Panzers south through the Ardennes Forest and over the Meuse River. A month later they were in Paris. Hitler had arrived on a four-hour victory visit and had done a jig of triumph and then gone home.

Tom had been mad with worry, imagining the worst. Because he knew Madeleine. She would not sit by and accept the invasion. She would get involved in whatever skulduggery was going on.

And then, amid his anxiety, the Special Operations Executive had come calling. They needed a specialist; French speaking with a background in the replicating of artifacts, to infiltrate France and help Mr Churchill win the war.

Tom had only one condition and they'd agreed.

Chapter 4

Christmas Day, 1945, in the morning Tom and Lucien gave each other a mumbled greeting, *Joyeux Noël*. Then Lucien surprised him when he grabbed Tom's shoulders, kissed him on both cheeks and hugged him. Tom could feel the older man's shoulders shaking and realised with horror that Lucien was crying.

"Forgive me, Tom," he said wiping his eyes. "I have lost so much through this war. Parents, friends. I cling to hope that Madeleine and the child have survived. At least I would have some family left."

"I know, I know." Tom didn't know. His words were hollow.

"Will you let me find them?" Lucien asked, still holding onto Tom. "I can help you. We can work together. Only then will my life begin to feel worthwhile again."

"I hadn't thought…"

"You'll want to come over soon, I imagine."

"I hadn't planned on returning to France."

"But you must. Of course you must. It is imperative. I can help. Please, you must let me help you."

There was little Tom could say. Would a quest to find Madeleine and the child ease this man's agony? Ease his own? They stood gazing at each other in forlorn despair.

There had been enough hot water for them to wash and shave. Afterwards they busied themselves, silently making tea and toast for a meagre breakfast. No croissants as they'd have had sitting in a café in Paris. The thought almost undid Tom, remembering Madeleine with him at a rickety table on some boulevard, laughing, her head thrown back with a sort of happy bravado. Madeleine had, has – he quickly corrected himself – a laugh like a gurgle that you might expect from a contented donkey. He'd told her and she only laughed more. He'd loved hearing that joyful sound.

On a bitterly cold Christmas morning in 1945, Tom and Lucien sat by the re-invigorated fire in the living room, each with a cup of tea and a plate of toast spread thinly with margarine and a slither of marmalade. Each held their thoughts close, unable to share the pain they felt for those dead or lost.

It's different, Tom thought. *Lucien can't feel the despair. The fear of living for the rest of his life alone, with only memories. Lucien can go on, marry and have children. I can't.*

Finally, Lucien put down his cup and turned to Tom. "You've read Madeleine's letter?"

"Yes. She gives me news of Sophie's birth."

"No information as to where we could find her?"

"No, sadly. She dated it February 1941 and says she's still in the apartment with Emily and Aaron Golding."

"I know she was with Emily and Aaron until July 1942," Lucien said. "She was there from 1939 when she left England. But then in the middle of July 1942 she disappears."

"Where did she go? What on earth was she doing? Why didn't she go home to your parents?"

"My mother had made it quite plain she was not welcome."

"Even with a child?"

"Especially with a child. Remember Sophie was your child, Tom, a disgraced Britisher. But at least it gives us a starting place. The *appartement* in Paris."

"The letter is dated nearly five years ago, Lucien. Much has happened since. Who is staying there now?"

"It's empty," Lucien said. "It has been since they all disappeared. I didn't rent it to anyone in case Madeleine came back and needed it."

"Disappeared? All of them? For God's sake, what happened? Were Emily and Aaron taken or did they get away?"

Lucien shrugged. "More likely arrested and afterwards, who knows. One of the death camps, perhaps. So, let's try to set out a timeline," he said, sitting up and beginning to count on his fingers. "March 1940 and you go back to Paris for a short while. Then December 1940 and a child is born. Emily and Aaron are living with Madeleine. Alright, one step back. The Germans were in Paris from June 1940. Madeleine had to earn money. Emily and Aaron were penniless. They had both lost their jobs. So, where did she go to work?"

"I wonder why they didn't get out. I remember the Spanish boy, Alego, had an open invitation for us all to join him in his orange orchard near Barcelona."

"We'll never know. Anyway, Madeleine was somehow keeping them alive. The Jews couldn't leave the apartment. At that time, Jews were being treated very badly. They could only shop in the afternoon between the hours of three and four. By then all the food would have been sold. They could ride on the Metro but only in the back carriage. No theatres, no cinema, not even the use of public telephones. So, Madeleine was doing all the heavy lifting while the couple kept house. She would be standing in queues from the early hours, as well as trying to hold a job down."

"Did you help her in any way?"

Lucien looked awkward. "She wanted her inheritance which was only due to her at the age of twenty-five, but I knew our father wouldn't agree. So, I gave her some money. Not enough, but at least enough for a few months."

"So, what happened next?"

"An edict. Jews had to be registered. October 1941, I think."

"Would Emily and Aaron have fallen for that malarkey? Surely it was obvious what the Germans had in mind for the French Jews?"

"You're using hindsight, Tom. At the time, French Jews were convinced they would not be in any danger. After all, both in the occupied zone and in the Vichy-controlled part of France, it was made perfectly clear only foreign Jews were in danger."

"So, they could have registered?"

"Which would have meant the Germans knew exactly where to pick them up. There was a big *rafle* in 1942. Thousands arrested. We don't know what happened to Emily and Aaron. I'm guessing…"

"And Madeleine could have been arrested as well?"

Lucien nodded "Perhaps."

Tom's lips felt tight as if the words he had to say were reluctant to leave. "Do you think Madeleine and the child might have been taken? The Foreign Office didn't say anything about a child, just that Madeleine had been arrested."

"I don't know, Tom. I only pray..." Lucien's face was gaunt and deadly white in the cold morning air. He stretched toward the fire, warming and then rubbing his hands together. "Let's be optimistic. Let us assume the very best. And believe they are alive somewhere in France."

"If they weren't caught up in the *rafle*, the round-up, then why the silence? Why did she lose touch with us?"

Lucien put his hands to his face and his voice was an anguished wail. "I don't know. As God is my witness, Tom, I don't know. All I know is we must find them."

Tom tamped down his anger. We? Did Lucien think he could drop everything and go to France in search of the impossible? But of course, he did. That was exactly why Lucien was here. Tom looked out the window. It was not yet ten o'clock in the morning and outside the snow was falling again in soft white cotton-wool flakes. If it keeps up this way, he thought, we'll be snowed in for another week or two.

They sat in silence watching the flames of the fire as they fell and flared up, teased by small draughts of air.

After a long and uneasy silence, Tom went to prepare Christmas lunch. He was more fortunate than most. Rationing was still in force throughout England.

37

Eggs, butter, meat were hard to get. But he had a contact here in the country, where food was a little more available. Twenty-five years ago, John Mason, the farmer down the road from his parent's house, had been the father-figure the small child had needed after his father had died. And Mason was still there for him all these years later.

The farmer had been a source of strength when the lost little boy had wandered onto his farm and was bowled over by an over-enthusiastic farm dog. The boy had been at a loss, not understanding why he was suddenly fatherless. Six year-old boys don't understand such things. Death was a mystery and would remain so for a while. Little Tommy Blake kept talking as if his father had gone on a trip and was expected back. Tom's mother did the best she could, and a father-figure such as John Mason was just what the boy needed. So, Mason took it upon himself to be available and had never stopped.

It was there on the farm young Tom had learned to milk cows and drive a tractor. He saw calves being born and felt the summer come and go with winter's breath on its back. John Mason and his wife, Lorna, were his surrogate grandparents, the ones he'd never had, his own biological grandparents having died in the 1918 influenza epidemic. Many years later, it was from John Mason, via the *maquis,* he had learned of his mother's last illness and her passing.

When Tom had come home, after VE Day, John Mason stood before him, twisting his hat and looking at his boots, his gnarled hands, anywhere but at Tom.

"She didn' wan' ye ta know she was ill, Tommy-lad. She knew ye was working hard to win the war an' didn' wan' ta worret ye."

His mother had died without him by her side. He grieved for her, guilty at his neglect, but he'd been in the mountains in France with the *maquis*, and therefore uncontactable.

Now the war was over, and Tom was home. Mr Mason made sure he was well-fed, at least as well-fed as possible in the bleak landscape of a recovering Britain.

The Masons had invited him to share their Christmas, but Tom assumed it would be chaotic with the Masons' four children, spouses and the grandchildren making it impossible to talk or even to sit comfortably. He had declined the invitation. There would be too much noise, too many bodies racing around, too many kindly questions, more than he could handle. Hypervigilance was exhausting and Tom had, of necessity, whittled down his human contact to one or two. John Mason understood, Lorna Mason less so.

But, thanks to the Masons' generosity, Tom would be able to give his guest a traditional Christmas lunch; a small roast beef, potatoes and a side dish of some locally grown vegetables; carrots, broccoli and winter kale. Mrs Mason had made sure there was a Christmas pudding, with thruppenny bits stuck in. She'd warned him, 'be careful with yer teeth, Tommy-lad'.

They talked over the cooking, Lucien carefully preparing the carrots. "I shall make you French vegetables to go with the English roast beef," he said. "You have olive oil?

Tom snorted.

"No matter. We can improvise. It seems England is in a bad way, *mon ami*. I see destroyed houses and factories everywhere."

"You came through Dover so you saw us at our worst."

"Yes. Terrible."

"Many cities and towns were heavily bombed," Tom said. "London's a mess. I understand something like twenty percent of all homes in Britain were destroyed, and a lot of people are now sleeping rough or staying in army camps or still in the Underground stations. We can't get the materials to fix things properly either, so it's going to be a long recovery. Food is still being rationed. We lost nearly two hundred of our merchant ships and two-thirds of our Navy, which makes it hard to get merchandise in. It'll take decades before we're anywhere near normal again."

"A costly war."

Tom thought not about the housing or the food rationing but about the people lost. A quarter of a million troops and about sixty thousand innocent civilians. And there was Madeleine.

And now another soul, a little girl called Sophie, and like her mother, she was lost somewhere in France.

Tom and Lucien sat in the living room, replete from a good Christmas lunch. Tom threw another log onto the fire and watched as the embers kicked into life again. The smoke from Lucien's Gitanes cigarette swirled in the air. Tom had never taken to Gitanes, their dark Turkish tobacco too strong for him. Instead, he sat with a pipe clamped between his teeth. Empty, as he hadn't been able to source pipe tobacco and the few ounces he'd brought back from France hadn't lasted a month.

"So, this was a typical English Christmas lunch?" Lucien asked, stretching out towards the fire.

"As far as I could make it, given the rationing."

"*Félicitations*, Tom. You are a genius."

"*Merci*, Lucien. I wanted to ask you if Madeleine had ever shown you the photos of our wedding?"

"No. I expect she felt I'd let her down, siding as I did with our parents. To be honest, Tom, I didn't think she'd made a good choice."

Tom laughed. "Quite right. I didn't deserve her."

He got up and went to a tall cabinet, pulled out a leather photo album and sat down again, the album on his knees. He hesitated. Should he show Lucien? Should he share this happiness with the brother who had, in the end, sided with her parents? But the Cona was erupting, and the aroma of coffee pervaded the room. In a flooding sense of cordiality and friendship he thought 'why not?' He opened the album and handed it to Lucien. "You look while I pour the coffee."

When he sat down again, he noticed Lucien was strangely silent. He looked over and saw, to his dismay, there were tears on Lucien's cheeks.

"I say, old boy, I didn't mean to make you sad."

"I am sad. I weep for you and Madeleine. You were married without a single family member by your side. Not my family, not your family. We deserted Madeleine. We abandoned you. There was no church ceremony, no bridal gown and veil, no father to walk her down the aisle. There should have been a great banquet at the chateau. A mother crying into her handkerchief, a father proud and upright. It is too much."

"But we were happy, Lucien. We were surrounded by friends. See here," Tom pointed out one photo. "There's Emily and Aaron. These two mischievous imps here were my first two Resistance workers. Emil and Michel. Before they died they helped hundreds of people by forging ration cards and IDs. And this girl here, Lucille, another *Resistant*. I believe she is also dead."

"So many died, Tom. Too many."

Lucien closed the photo album and handed it back to Tom who placed it back in the drawer, wishing he'd never opened it. To see Madeleine's face, so full of joy and love, was hard. And to think he had thrown it all away. All that happiness, and contentment, all the dreams of a future together. On what? Hubris? He'd thought he was cleverer than anyone else; that he could fool anyone. He burned with shame. Yes, she definitely deserved better.

The two men settled into soft armchairs, a brandy by their side and each feeling quietly complete. Tom felt dozy and noticed Lucien's eyes were at half-mast too.

"So, how did all this begin for you, Tom? I know you were in France…"

"I was recruited."

Lucien laughed, a bark of amusement. "Into the Army?"

"No."

"*Mon Dieu*. The English saying, 'scraping the bottom of the barrel' comes to mind. My apologies, Tom."

Tom smiled. "I take no offence. There were all sorts called to serve their country and they did well in the SOE."

"SOE?"

"Intelligence. Special Ops. We'd been tasked by Churchill to set Europe ablaze."

"Ah, so not the Army or Navy but the secret service. And did you set Europe ablaze?"

"In our own small way, I suppose we did."

"Go on."

Tom automatically knocked out the non-existent dottle from his pipe. "There were some shady characters recruited, but when faced with the challenge, they did well. There were some in prison who were released to serve in the war. I once met up with a cat burglar who could open safes with a hairpin. He was that good. They recruited him to teach blokes the art of safe cracking. I believe he got some medal at the end of the war for services rendered."

"You say you were recruited. How did it happen?"

"Obviously, I wasn't present at the early meetings, so let me extrapolate and embroider a little. Let's call it narrative non-fiction." He settled back into the softness of the armchair. "It all began sometime in 1940, Brigadier Allan Forester of the newly formed Special Operations Executive had been tasked, as I said, by Winston Churchill to 'set Europe ablaze'. So far, the only thing set ablaze, I should imagine, was the end of his cigar. I learned later there was rivalry between SOE, the SIS or Secret Intelligence Service and Military

Intelligence and it was putting a dampener on any fires they might light in Europe. So, progress was slow.

"In the small office from where so much was going to be achieved, and facing Forester was a portly man in a navy suit. I saw him once but never found out his name. Secrecy and all that, but he popped up every now and again like an insurance salesman," Tom said. "They were already forecasting scenarios, one of which was getting captured Allied troops out of occupied France. The BEF…"

"BEF?"

"British Expeditionary Force, those poor buggers sent in the day after war was declared with a lot of training but hardly any weapons. Cannon fodder."

"That was before Dunkirk," Lucien said mildly.

"Indeed. They fought well and hard, but nothing could stop the *blitzkrieg*. Of the forty-one thousand men missing or wounded in that debacle, many were captured but a lot of them evaded capture and were floating around France. Churchill was determined to get them out. The French could melt into the population or merely go home. But the Brits needed to be hidden, clothed and given new documents. Forester wanted trained forgers to create documents for all those escapees. And that's where I came in."

"Go on with your elaboration, Tom. I'm enjoying the fiction."

"Not fiction, Lucien. I promise. Merely an imagining of the events. Let's see, where were we? Forester asked the pompous and mysterious civilian, 'Do we have anyone we can train and send over?'

"I do have one chappie whom I think would be ideal, sir," the man said.

"Why not bring him here and we'll talk to him. See if he's suitable."

"Bit of a problem, sir."

"Why?"

"A friend suggested him, Freedman from the Victoria & Albert Museum. The chap's in Wandsworth."

"Wandsworth Prison?"

The man nodded. "Only Wandsworth I know."

"Well, can't you get him out? We can't have His Majesty's Prisons holding things up. We've got work to do. What's he in for? I'd draw a line at murder."

"Nothing like that, fortunately, sir. Forgery is his game. Something to do with medieval manuscripts. Which is why I think he'll do. Did a post-grad on medieval art restoration at the Sorbonne in Paris and must have got a taste for it, the fiddling, I mean. He got caught making what looked for all the world like a genuine medieval document and sold it to the V&A. Said his caper was a lark, but the people he sold it to thought differently. Hence the prison sentence. Man's fluent in French. Lived in France for a number of years. Has a French wife."

"Well, if he can forge a medieval document and pull the wool over the eyes of experts at the V & A, then he can forge identity cards. He's our man, just get him out and bring him here. Tomorrow if you can. Who is he, by the way?"

"Chappie by the name of Thomas Blake."

"At least that's how I imagined it going down," Tom said.

"They were quite desperate if you were their only choice."

Tom laughed. "Yes, I expect so. But it was the making of me, Lucien. I went in to prison an undisciplined arrogant boy and came out of it all, prison and the spy agency, a man. A great way to bring a man to his senses."

"Bravo, Tom."

Chapter 5

Wandsworth had been a lesson in and of itself. Thomas Edward Blake was a total outsider in a place where most of the men were illiterate, brutish and brutalised and, for the most part, unrepentant. Or innocent, to their way of thinking. Someone else was always to blame. In the first few days he'd been on his own in a grey cement cell, staring at the walls. On the fourth day he was placed in a two-man cell with a man who boasted about how he had killed his wife.

"Slit her froat, dinn I, frum side ta side. Her neck openin' like a second mouf. No one cheats on me, buster, an' gets away wiv it."

A warning? Tom wondered how he was going to survive, especially when it came time to shower.

After a few dreadful months made worse by no communication from Madeleine, salvation came when the Head Warden ordered him to present himself at the office. He could read and write; he would therefore be in charge of the library. He found solace in the small room with its collection of ragged books and bowed shelves. Every few months another carton of donated books arrived, and he had the pleasure of placing them in the right order next to their compatriots. Louis L'Amour's cowboy stories were among the favourites with the inmates. Conan Doyle and other crime novels were also popular; the prisoners perhaps thinking to sharpen their skills.

After a year in the so-called library, Tom had decided it needed a spruce-up. He requested paint and a paint brush and spent one whole day painting the walls and strengthening the shelves. The Head Warden took a kindly interest and found a couple of old film posters which Tom glued to the one wall. He commandeered two chairs and a small table from the chapel and, suddenly the library looked like a library.

It was when he'd cleaned out the shelves to repack the books he found the slim volume of poems, a rather posh-looking book with a cover in black and gold. It was a love poem translated from eleventh century Sanskrit and he couldn't imagine how the hell it ever got into a prison library. He opened it at random, and as he read a few lines, he slid to the floor and for the first time since the police knocked on the door of their flat, he began to weep.

Even now
I seem to see my prison walls come close
Built up of darkness, and against that darkness
A girl, no taller than my breast...

It came to him in those darkest of hours, that because of his stupid arrogance, he had lost everything.

The end came one grey morning when he was in the dining hall with his breakfast on a tray in front of him. He usually managed to shut out the noise thundering around but, on that day, he was feeling particularly wretched. It was Madeleine's birthday. There was the usual grey glue passing for porridge, the usual cold, tired toast with a smear of jam and a cup of brown water called coffee. He longed for the real deal; porridge made by his mother with loads of cream slathered on the top and a dab of butter slowly melting over it like the ice cap of a mountain in spring. Toast with marmalade so thick you had to look to find the bread. And coffee. He'd got a taste of real coffee in France and longed again for its rich flavour and aroma. A *demitasse* of heaven.

He hadn't seen anything remotely resembling civilised life for more than two years. A very long two years with another six to go. Each day he wondered why he'd been such a fool. He dug the spoon into the porridge and the spoon stayed upright. He pushed the tray away and wondered briefly what dying of starvation would be like.

His miserable thoughts were broken by a guard looming over him. "Blake, go to your cell and collect your stuff."

He'd learned not to ask questions. What the guards said, you jumped to it promptly or you had a short jab with a truncheon in the kidneys. So, he left his uneaten breakfast and went to collect his things. Another cell, another prison. Well, they all looked the same. The guards all looked the same. All prisons were unofficially run by the same vicious uber-convicts who grabbed whomever they wanted for a little bareback in the shower. His size had prevented him from becoming someone's girlfriend but who knew what lunatic gorilla he'd have to face in the new place.

He packed quickly, stuffing clothes and toiletries into the duffel bag thrown to him by the guard.

Tom stopped packing when he found the book of poems. Outside, he would have laughed and shoved the little book onto a bookshelf. But in here, between grey walls, barred windows and illiterate yelling thugs, he lived again with Madeleine through the words of a Middle eastern eleven-century poet.

Even now
I remember that you made answer very softly,
We being one soul,

He knew the whole damned thing, all fifty stanzas, almost by heart. Each word a song to Madeleine. Each an excoriating damnation of his foolishness. He shoved the book under his toiletries and zipped up the duffel bag.

One guard took his bag while another slipped handcuffs on his wrists. At the prison gate the Head Warden stood waiting. A last farewell perhaps. He'd been a fair man, tired from the constant flow of evil men who never seemed to learn. Perhaps he thought Tom Blake would be the exception. And he was right. He led them out beyond the prison walls. There was no prison van. Instead, a sleek black Pontiac limousine with the rear door held open by a uniformed chauffeur.

Even the Head Warden was shocked. "What the…?"

"Service for Mr Blake, sir," the chauffeur said, his face blank.

"Seems like we're going somewhere in style, Blake," the guard on the other end of his handcuffs grunted his surprise. "Who do you know?"

Tom was as much at a loss as the guard. They climbed in and the limousine slipped silently through London's morning traffic. Almost brought to tears at the sight of cars and people walking by Tom, stretched out his legs as far as he could and stared around drinking in the scenes as they went past.

The vehicle stopped at a small hotel, St Ermin's in Caxton Street. They slid out of the limousine, a convicted forger and a prison guard, who was sensitive enough to cover the handcuffs with his coat. They walked up an ornate central staircase and to Room 106, the guard so close Tom could hear his breathing. On the bed was a suit, shirt and tie. Polished shoes on the floor by the bed. His own. What the hell was going on? And where the hell had they got his clothes from? As far as he knew, everything had been packed up and put it into storage at his mother's house in Kent.

While he changed, the guard took out an envelope and read it. He was instructed to take Prisoner #74378 to an address in London. Tom changed quickly, found the suit hanging a little. He'd lost weight. He reluctantly accepted the handcuffs once again and was hurried out of the room and down the stairs. The limousine was still waiting at the door.

Weirder and weirder.

A short distance past the grey sand-bagged buildings, the limousine stopped again. The chauffeur got out, opened the rear door and they shuffled out and into an anonymous-looking building in Baker Street.

"Do you know the hell what's going on?" Tom asked.

"Not a clue, mate, but it looks cushy, so enjoy it while you can."

A shuddering elevator with metallic lacy side walls took them to an austere office. The guard unlocked the handcuffs and told Tom to wait. Then he left the room. A few minutes later a tall man in uniform bustled in and sat down without looking at Tom.

"My name is Forester," the man finally said looking down at a file. "And you are Blake. Thomas Edward Blake. Graduate of Bath University and the Sorbonne in Paris. Aged twenty-seven. Married to Madeleine Aubert. You were convicted of a crime and are presently serving an eight-year sentence."

"Yes, sir." Tom nodded, not yet sure why he was there or in fact where he was. The sight of Big Ben through the window assured him he was still in London and that was about all.

"You don't look like a criminal," the man said.

"What does a criminal look like?"

"You were found guilty."

"Yes, sir."

"Well, sit down, man, sit down. I don't like people looming over me."

Tom sat and waited while the man read from a file. Tom was pretty certain the man had read his file before, probably more than once. This was theatre.

"Born 1912, father, Hector a parish vicar, mother is Evelyne, housewife."

"Yes, sir."

"You're a classical historian specialising in repairing ancient manuscripts." The man looked up. "And your French is fluent."

"Yes, sir."

"Your degree, a masters, I see. What exactly did it qualify you to do?"

"Nothing much, sir. Forging old manuscripts, I suppose."

"Hmm, I see," Forester said dryly. "Didn't get you far, did it?"

"No, sir."

"So, from the time you graduated cum laude or whatever they do at the Sorbonne, what did you do?"

"I swanned about France mainly. Digging things up with my girlfriend, Madeleine Aubert and a team of other amateurs. She's into the Cathars and Knights Templar, that sort of thing, so we dug around in Cathar country in southern France."

"You were looking for the Holy Grail?"

"Yes, I suppose so. Sounds rather adolescent now but at the time we believed in the legends. Didn't find anything, of course. Then we married and came to London. I got a job in a bank. Bloody boring."

"I'm curious, Blake. What exactly were you looking for out there in Cathar country?"

"As I said, the Holy Grail."

"Ah, come now, young man."

"My wife and I are Medievalists, sir. There is definitely something down there. We've seen statements made by people who should know. A lot of treasure is reputed to be hidden in the south of France near Rennesle-Chateau. We dug around in some sites, all rather superficially I'm afraid. But we were students and having fun more than anything else. There was a rumour going round at the time that Hitler wanted to find stuff to enhance his stature. Like the Grail. Or the Ark of the Covenant. A weird little chappie called Otto Rahn was down there more or less when we were. Apparently, he was Himmler's blue-eyed boy, in more ways than one. It would have been quite nice to find something significant and stop him in his tracks. At least we made it our motive, a sort of one-for-all type of gesture. Anyway, if we'd found anything, even a medieval coin, Maddie would have been ecstatic."

Forester nodded. "I should imagine so." He looked down at my file. "Madeleine Claudine Aubert? Your wife?"

"Yes."

"How is she, by the way?"

Tom didn't know so he kept silent.

"Do you know where she is?"

"No, sir. She left me when I was convicted. I presume she went back to France, but I don't know."

"She's never written to you, or visited?"

"No, sir."

"Do you regret what you did?"

"More than you'll ever know."

"You any good at forgery?"

"Good enough to fool the Medievalists at the Victoria and Albert."

"How did it unfold? Who sussed you out?"

"There was never any thought of cashing in on it, I assure you. From the start it was a caper. In the basement of the university, I'd found an old manuscript with several blank pages at the back. It was quite often the case; they'd leave several blank pages at the back. Anyway, at the time I hadn't thought anything of it but I cut one page out with a scalpel and then went to work. I thought it quite splendid at the time, working with all those wonderful colours, red, gold, hunter's green. So busy thinking how brilliant I was, I let the whole thing get away from me. Someone offered a bet that I could fool the experts. I went to the V&A and offered it. Trouble was, they wanted provenance which, of course, I couldn't give them. They grew suspicious and before I could tell them it was a fake and I had won a bet I could fool them, they had me arrested. I have no excuse, sir. I was an idiot."

"So, you were good enough to fool the experts."

"Yes." Tom still felt a frisson of satisfaction. He was good at something, even if it was only at forgery.

"How much?"

"Sir?"

"How much did you win? Your bet?"

"Twenty pounds, sir. Didn't even cover my lawyer's fees."

"I should think not. And in the end, you paid a high price." Forester opened a drawer and pulled out a French identity card. He threw it over the table and Tom caught it. "Could you forge this?"

Tom turned it over, examined the back, checked the thickness of the card, looked at the edges, the font, the weight of the paper, and set it down on the table.

"Yes, easily. Given the right paper and inks. The stamps would be quite simple to make. Heck, you could carve a potato and make a stamp like this."

"We're going to need documents for agents we might send in. Refugees coming into France from the Low Countries. Jews coming from east Europe. Even possibly Allied soldiers escaping POW camps. At the moment, we can't help them. It's worrying the Old Man."

"Churchill, sir?"

"Any other Old Man we should be talking about?"

"What can I do to help?"

"I want you to go to Paris and set up a forgery section to make the documents we need. We don't have anyone now, so you'll have to recruit your own team. It won't be a picnic, Blake. The German Army may not be in Paris now, but we are at war, and we have it on good authority their influence is already being felt. Which means, if arrested, you could be subjected to some very bad things to get information out of you."

"I can imagine."

"No, you can't, believe me."

"I don't think…"

"You don't want to go?"

"It's not…"

"Would you prefer to go back to prison?"

"Is that the alternative?"

"I rather imagine so." Forester stood up. "Decision time, young man. I can't promise you a safe ride. We'll train you up, of course. Forgery you're good at, but you need to know other things like how to kill.

Silently and with your bare hands. How to blow up a bridge or derail a train. How to send coded messages. That sort of thing. Then we'll drop you into France by parachute or send you by submarine and then fishing boat to some beach or the other. You will create something out of nothing. The Germans will arrive in France, sooner rather than later. There's a good chance once they're there, you could be arrested, then you'll be tortured and probably shot. You have five minutes to decide. Anything further and you'll have to sign a secrecy form or go back and serve your sentence."

"Sounds like fun. I'll sign. With one proviso."

Forester looked grim. "We don't do deals, Blake."

"I want a pardon."

Forester was silent. "And I'll want some evidence you'll do as you're instructed at all times and do it well enough to fool the Jerries. Then we'll talk again."

"Is it the best you can do? How about an IOU?"

Forester laughed. "You're a persistent bugger, Blake. I'll give you that. I like that, someone who doesn't give up. I'm dropping you in a bucketload of you-know-what and you want the crown jewels before your feet have touched the bottom."

"Yes, sir."

"Very well, I'll get the ball rolling. The day you come back from France, having set up a sound organisation and got it going, you'll be a free man."

As he was leaving Brigadier Forester spoke again. "By the way, Blake, did you really?"

"Did I what, sir?"

"Did you really fool that old fartbag Freeman at the V & A?"

"Well, yes, sir. I did."

"I think you'll fit in nicely into the Ministry of Ungentlemanly Warfare."

"Is that what I've signed up for, sir?"

"It isn't for the bloody 1940 Tiddly-Winks championship."

Chapter 6

Lucien laughed. "So, that is the story. I wondered at the time. All I knew was Madeleine came storming back to France with her mouth tight like a spinster's purse. You were a fool, Tom. To throw it all away."

"I know, and on a silly bet." Tom poured another dram of whisky into their glasses. "Something I'll regret to my dying day."

"Continue, Tom. As they say, I'm all ears."

"After the meeting, I lay there on a very comfortable bed in St. Ermin's Hotel, watching my cigarette smoke spiralling up to the ceiling. Life had taken a surprising turn. That very morning I'd been shovelling gluey porridge down my throat in one of His Majesty's Prisons, or trying to, and by evening I was lying on a luxury bed in a London hotel. A free man. Well, almost. All I had to do now was go to France and find Maddie. No problem. I would persuade her to come back with me. And I'd already convinced myself she would. I was a changed man. Two years in the nick had wiped away my youthful irresponsibility and taught me a few hard lessons. I had grown up and, as Maddie would probably say, about time."

"And what about the job Churchill was expecting from you?"

"Piece of cake, old man. At least so I thought at the time. A bit of danger, a bit of derring-do, get the youthful enthusiasms out of my system and become the man Maddie wanted me to be. I could pay back what I owed to society. Perhaps pay forward as well. But most of all I wanted to find Maddie and make it right with her."

*****

Back in his room at the unobtrusive little hotel, Tom looked out the window, wondering what the heck the interview had been all about. He'd signed up for something very big and very important, but what the hell it was, he still had no idea. Ungentlemanly Warfare? What in God's name was that?

He was still trying to absorb the events when someone knocked on the door. A waiter stood there smiling. "Mr Blake? Room service."

Room Service? If that didn't take the bally cake, he thought, then I'm an Irishman.

In front of him a large trolley held several dishes under silver hoods each covering something steaming and fragrant. He took some small change from the stash given to him by Forester and handed it to the waiter, who counted it, smirked and sauntered off. He'd obviously over-tipped him, but what the heck. Not his money. He was out of prison and on another adventure.

Tom lifted the covers. Soup, a plate of sliced beef and roast potatoes and another smaller one revealed a chocolate dessert. There was a glass of what tasted like a very good red wine.

*****

"A remarkable meal for wartime Britain," Lucien said.

"More like the final meal before execution, my friend. To continue, the last thing Brigadier Forester had said was, 'You stay in the hotel, Blake. We'll send for you in two days' time. You put a foot out of your room, and I'll have you arrested as an escaped prisoner. I promise you, if you go AWOL, you'll never see the light of day again.'"

"A threat like that would keep you grounded," Lucien said.

"Indeed, it did. I later heard men got shot for less. So, there I was, lying in the darkness. By then the lights of London had been turned off, in case of German bombers. It was pretty dark in the streets, just vague shadows walking by with their gas masks over their shoulders. A bicycle or two with shaded lamps. In the background the search lights criss-crossing the sky. But I was in a comfy room with a full stomach and a head nodding off after a glass of wine and suddenly there's this soft knock on the door.

"Mr Blake, sir?" A young woman in a Wren uniform stood outside my door, looking very serious. "You're needed upstairs. Please come with me."

I reached for my jacket. "Upstairs? What the heck is there upstairs?"

"I can't say, sir."

"Can't or won't?"

The woman said nothing, just smiled and started up the stairs to the floor above. She led me to an office, asked me to wait and closed the door. I sat down wondering what the hell was going on.

When the door finally opened, the man who walked in didn't look at all military. He was dressed in an awful olive green tweed suit, with a slight paunch showing under his waistcoat. A small head from which his hair had begun the slow retreat of late-middle age. He appeared pompous, rather too self-assured. I wondered what I could do to take this man down. Some snide comment. Then stopped. This wasn't a game. This was it, real life.

"Names are unnecessary," the man said, gesturing me to sit on the other side of the desk. "I'm here to ask a few rather intrusive questions. Sorry about this but we need to know if you're the right material for the job."

"I jolly well need to be if I don't want to go back…" I stopped, rather hoping he didn't know.

"To prison? Quite. Shall we start?"

I soon realised the large dinner and the glass of wine was doing as intended, making me a little less on guard. The questionnaire was lengthy and detailed. And it was personal. Even asked if I'd kissed or been kissed by a man. I answered, 'yes, my father'. And had I any bad sexual experiences in prison. Or good. I think he was trying to find out if I was a pansy. I told him any man who'd laid a finger on me would have regretted it. Heck, I'm a married man."

"So was Oscar Wilde," Lucien said.

"True. Anyway, I answered all the questions as best I could. The one that stumped me was, 'Would you kill your mother if ordered to do so?' I wrote, 'Yes.' I wouldn't, of course. Mum was rather a jolly old bird who knitted socks for soldiers and wrote some awful rhyming poetry. I had no reason to kill her. In fact, I was rather fond of the old duck, she was the only one who visited me in Wandsworth. What a question!" Tom smiled. "Still don't know if it was the right answer.

"When I handed back the questionnaire, the gentleman, who still hadn't given a name, said, 'Very well, you may go.'

"I allowed myself to be guided down the stairs and to my room by the same silent woman. I thought it was all rather strange. It got stranger when she asked me quite bluntly if I would like her to stay the night. I politely thanked her but said I'd rather not."

"A trick?" Lucien asked.

"I thought so at the time. Besides, there's always Madeleine."

In the morning, I was told to pack my bag, given a train ticket and taken to the station. It appeared I was on my way to a training camp in Scotland.

Chapter 7

Christmas lunch was over, their wine glasses added to the pile of dishes. Tom stood at the sink washing with Lucien by his side, drying the cutlery with a dish towel. Afterwards they again sat silently by the fire while coffee slowly filtered through the Cona, each with a glass of an ancient liquor Tom found in the back of a cupboard. It was sweet, almost sugary but still pleasant. He threw another log onto the fire and watched the embers dance.

Outside the snow hadn't let up. It was still falling, quiet as confetti. His Austin almost nowhere to be seen. Just a lump beside the garden gate. Tom's mind flashed to a night when Maddie slept by his side, her hip a silver mound lit by moonlight, her blonde hair tumbling over her face. He'd run his hand down her body, amazed she had consented to be his wife. She turned as if wakened by his touch. 'You're not allowed to watch me when I sleep,' she said. 'Why not?' 'You'll learn secrets I'm not ready to share.'

What secrets, he now wondered.

Even now
I see her fair face blonde like gold
Rich with small lights, and tinted shadows surprised
Over and over all of her...

"I see you have a gift for Madeleine," Lucien said, pointing to the little tree. "You obviously believe she will return."

"Yes." A forlorn hope, all that was keeping him from walking into the sea with a pocketful of pebbles.

"I should leave tomorrow, Tom, if the weather lets up. Now, this is the issue. I want you to come back to France with me. With the two of us working together, I believe we can find both your wife and your daughter."

"Steady on, old chap. You said there was more to tell me. Why not begin at the beginning before we go haring off. When was the last time you saw her?"

"I saw her in September 1940. Things were getting hard in Paris. The Germans were there. Emily and Aaron were still in the *appartement* with her. She wanted to work to make money to feed her friends. It was *les vendanges*, the grape harvest. She was going to pick grapes, but I could see she was pregnant, and I wouldn't allow her to work in the fields. Instead, she kept records and supervised. Starting to show her pregnancy, slim with this tiny protrusion that would become her child, and beautiful with it, Tom. Radiant. More beautiful than I'd ever seen her."

"How did your parents react?"

"Badly. A child by a disgraced 'rosbif'. Eventually, I hid her in one of the workers' cottages. She was content just to be back among the vines. She said it was a healing process for her. By that time the Germans had been in Paris for three months and things were getting nasty, especially for the Jews. She said Emily and Aaron had wanted to leave before the Germans arrived but had left it too late and they were stuck."

65

Tom got up to pour the coffee. "I remember when I was there in the April they were planning to go to Spain."

"Not easy, even then. A trip over the Pyrenees is never easy, even in summer."

"I know, I did it once or twice." Memory flooded over him.

The lower reaches of the Pyrenees were manageable. The further up they went the harder it was. Snow, hidden rocks and fissures. The first time he'd undertaken the journey with an experienced Basque *passeur* or guide, sometime in the second or third day, they'd lost their first refugee, an old Jewish man with a large suitcase to which he clung as if his whole life was inside. And perhaps it was. As he lay in the snow, clutching the suitcase, each person stepped over him and walked on. He looked up with glassy surrendering eyes. And they had left him. He wandered now how long it had taken the old man to die.

It had been a difficult journey. Each escapee walked in the footprints of the man or woman before them, sometimes clinging to each other's coats as they traversed a narrow ledge. Tom's memory was only of those footprints, on and on through the white blistering cold. One step, then another and another.

It came back to him at night, walking over the old man and leaving him. And woke him up sweating.

"And Madeleine went back to Paris after visiting your vineyard and having been rebuffed by her parents. And then had a baby? I'm trying to imagine her thought-process. Was she angry at the rejection, sad? Did she want to come home to England?"

Lucien nodded. "Once she found out she was pregnant, she wanted to leave France, to go back to London, but it became impossible. Travel issues, you understand. The ferries had long been stopped. The only way was through Spain, and you know what that meant. All sorts of permits and identification."

"I know, my friends were forging them. I also managed to get her some extra ration cards that weekend I was there. They were our first batch and they were good."

"Ah, yes, of course," Lucien said. "I'd forgotten. I suspect she decided, if she couldn't get to London, the next best thing was to work at whatever she could do. The sooner victory over the Germans, the sooner she could return to London. There were very few who worked against the Germans in those early days. Most either stood back or collaborated. The only way to live in a tyranny is you either stand back or stand up. Naturally, Madeleine stood up."

"But with a child?"

Lucien shrugged. "The last time I saw her, she told me Emily and Aaron were keeping a low profile after both had lost their jobs. I suspect the plan was for Madeleine to work and Emily to babysit. You saw them in the apartment. What did you think at the time?"

"They were really desperate. They couldn't work and I wondered how they were managing to survive. I can understand why Madeleine found it difficult to leave Paris. It would have been a betrayal of her friends. I got the feeling she would have gone with me back to London except for the Goldbergs. I'm sure I could have got her out."

And there it was, the source of the pain.

That weekend, he'd asked her to go home with him. And she'd refused.

Said she had obligations. At the time he'd thought she meant her family, but it was Emily and Aaron to whom she showed allegiance.

"Where was she working?" Tom asked.

"You remember Phillipe Moreau? He worked at the Louvre, and he employed Madeleine when they were packing up in 1939. She did some night shift work, recording what was leaving the museum and where it was going. Most of the treasures went to the Loire valley, to the chateaux where they were safe from bombing. In the end it wasn't bombing they were safe from, but Germans looting every artwork they could lay their greedy, dirty little hands on. Now, I hear people are bringing the treasures back to Paris. The Louvre is buzzing again and will soon open to visitors. Soon we'll be able to go and see our treasures in their full glory, back where they were meant to be. It's an exciting time, Tom."

Tom felt a pang of jealousy. "Phillipe always had a thing for Madeleine."

"There was only one man in her life, Tom. You know that."

Tom felt embarrassed. Lucien could read him well.

"So, what is it to be? Will you come back with me?"

Tom felt himself shrinking into the big armchair. He didn't want to go back to France, to see the streets where he'd walked with Madeleine, the cafes and bistros where they'd eaten, the parks where they'd lain on the sweet grass and dreamed of a future together. He didn't want to feel the agony of wondering where she was, whether she was dead or alive. He had closed off the part of his heart where she lived. It was safer so.

And there was that other France he could not face. The dirty inns where he sat drinking with the local *maquis,* trying to persuade a decrepit bunch of locals that banding together under a British SOE agent who could guarantee armaments, would have better results than a bunch of ill-armed, ill-prepared yokels. Not always successful. Those who had worked with him had suffered. Many had died. How many were left? He couldn't say.

But there was always Madeleine. She was a courageous woman, one who would not have stood aside when the Germans invaded. Although she'd not said anything to him on the weekend they spent together, he was sure she would have been involved.

According to the Foreign Office she had been taken by the Germans. Had they executed her? Had she been tortured? He couldn't bear to face those questions.

"Was she in the Resistance?" he asked, afraid of the answer.

"You know Madeleine."

"That would be why she was taken by the Gestapo."

"It's something we must face. She could be dead."

"We shouldn't underestimate her," Tom said quickly. "We always underestimate our women, their courage, their intelligence, their ability to survive. Better than most men, I found."

"Yes, we saw it, didn't we? The women were far braver than us, could withstand torture while many men just crumbled. As for Madeleine," Lucien shrugged. "She could very well have survived. I'm optimistic. I believe we'll find her."

Tom felt pressure building up behind his eyes. A bomb ready to explode. A decision to be made. And soon.

A flash of memory.

The past looming up.

A girl, the same age as Madeleine, lying on the ground. Half her head... German tanks leaving. The girl had got in the way.

Tom dragged himself back. Lucien was speaking again. "And the child, of course. They may be together somewhere. I'm in touch with the Red Cross. They are busy tracing displaced persons. Madeleine and the child may very well be together in a small village somewhere, waiting it out. The Red Cross are also recording survivors from the camps, making sure they get home or go to hospital. Survivors are coming back in a trickle, those poor souls, so few, you cannot believe. So, it's a work in progress. If she was in a concentration camp and if she survived, they'll let me know."

"So, if she was arrested by the Gestapo, we could assume the child would have been taken too."

Lucien stirred uneasily. "French children didn't survive, Tom. They were immediately exterminated. We have stories about them being put naked into cattle trucks on trains. There was quicklime on the floors. Most of the children were dead when they arrived at the crematoria."

Tom shrunk back in his chair. "You think my child was one of them?"

Lucien shrugged. Shook his head.

"How many were taken to the camps?"

"More than eleven thousand children."

"How many came back?"

"None."

Tom leant back in his chair, the weight of a terrible sorrow pushing at him. "Then the child is dead."

Lucien bent forward his hands near the fire. "You mustn't think like that, Tom. There's every possibility she survived. There are any number of orphanages where Sophie could be. Please, close your cottage and come back with me."

"Yes. Yes, of course." Tom got up slowly, his limbs feeling like those of a frail old man. Of course, he must find this child. She was all that was left, the culmination of their love. If the child was still alive and he could rescue her, he would have at least part of Madeleine back.

He would be doing it for Maddie too.

"I'll ask my neighbours to keep an eye on things," Tom said. "We'll have breakfast and …"

Tom's thoughts trailed off. He was going back to a war-ravaged France. It would be a different sort of damage. England had been blasted from the air by the Luftwaffe whereas France had been the site of battles. German troops had trampled all over its soil, destroyed its villages and fields, put people into churches and set the churches on fire. What was left? Would he be able to

71

contact old friends, colleagues, fellow conspirators in the Resistance who may know something? Where would they begin to look for Madeleine or the child?

Lucien stood up smiling, his exhaustion a thing of the past.

"We'll find them, Tom," he said stretching out his hand to Tom. "Together, we'll find them, I have no doubt."

Chapter 8

Tom was secretly pleased. Snow had fallen heavily on the night of Christmas and for days afterwards. It meant he could put off for a few more hours at least, the idea of returning to Paris where he and Madeleine had been so happy.

Of course, he had to go back. It was the right thing to do. This little child, this Sophie, was the sum total of their love and she had been lost for three years. He tried to imagine what a child might experience in those dreadful days. Lost and alone.

Lucien was impatient to get away, moping and grumbling and striding across the little living room, caged by the weather and his anxiety to be away and doing something.

The third morning and the snow was still falling. Tom got out a shovel and cleared a path to the woodshed, his boots squeaking through the crusty snow. Soon his wellingtons were filled with cold wet sludge. Once the fire was going, he made a simple meal, a macaroni cheese dish his mother used to make which Lucien poked and looked at questioningly.

"Sorry, *mon ami*," Tom said. "We're getting short on rations. We'll have to be careful until I can get to my neighbours. You better eat it, there's little else."

"We go tomorrow, no matter what," Lucien said.

"We'll see what the weather does."

Lucien had begun to mutter, something about having to eat glue, slamming his fist into his cupped hand. As he shovelled the food into his mouth, he stared out of the window where snow had piled up along the low wall between the garden and the road. Beyond the wall, Tom's little Austin was completely hidden in a mantle of white.

"Alright, I confess," Lucien said as he laid down his knife and fork. "It wasn't as awful as it looked. Your English food is dull when compared to French *cuisine*. My soul cries for *coq au vin, boeuf bourguignon, quiche Lorraine*. And perhaps a good French onion soup topped with cheese and toasted *baguette* slices." Lucien kissed his fingers in remembrance.

There was enough 'dull' English food for a few days. Tom began to worry. If the snow continued for much longer, he would have to find a way to Mason's farm for eggs and milk and what vegetables they could spare. It was not a comfortable thought, wading through a waist-deep blanket of icy blinding white.

Finally, on New Year's Eve the snow let up and they decided to leave the following morning. With a small suitcase by his side, Tom gave one last look at the living room with its fading little Christmas tree. 'You'll have to wait 'til I get back,' he said to it. 'I won't be long.'

He stepped out of the cottage, locked the door and walked to the Austin. They had dug out the snow from her sides the day before and released her from winter's icy grip. They were now ready to go.

"She will get us to Dover?" Lucien looked doubtful.

"She's British-made, of course she will."

Lucien wedged himself into the passenger seat. "I am not reassured, Tom."

"A little English rust, Lucien. Don't be afraid. We proved ourselves, didn't we? Rust and all."

Lucien gave a small snort. Tom ignored him, concentrating instead on the road.

The trip to Dover was dismal, the Austin battling valiantly along roads barely visible under their snowy covering. Petrol was still rationed and, although Tom had sufficient ration tickets, it was not always possible to buy fuel when needed. As it was, they limped into Dover with the gauge hovering on empty. He parked the car in the back yard of a friend's home with a note stuck through the letterbox, explaining the situation. He'd pushed the keys through the letterbox as well, thereby sealing off any escape route he may have thought of.

A half-empty ramshackle bus puffing oily smoke took them to the Harbour where they waited for the ferry in a warm tea shop where condensation ran down the windows in streams. Even hot tea and toast did little to cheer Tom up.

This was all a terrible mistake. What did he think he would find? Even if he found proof Madeleine was dead, would it make his life any easier? And what of this child? What was the point, this digging into the past? All it would do was reignite emotions he'd rather stay buried. Tom finally admitted to himself, he didn't want to feel anything ever again.

He tried to explain to Lucien this fear of finding out the truth.

"Poor little girl," Lucien murmured.

"What do you mean?"

"Sophie has a father who is afraid to love her."

"You don't even know if she's alive," said Tom. He'd rather been hoping for some sympathy from Lucien and was aggrieved none was forthcoming.

The ferry dipped and dived its way to France as if reluctant to make the icy journey. Tom began to feel seasick and found an isolated nook where he could lie down and feel sorry for himself.

They arrived with a loud thump at the dockside and soft falling sleet. The damage to Calais harbour was depressing. British army trucks revved in the still air creating curls of exhaust fumes. Workers drifted in and out of the debris left behind by the Germans, carrying bits of wood, scaffolding, lengths of pipe. Their wandering seemed directionless, as if they were merely transferring the same bit of broken masonry from here to there and back again. Even the fishing boats had been damaged. Surely, Calais would never return to the famous port of the past?

"We'll build it again," Lucien said seeing Tom's dismay. "Only a matter of time. Come along. If we hurry, we'll just catch the train to Paris." Lucien took Tom's arm and dragged him half-running to the railway station where several awaiting passengers stood on the platform, against a background of twisted iron beams and burnt wooden walls.

"This platform has only recently been repaired." He waved his arm around. "We've had to fix the railway lines as well. Top priority. You can't have an economy without good transport. Good roads and railways, very important."

"This your work, the damage?"

Lucien shook his head. "No. I was too busy trying to keep heart, mind and soul together. In other words, the vineyard. I heard of men who blew up trains, but usually inside a tunnel with a delayed fuse where damage would be extreme. The retreating Germans did the rest, I'm afraid. I think some sixty percent of the buildings ruined, all the work of *les Boches*. Very much like Dover. A long, long recovery, *mon ami*. Come along, this one takes us via Abbeville."

"I heard Hitler had ordered the total destruction of Paris. Was it badly damaged?"

They clambered onto the train and found a quiet carriage. "Paris is not physically damaged," Lucien said. "We have the German commander of Paris to thank for that. He disobeyed Hitler's orders to level Paris to the ground. The first time in his life, Dietrich von Choltitz acted according to his own conscience. Initially, Hitler was going to use Paris as his headquarters, so damage was kept to a minimum. Later it was designated a holiday resort for his tired soldiers. Oh, the poor darlings!" Lucien put his hand to his brow, mocking the 20s starlets. "It worked for a while. Besides, French people have too much respect for their heritage, so there was no sabotage. But I think many people are still trying to come to terms with what happened. What they did or didn't do."

The train began to jerk away from the station. "Most cities were unharmed. Towns and villages were ruined when Germans soldiers took out their frustrations

77

at being defeated," Lucien said. "It is not only the various locations around France damaged or destroyed, but also our inner landscape. Our souls." Lucien gently touched his chest. "We collaborated, Tom. Vichy collaborated. We were in a marriage of convenience with the Germans. We must live with the knowledge, we collaborated."

"It wasn't only France. There were other countries, Lucien."

"No comfort. A stain on our national character I personally can't forget."

"De Gaulle..."

"De Gaulle?" Lucien spat out the name. "That man. He hated the English but was perfectly happy to be their guest while the war was on. He made a big fuss when he arrived in Paris in 1945, telling the French they had won the war on their own. We didn't. It was a lie to make people feel better about themselves; to forget they allowed the Germans to walk all over them."

Tom thought it wiser to remain silent. Lucien could criticise his own but, as a foreigner, Tom dared not, although he had his own ideas about who won the war. And how it was done. We did it, he thought proudly. Us blimmin' Brits, the grocers, the loud boys, the schoolteachers, the ordinary blokes in the pubs. We all put on the uniform and marched out. We won the bloody war. We beat the flamin' Jerry. May they rot in hell.

The train chugged slowly on as if reluctant to arrive at a city whose heart had been torn out. A long journey, a tiring one. Tom fell asleep, his head against the window. They had a meal on an anonymous station, some poor wretch of a women selling food. Cheap, hot, restoring. They paid more than the price asked. The smile lighting up her tired eyes was their reward.

Another railway station, this time in the heart of Paris. Gare de Lyon, where both men jumped down onto the platform.

Paris looked shabby, down-at-heel. The people walking past, clomping by in worn shoes or wooden clogs, kept their heads down, their gaze inward.

"This is where we part company, Tom. I to Lyon and then to the vineyard and you to the *appartement*." Lucien put out a gloved hand.

Tom was surprised. He'd assumed he and Lucien were going to tackle the apartment together. It was, after all, Lucien's idea.

"Don't look so shocked, Tom. You don't need a babysitter. You can take the Metro from here. It'll take you almost to the street. Some of the stations were closed off during the war, but this one is still open. As for me, I need to go back to the farm. I have some issues to sort out. You go to the *appartement* and settle in." He pulled out a key ring from his coat pocket and disentangled one large key. "Stay there until I come. About a fortnight. If you think of anyone who might know something, go and see them. Your forgery people, for example. Anyone who was in the Resistance. Go to the Louvre and speak to Phillipe. Yes, I can see by your face he's the last one you would want to visit, but Madeleine worked at the museum, so he must know something. Or there may be women she made friends with. When I get back, we can combine our energies. Double the power, my friend. *Adieu*."

Tom watched as the train carrying Lucien pulled away. He stood on the station until it was a small smoking shadow on the tracks. He felt exhausted from the journey, the onrushing scenery, the desperation on people's thin faces and the monumental task ahead. It would be a relief to get to the apartment, sink into a bed and sleep.

He would avoid the Metro. The thought of being closed in underground raised horrific memories. Instead, he looked for a taxi. But there were no taxis, he was cheerily assured by a street sweeper. But a bus would be by soon. Not many of those either, the man said, but it's your lucky day. Tom made it the sweeper's lucky day too with a full packet of Lucien's Gitanes.

When the bus came Tom settled as far away from the other passengers as possible. In England, he'd become a recluse, too much alone, too much in his own company which he far preferred to that of humankind. A bad move really. He'd have to emerge and engage sometime. But not on a bus full of dodgy-smelling Parisians.

The bus's interior stank of cigarette smoke, the seats were torn and patched. Tom sat with his suitcase on his knees, hanging onto the seat in front as the driver doggedly wove his way through what little traffic there was. Tom remembered the general street cacophony added by the joyful hooting of bus drivers. He was in Paris. Again.

As they chugged along the narrow streets between shabby shuttered houses, Tom roused himself. He'd been in a fugue state since leaving Kent, not wanting to think about the enormous task ahead. Instead, he thought about the future of France, of Lucien and what the French people faced with rebuilding a shattered nation. He wondered what lay ahead for himself. He had been so focussed on being one of the 'Baker Street Irregulars', as the agents were called, that a future was too far ahead to be thought of. Many of the men and women he worked with had no future. He thought of the forty-one women sent over by Vera Atkins of the SOE. Only twenty-five came home. Some had died in Hitler's gas chambers. Few of the men sent over to Europe lived to return. He was one of the lucky ones. No wonder they had all learned to live in the present with no past and no future. Only the present, however awful that was.

On the train he'd raised the subject with Lucien.

"What are you plans for the future, Lucien?"

"You mean after we find Madeleine and Sophie? I must decide," he said. "Do I want to go back to architecture, or do I want to be a *vigneron?* Did you know Madeleine had given some serious thought to taking over the farm, training to become a *vigneron.* Learning about the grapes."

"I didn't know."

"She spoke to me about the possibility. Our father would have been shocked had she broached the subject with him before the war. It would never have occurred to him. Not too many women *vignerons* around, you see. Although the few I know are talented, winemaking is traditionally a man's occupation."

Madeleine had been looking to a future without him. And who could blame her after he'd stuffed up so royally.

Chapter 9

The bus left Tom in a street not far from the *porte-cochères* that led to the apartment. The entrance to the courtyard was still imposing, although five years of neglect were beginning to show.

A carved stone archway held up by Doric pillars and a wrought-iron gate, the impression was of an entrance to a large baronial residence. In its heyday the building had been the home of an aristocrat but had been sold and chopped into apartments after the Great War. Or the one before that. It was in an area no longer part of fashionable Paris and had slid into a semi-respectable suburb for blue-collar workers. Before the war came and disrupted everything, it was along the street women had brought out chairs and sat knitting, soaking up the sun and exchanging gossip, their fingers making as much conversation as their mouths. But today and in the dead of winter, the street was silent.

On either side of the entrance were two shops. On the left a dressmaker, a little dusty and, in the window, a few blank-eyed mannequins gazed out impassively, their pre-war dresses hanging forlorn from their shoulders. On the right a book seller, the gilded name on the window glowing in the evening light.

What Tom could see of the courtyard beyond the *porte-cochères* looked grim, damp and neglected. The concierge's small vegetable patch now a sea of weeds.

He looked around for her, remembered the woman with thin lips and narrowed eyes who sat at the entrance knitting and watching with silent disapproval as tenants walked past. They had called her Madame Defarge after the Dickens character who sat knitting at the guillotine. This concierge had also missed nothing.

The book shop to the right of the entrance was closed, but Tom could see through the glass, someone was moving about. He'd call in, have a chat. The dress shop to the left was also closed and dark. Madeleine used to buy clothes there. He would speak to the *couturière* who might remember his wife.

He trudged up the stairs, his suitcase pulling at his tired shoulders, thinking about the last time he had walked there.

At the end of March 1940. In the middle of the Phoney War when nothing was happening, but everyone was tensely waiting.

He remembered the apprehension he felt, the tightening of stomach muscles, wondering if Madeleine was there in the apartment where they had lived as students. If she was, would she accept him or turn him away. He was, after all, supposed to be inside one of His Majesty's prisons, not out cavorting around Paris at the request of the SOE. To his relief, after her first shock at seeing him, Madeleine had forgiven him. And Sophie had been conceived.

Five years later, here he was again, hesitating as he climbed the steps. At the front door, Emily's bicycle leaned against the wall, tyres deflated and the basket forlorn and broken. The door, once an inviting blue, had faded to dish-water grey.

Tom unlocked the door and stepped in.

The apartment was obviously uninhabited, the air stale and dust on every surface. He closed the door behind him and stepped over a small pile of letters that had been shoved through the brass letterbox. He knew which was Madeleine's room, on the right. Beyond that was Emily and Aaron's bedroom and further down the passage the one Tom had used. Alego, and the girl from Normandy whose name he could no longer remember were upstairs in the two attic rooms. There had been a few others in other rooms further down the passage whose faces were blurred in his memory. They came and went as their studies ended, they graduated and left Paris. They had all, as students with carefree hearts, lived in a sort of chaotic joy with books and wine and cheap restaurants. Coupling and uncoupling with no malice or grievance. Pairing up and then unpairing. Emily and Aaron Golding had obviously lasted, as had he and Madeleine. He wondered where they all were. What had happened to them? Emily and Aaron were the ones who troubled him the most. He'd heard stories, bad ones, of the fate of France's Jews. Perhaps they had also been taken to the concentration camps like other Jews across Europe. Perhaps they ended in a gas chamber. Or perhaps they got out and were busy picking Alego's oranges in sunny Spain. He could only hope so.

He put his small case down. Before boarding the bus at Gare de Lyon he'd bought a fresh baguette, some cheese and a bottle of wine. It would be a meagre meal, but sufficient. He found plates and glasses where they'd always been. Dusty and unused for three years. Rinsed off, Tom laid out thick slices of bread and cheese. A glass of wine. And then another.

He was putting off going into Madeleine's bedroom, afraid of what images might arise. Finally, he picked up his suitcase and opened the door.

It was worse than he could ever have imagined. The air seemed to be permeated with her essence. Madeleine could have been there, lying in the bed waiting for him.

It was neatly made with a pink chenille cover firmly tucked in. On the dressing table were a few of Madeleine's cosmetics, dried-up and stale but still hers. He bent over them taking a deep breath, afraid to touch but needing the aroma, and the nearness of Madeleine emanating from the powder and perfume and lipsticks.

He opened the drawers. Madeleine's clothes. It was the bottom drawer that held his startled attention, full of small garments in white, cream and blue. Baby clothes.

He slammed the drawer shut with a muted cry of anguish. Then slowly opened it again and stared. So, she was real. It wasn't just something Lucien had made up. The child was real. Here were her clothes. Here were her vests, her shawls, her bonnets, and her socks so small they could have easily fitted over his thumb.

He took one item out, a cream blouse with lace at the collar and lay down on the bed. "I promise you. I promise you," he murmured, clutching it to his heart. Not knowing what he was promising, only that if he was ever to be complete, he must find her and take her home.

Please God he would have the courage to go through with this, a man convicted by his own hubris, and a jailbird and a man trained to kill for 'King and Country'. Above all, a man damaged by circumstances and made into a shell of his old self. Ironic they had to kill people to maintain peace. *But it was ever thus*, Tom thought. But it wasn't his time in prison that haunted him and brought him to his knees. He had the fighting in France to thank for that. It had drained him of any courage he ever had and all he wanted was for it, his life, to stop. What sort of a father would he, could he, ever be?

He thought of the small cottage in the Kentish countryside, the Christmas tree standing forlorn, waiting alone amid the clumsily wrapped presents. None for Sophie. He would remedy the empty space the moment he, they, got home. A teddy bear, some books, a skipping rope. Some new clothes. He imagined the small bedroom at the back which had once been his. He'd paint it white and put prints of animals or flowers on the walls and a small bed covered with pink chenille, just like her mother's. There would be someone in his life, someone to give him purpose. At last.

Still holding the small blouse, Tom Blake fell asleep.

At close to midnight he awoke, found himself on top of the bed shivering with cold. He smoothed over the satin feel of the clothing in his hands and for a moment Tom wondered if it were possible to survive such heartache. He felt drenched in pain, physical and emotional. It ran through him and weakened his muscles so that he sat on the side of the bed, holding Sophie's blouse like a life belt in a stormy sea.

He placed it gently on the pillow, took off his shoes and jacket and crawled under the blankets, the small blouse close to his cheek.

*****

Tom woke to a bleak and cold morning. The apartment was like an ice chest, and he quickly got the boiler working. When the water was tepid, he had a short wash and vigorously rubbed himself dry. He drank water straight from the tap and instantly regretted the rancid taste. There was a little of the bread and cheese left over from the night before, but what he needed most was a cup of coffee. He wondered where food would be available in a Paris still reeling from the war.

But first he would set out a plan to discover what had happened to his wife and child. He wrote down a few points to remember; see the book seller downstairs, see the dressmaker and, reluctantly, see Phillipe Moreau at the Louvre. Who else? Find any of the people he'd set up in Paris to forge documents for the Underground. Emile and Michel, if they were still alive. Then, finally, wait for Lucien to return from the vineyard. He'd been given a fortnight. In that time, he promised Sophie, he would know where to find her.

But first, the concierge. It was axiomatic, the concierge of any apartment building would know everything about everyone. They were the first to know who was a drunk, who beat his wife or who was an irregular payee of rent. Madame Defarge or whatever her real name was, used to sit in the foyer of the apartments with her knitting. A slow progression of greying garments crept from her needles as her sharp eyes schemed, calculated, condemned and missed nothing. She would be the first to answer some questions.

Tom finished dressing, and then made his way down the stairs and to the small apartment on the lower floor where the concierge lived.

He lifted the brass knocker and let it fall. No answer. He waited. Knocked hard this time. Waiting with a sense of urgency, he finally heard the soft shuffling of footsteps from beyond the door. It creaked open and a pair of bloodshot eyes peered out at him. It was a young man in a ragged grey vest and trousers concertinaed to his waist with a leather belt. His feet were bare.

"I'm looking for the concierge." Tom was pleasantly surprised at how easily the French language slipped from his tongue.

"Why?"

Well, it's not to invite her to lunch. "I need to ask her some questions. About events in 1940."

"She's not here."

"When will she be here? I need to speak with her rather urgently."

The door opened fully, and a young man stood there. He was emaciated, his chest a web of ribs.

Camp survivor? Or from prison. Poor man. The 'poor man' clung to the jamb as if without its firm support, he would fall over.

"I am her son, Monsieur. She is not here."

"I need to ask her about events during the war."

"My mother is dead."

Tom felt a lurch of disappointment. "I'm so sorry. When did this happen?"

"At the end of the war."

Oh God. The tragedy never ends.

"She was executed. Here." The man waved his hand vaguely towards the courtyard.

"Why?"

"Why was anyone executed right after the war ended? She was accused of collaboration. It was a time of great revenge, mainly against women."

"And your mother?"

The man jerked his head in a gesture of impatience. "I was arrested for the act of intercourse. The Gestapo promised to release me in exchange for information. Of course, my mother agreed and did what they asked."

"I bet they never released you," Tom said.

"No. I was sent to a camp. There I was forced to wear a pink triangle."

A homosexual. Tom felt profound compassion for this man, living in the shadows and then being punished for it.

"It was remarkable my mother ever believed them. But those were desperate times, *monsieur*, and she would have done anything for her only son."

"How can you bear to live here in this place where your mother was executed?"

The man shrugged. "Where would I go?"

Tom nodded. He must help him, bring this man some food or medicine or something. "So, you know nothing about what happened here in the apartments."

"No, not really."

With a small muttering of condolences Tom left the young man still hanging onto the door jamb and went back upstairs.

He ate the heel of the baguette and had a sip of wine. As he chewed on the bread, he picked up the small pile of letters still lying at the front door, put them on the table. The top one was addressed to Lucien, and he thought he would remind him to take them with him when he returned to Paris in a fortnight.

Then he left, pocketing the heavy front door key. He stood at the bookshop window, pressed his face to the shadowy glass and noted there was a dim light glowing at the back. He pushed open the door to the faint tinkle of a bell. Around him were memories of the time he and other students had browsed the shelves, looking for something cheap and interesting, or a long-lost masterpiece. The over-filled bookshelves bent under the weight of paper and magic. A corridor between rows of shelves led down into a murky shadowy interior. The air was musty as if it had not been disturbed for a long time.

Tom remembered a friend once stating, Paris was the only city in the world where a river ran between two rows of books. And here, in this small space was the whole of Paris in miniature.

The floorboards creaked, and a man walked down between the rows of books. He was elderly, gaunt and grey-faced, his eyes deep-set.

"May I help you?"

"*Merci*," said Tom. "I am Tom Blake and before the war I lived in apartment number three upstairs. I'm trying to find my wife who lived there during the war. I went to England at the start and haven't been back until now." Tom found the lies tripped easily off his tongue. "Madeleine was supposed to follow me, but the Germans came."

"Ah, yes, terrible times."

"I thought the concierge would know but I hear she died."

The books seller's mouth tightened. "She was shot as a collaborator. The Resistance came for her. They took her out into the street, shaved her head and then shot her for betraying Jews."

"Yes, her son told me so."

"She was a dreadful woman," the book seller said, and Tom wondered if he was the one who'd told the Resistance about this woman and her collaboration. If the story of her allegiance to the Germans was true, Emily and Aaron could have been her victims. And Madeleine. And the child.

"Do you ever wonder," he blurted out. "When someone comes into your shop, what they did during the Occupation?"

"Yes, and I suspect it will be the hidden question for the next generation at least."

"My wife, Madeleine Aubert, lived upstairs."

"Ah, yes. Lucien Aubert's apartment. I remember."

Tom felt a shiver of anticipation. "Do you know what happened to her, to the occupants?"

The old man's eyes closed briefly. "The same thing that happened to all the Jews."

"My wife wasn't Jewish," Tom said, sick at heart for sounding a bit like the apostle Peter betraying Jesus.

"They were taken away. Most of them in one raid in 1942. A terrible day. The Jews were the ones who bought my books. They treasure knowledge, those Jews, it's part of their culture. People said they're too clever by half. But in my opinion, the Jews know what is important in life. Education. Knowledge. Books. And from knowledge and education comes wisdom. And all from the source, books. But, of course, during the war, there was little money for anything but food. In times of strife, books are a luxury. People still came in, but seldom bought anything. They'd stand and read and leave empty-handed. As for your wife, Madeleine, I'm sorry, I know nothing." He turned away, then turned back, looking closely at Tom's face. "Wait. I remember you. You're the Englishman who lived upstairs before the war," he said glowering. "You once stole a book from me."

Tom remembered it well. Alego had taunted him, calling him a coward for not shoplifting. The book he'd taken and shoved under his pullover was a translation of Plato, not something that held his interest but small enough to hide successfully. He reached for his wallet.

"You have a good memory, *Monsieur*. Yes, I stole a book," he said. "I apologise. It was a silly student prank. I can pay for it now." He dragged out a couple of hundred francs and place them on the counter. "Will this do?"

The old man gathered them up, not counting them and nodded.

"Now that's settled, what do you want from me?"

"I've come from England to find my wife, Madeleine Aubert," Tom said.

"You should talk to Madame Durand. They were friends."

"You mean…" Tom pointed to the shop across the entrance.

The man nodded once again. "They closed up around '43 or '44 but occasionally I see someone coming and going there. You might be lucky. Your wife you say? The one with the baby?"

Tom nodded, not trusting his voice.

"You definitely must try Madame Durand. She will know, if you can find her."

Tom felt an obligation to the old man. He gazed around, saw a book of Grimm's fairy tales. It was beautifully illustrated on thick paper the colour of Swiss cheese, the leather cover a deep crimson embossed with gold fairies and grim-looking ogres. Perhaps it was something a little girl of five might enjoy. He dug out his wallet again.

With the book safely wrapped in brown paper and string and a promise to return if he had news, Tom walked to the dressmaker's shop. He rattled the handle, but the door was locked. Tom pressed his face to the window, gazing past the mist of his breath, and the drooping mannequins. Clothes hung higgledy-piggledy from the rails, some trailing onto the dusty floor. Tom imagined German soldiers coming in with their lustful eyes, and thick fingers more used to triggers than silk, fingering the smooth taffeta and chiffon dresses. Gazing at the shining diamantes woven into the fabric, eyeing the costume jewellery. He'd heard tales of soldiers buying up everything and sending it all home to their fat *freundinnen*.

By the layers of dust on the counters, the shop obviously hadn't been open for a while. He'd write a letter and stick it in the door frame asking Madame Durand to contact him. In the meantime, he would go and see Phillipe Moreau at the Louvre and find out what he knew. He may very well discover Madeleine there, ensconced as Phillipe's lover. His fingers itched. He imagined giving the tall, spiderly man a good thrashing.

Tom hunched his shoulders, bending to the wind and sleet and began to walk to the Louvre.

Chapter 10

At the museum there was much hustle and bustle with staff walking swifty and with purpose, carrying paintings or small *objet d'art*. Straw and wrappings lay everywhere. Some people wandered around with clipboards and worried expressions. Eyes slid away as he came towards them. Most ignored him, a few muttered when he tried to engage them and shook off his hand from their shoulders. He approached a young woman carrying a decorative vase. Clearly the artefacts were being brought home from their temporary accommodation in chateaux in the Loire valley. Soon, Tom was sure, everything would be back in place and the public would flood in, grateful the German looters had not got hold of their treasures. He grabbed hold of the arm of the passing woman.

"*Excusez-moi*, could you please tell me where I could find Phillipe Moreau?"

She pointed vaguely up the stairs and mumbled what Tom thought was a room number. She was curt, close to brutal, concentrating instead on her clipboard. They should be pleased to have a job, Tom thought. Pleased they saved so many of France's treasures. What's the matter with them? Perhaps they still felt the weight of their guilt. These people had sat back while France's Jews were transported to their deaths. There was blood on their hands even if they could not see it.

Tom had once seen a trainload of humans, passing slowly through a train station with hands outstretched, voices begging for water. He'd run for a tap but had been knocked down by a German soldier who snarled some expletive at him as the train lumbered away. It had made him fight all the harder, because the locals didn't.

The door to Philipe Moreau's office was ajar. The man he'd come to see was with a colleague, both hunched over a desk pointing to documents lying between them. Tom knocked softly. Neither man responded and so he knocked again. Louder this time.

Moreau started up and said roughly, "Yes, what is it? What do you want?"

"A moment of your time, *Monsieur* Moreau," Tom said.

"I have no time for you, I'm afraid. I'm busy." He looked closer at Tom's face. "Wait, who are you? Your face is familiar." Moreau was a stern man gaunt to the point of emaciation, greying at the temples and with deep frown lines on his forehead.

"I am Thomas Blake, Madeleine Aubert's husband. I'm trying to find her."

"Ah. A moment." Moreau exchanged a few muttered words with the colleague who picked up the papers and retreated. "Come in. Please sit. Forgive my curtness, I am no longer used to being polite."

Tom cleared a chair and placed it on the side of Moreau's desk. He sat down and gazed at the man who lusted after his wife. "My wife's brother and I are looking for Madeleine. I wondered if you might know where she is."

96

"I haven't seen your wife lately. She worked here in '39. After that, who knows?"

"What did she do here?"

"She worked as night custodian when we were packing up the treasures of the Louvre, preparing to transport them out of Paris before the Germans arrived. It was, as they say, a frantic time, just after war was declared. But later... How much do you know about what was happening in France during the occupation?"

"I spent more time in France than back home in England," Tom said.

Moreau nodded. "Madeleine worked here for a while and when we'd sent all we could to the Loire valley, I directed her to another job in a different museum. I couldn't have her here any longer than necessary."

"Why not?"

Moreau was restless. His hands, white like flaccid fish, slid across his desk, found nothing to touch, slid back. "I believe you may know how I felt about your wife. I would have married her in an instant. I thought she was mine, that I had a chance, but then you came along. An Englishman." There was a sneer in his voice Tom decided to ignore. "When she came back to France after your trial and imprisonment, I once again believed..." He held up his hand. "I apologise. I made it my business to find out. I hoped she would consider divorce and look in my direction. But, sadly for me, she didn't. It was hard to see her every day and know... So, I asked her to leave."

"I see. You weren't concerned that she needed to feed herself and two of her friends?"

"I was, so I sent her to work for someone I knew well and who could be trusted. You must understand, Mr Blake, by the time the Germans were advancing on Paris we were frantic, trying to save our treasures. We here at the Louvre, day and night, had packed almost everything and sent our treasures into safekeeping. There were other museums and art collections that were similarly being sent out. Or hidden away. A colleague of mine, Jeanne Bonnet, worked in the library at the *Musée National des Arts* and I knew she was trying to save as much of her collection as possible. I thought Jeanne could do with some help. So, I sent Madeleine to her."

"When was this?"

"Let me see," Moreau said. "January 1940, she came here. We were packing up the last of the art works. She worked here until the beginning of May. After that, I don't know."

She was working here when he'd come over from England. Madeleine hadn't mentioned it. Tom felt a welling up of resentment. This man had seen Madeleine, had been in her company and yet he knew nothing.

"May I use your name when I go to speak to this Mme Bonnet?"

"Of course. Wait while I write a note. I can't be sure she'll be there, but you should try."

"Did you see Madeleine after she left the Louvre?"

"I never saw her again."

If he had been sexually overbearing Tom was certain Madeleine would have kept her distance.

"Thank you for your time, and for the note. If you can think of anything more, please contact Lucien or me."

Tom scribbled down the address of the apartment, hoping that Moreau would never have to use it.

And so, Tom Blake left the Louvre no further forward, although he had a thin lead, a name, Jeanne Bonnet. And a location. It would be the next step, and Tom was afraid he would soon run out of steps.

*****

The next day broke cold and wet. Tom lay in Madeleine's bed hugging the blankets around him and wishing he were back home in Kent where he could start a fire in the living room grate and stay hunched over it for the rest of the day. Reading, smoking a cigarette or daydreaming. But here he was in Paris, the city shabbier than he remembered and, while there was little physical damage, it was populated with people who seemed shell-shocked. He hadn't found anywhere to eat, except the previous evening near the Louvre he'd come across a small untidy bistro serving the smallest crepes he'd ever seen.

There were two visits on his list for today. One was to the *Musée National des Arts* in the *Palais de Chaillot*. If Madeleine went to work there, perhaps someone may remember. If Jeanne Bonnet was still there, he would be most fortunate.

The other was to track down Mme Durand, the dressmaker.

The bus service would be erratic if only two buses served the entire city. A city the size of Paris and only two buses? One passed him. It was so full that several young men were standing on the plate outside the folding door, hanging on it seemed by their fingernails. If Tom was to get to the Palais de Chaillot in the Trocadero area of the 16th *arrondissement*, he would have to use shanks' pony and just slog it out in the grey sludge passing for snow this morning. He gave thanks for the sturdy boots he wore.

The courtyard of the *Palais de Chaillot* had bad memories for Parisians. It was here that Hitler stood looking out over his latest conquest, gazing at the Eiffel Tower and doing a little victory jig. And yet in the light of the mid-morning sun, everything around the Palais shone with misty golden brilliance. Tom stood for a moment, giving thanks he had been part of the defeat of that dreadful monster who stood in this very place four years ago and gloated.

He hoped there was a special place in hell for men like that.

Inside, the *Palais* had the feel of a dirge being played on a harmonica. A forlorn song of hollowness, of empty corridors and dirt encrusted windows. Tom made his way past dark marble pillars, up wide shallow stairs, through empty hallways and along dim passages. Every now and again he called, 'is there anyone here?', but his voice echoed back at him. He paused to admire the vaulted ceilings letting in fractured light, and the marble inlaid floor. A magnificent building, which appeared to have been deserted.

The large oak door to the library was closed. He pushed, then knocked, the sound of his knuckles breaking through the eggshell of silence. Behind him he heard someone cough. Tom peered into the gloom. A man stood there with a mop in one hand and a bucket in the other. His back was stooped, and his grey head bent to one side like a chirpy sparrow.

"*Excusez-moi, m'sieur*, are you looking for someone?"

Tom stretched out a hand. It was taken by the man's damp gnarled fingers and quickly released. "Yes, I am," he said. "A lady called Jeanne Bonnet. I believe she works here in the library."

"Ah, *monsieur*, you are about four years too late. *Professeur* Bonnet worked here during the war. Now," the man gave an eloquent shrug. "Who knows where she is."

"Is there anyone here who would know where I can find her?"

"In in connection with what, may I ask?"

"There was a young woman who worked for her during the war. Madeleine Aubert. A casual worker, I think."

"And why are you asking? Forgive me, *m'sieur*, but even now it is necessary to guard one's words."

"Of course. Madame Aubert was, is, my wife."

"You are the Englishman," the man said smiling. "Forgive me, I overheard the *Professeur* saying something to a colleague."

Tom nodded. "We were separated by the war and now I'm trying to find her."

The man was silent. After a small hesitation, he dug inside his pocket and pulled out a large key. "We can speak more easily in the library," he said as he inserted the key into the oak door and opened it. There was a rush of stale air and dust mites danced in the thin light that speared down from a skylight onto a long central table stretching the length of the large room.

"This is the library of architecture," the man said gesturing at the empty shelves. "This was where *Professeur* Bonnet worked. She packed up most of the volumes herself and dragged them to the basement. I believe she had outside help but she did most of it on her own."

"And she hasn't returned to the library?"

"No, sir, not yet."

"You know the story of what happened here." It was a statement. This man was not only a janitor and a cleaner, but he was also a keeper of secrets. Tom understood these things and these kinds of people. He was one himself. "You know things, *M'sieur,* because you understand the need for secrecy."

"I do, sir."

"Then I appeal to your good heart. I need to find my wife. I need to know if she's still alive or..." Tom could not bring himself to speak the words.

"Indeed, sir. I know all too well. My son is still missing, so I do understand. If we sit here, I'll tell you what I know."

"In June 1940 the Germans had broken through the Ardennes and were approaching Paris. They had bypassed our impregnable Maginot Line. This you probably know." The janitor shook his head. "What fools we were! Thinking a pile of stones and a few rifles would keep *les Allemands* out. We had a good army but spread too thinly. The strategy at the time was still mired in the Great War, trench warfare had gone but our leaders still believed in it." Tom nodded. No one in the French military hierarchy understood de Gaulle's book on lightning warfare. But in Germany it was studied and implemented. Tragic that the *blitzkrieg* had, ironically, been de Gaulle's idea at a time when French army strategists were still bound by the trench warfare ideology.

"We were afraid," the janitor said. "All of us. We began to hear about other countries. About Poland. We thought we knew what to expect. Madame Bonnet feared the volumes by Jewish authors and plans by Jewish architects would fall into the hands of the Germans and be destroyed."

The man hesitated. Tom could see he was overwhelmed by harsh memories of those early days. He felt in his pocket and pulled out a packet of Gitanes, snipped it open with his thumbnail. They were intended for the young son of the *concierge*, but he would have to go with one packet less. The man took it gratefully. He began to speak again after the first coil of smoke left his nostrils. Tom pushed the packet towards him, and he gratefully pocketed it.

"I only surmise *Professeur* Bonnet had an underground group going. There were meetings here, whispers, nods of the heads. Handshakes. They had a sense of jollity about them, like children playing a game.

Perhaps, they were careless. It was all very new, this kind of thing."

"And then?"

"And then the Gestapo came. They took the *Professeur* and her colleagues away. She has not yet returned."

"When was that?"

"Sometime in 1943."

Tom felt his lips were too stiff to ask. "And the others?"

"I understand the men in the group were all executed. The two young women who worked with Mme Bonnet were taken as well. At least, I assume so, because I never saw them again."

"Who were they? Do you know their names?"

The man shook his head. "Perhaps *Professeur* Bonnet's brother may know more. He lives in Lyon. You should go there and ask him."

Chapter 11

Tom walked away from the museum as the day closed in around him. It felt as if his chances of finding Madeleine were fading. The man he thought of as the keeper of secrets had little more to tell him, other than the name of the brother of *Professeur* Bonnet who might be able to help. Hugo Bonnet, who lived somewhere in Lyon. Tom had asked for an address, but the janitor had just shrugged.

If the men in Jeanne Bonnet's ring had been executed, then what had happened to the women? The three women, Jeanne, Madeleine and one other, could have been taken to one of the concentration camps. Had the Red Cross any record of Jeanne Bonnet? Had she come home? If so, perhaps Madeleine had as well.

If Madeleine had survived, the Red Cross or some other organisation would surely have contacted him or Lucien.

They hadn't.

Ergo, Madeleine was dead.

It was all too much. He'd go back to the apartment, try to sleep, and later make his way to Lucien. Then to England. There was nothing more France could give him. His child was lost. Madeleine was probably dead. All he wanted now was home. He'd done enough, seen enough, had the nightmares to prove it. How much more could he give to this war? There was such an exhaustion in the whole process of trying to be normal, trying to act as if he'd come unscathed through this business of murdering, of seeing murder, seeing the burnt corpses of women and children, witnessing the crucified men. It had to stop somewhere. It had to stop. Because slowly, slowly it was claiming him.

Surely if he could just get home to his cottage with the worn-out sofa and the dead Christmas tree and just sleep and read and not have such vivid dreams of what he had become. Surely, by the grace of God and time, he could heal.

It had become colder, and Tom shrugged deeper into his jacket and pulled his scarf across the lower half of his face. People as vague as ghosts hurried past him, their breath coming in clouds and the snow as it fell turned to grey sludge beneath their feet. At a small bistro he stopped for a glass of wine and some nuts from a glass bowl. Further down the street there was a *boulangerie* from which the tantalising aroma of fresh bread suddenly erupted into the frigid air. He waited at the end of a queue, nodding politely as, one by one, patrons came out clutching bread. Then his turn. He went in and bought a *baguette* for himself and, as an afterthought one for the boy in the apartment below. He added some pale-looking cheese to his purchase from the *crèmerie* next door and walked back to the apartment, surprised that he could actually buy enough food for two. Parisians were still starving, and he had found two places to buy food.

He must have woken the young man up for he appeared in the doorway dishevelled and sleepy-eyed.

"I'm sorry, *monsieur*. I haven't thought of anything more. I have been asleep."

"It's alright. Here," Tom thrust the baguette and cheese at him. "Take this. I'll see you tomorrow perhaps."

The man took the food clumsily as if unaccustomed to receiving gifts. "*Merci.*"

Tom walked up the stairs, every step slow, almost ponderous. What next? Where to next? He must speak to Lucien and perhaps they could go to Lyon together. It felt too arduous a journey to make on his own.

It was beginning to feel like a quest. The sort of journey he needed to undertake in order to get through to the other side.

What other side, you dolt?

He couldn't say, but he remembered the myths and legends written in Latin in the medieval documents he perused. Beautiful paintings of adventurers in search of... something. He couldn't remember precisely what they were searching for. The Holy Grail? Was Madeleine his Holy Grail?

He unlocked the door, closed it behind him and went to sit at the table. Utterly spent, Tom pushed aside the pile of letters and put his head on the table. He wanted to weep. It was all so hopeless. He was tilting at windmills. Should he return to England and live with his loss? No Madeleine, no Sophie with angel wings on her back. Just Tom Blake.

Wearily he went to the kitchen, cut some of the baguette and cheese and put it on a plate and went back to the table with his paltry meal.

Tomorrow he would go to the vineyard and speak to Lucien, tell him it was hopeless.

He put his plate down and began to eat, idly sorting through the letters.

It was only then he saw one addressed to Madeleine Aubert. Not franked, nor stamped, but delivered by hand, pushed through the letterbox. He slid his finger under the flap, opened it.

And let out a howl. Not of anguish but of hope. More like a war cry than one of despair. He read the letter and read it again. It was from Antoinette Durand, the dressmaker downstairs. Only one line and her signature.

I have your daughter. Please come to the shop to collect her

Antoinette Durand

Sophie was downstairs? Was it that easy?

The note had lain under his feet, and he hadn't bothered to look at the collection of letters at the door. Dear God, what a fool he was. He didn't stop to think the letter was addressed to Madeleine. Surely, everyone knew Madeleine hadn't been back here for years. Why had the dressmaker sent this letter to someone she knew hadn't been here since 1942? Had she perhaps heard someone in the apartment and just assumed it was Madeleine? And, above all, why did the dressmaker have Sophie?

It also likely meant she knew Madeleine was alive and, hearing noises in the apartment upstairs, had assumed she was back in Paris.

He wanted to dance. He wanted to sing. He wanted to shout. At last. Something solid. The dressmaker downstairs had Sophie. He'd go... no, it was too late to go tonight. Tomorrow he would go to the dress shop and claim her. He dug into the small kitchen cupboard serving as the wine cellar when he lived there. Three bottles of wine, dusty, lay side by side. He took one, opened it and slugged wine from the bottle before pouring a glassful.

As he did so there was a knock on the door. A timid sound, one he was tempted to ignore. Again, another knock. The dressmaker!

Tom rushed to the door, opened it.

It was the concierge's son.

"I've remembered something, Monsieur. Perhaps I may come in and tell you?"

"Of course." Tom could afford to be magnanimous. He was about to rescue his child. "Come and have a glass of wine. We'll have some of the bread. Have you eaten?"

"Not yet, Monsieur." He settled into a chair at the table as while Tom fussed with the bread and cheese. "My name is Francois. My mother was widowed in the war. Not this one but the one everyone said would end all wars. I was still a child when I heard my father had died. When you are very young, death has no meaning. I kept expecting him to return, I kept asking for him, 'when will Papa come home?', and when he didn't come back, I couldn't understand it. Surely, if I was a very good boy, he would come back. But, of course, no matter how hard I tried, he never came home."

For just a moment Tom felt stunned. This was exactly what he had felt when his father had died. "I'm so sorry. There were many men who didn't return. But to live without your father, I know. I lost my father too."

"*Oui*, Monsieur. I know I was not alone in my grief. I understand that now, but for each child their sorrow is unique." He drank greedily of the wine, grabbed a piece of baguette and cheese and ate hungrily. "My mother was embittered. She felt the government should have done more for war widows. My mother was a hard woman, quick to take offence. Bitter because of ill-treatment she only perceived. She had a small pension and this job. She was alright."

He tore another piece off the baguette, speared a piece of cheese and ate. "No excuse, Monsieur. I am not here for judgement. It was as it was."

"We cannot judge. We weren't in her shoes," Tom said, nodding and eating his bread. He wanted to judge her. How many Jews had that woman betrayed? Was there forgiveness for such an act and who would give it? He couldn't absolve Francois' mother for a deed not done to him directly. Only those she had betrayed, and they were all dead. And did any human have the right to forgive? Should he be asking for forgiveness for those German boys he helped to kill? Surely, only God could do that. Would he feel better if he asked them for forgiveness or would that just absolve him from justified suffering for what he did?

"You say your mother was bribed by the Gestapo?"

"Yes, they wanted to know who in the apartment was Jewish. I understand that two of the tenants in this apartment were Israelites. My mother said they hadn't registered and so were illegal. There were others in the building next door. My mother was caretaker there as well, you see."

Emily and Aaron, Tom thought. He'd hoped they had left, gone south to Spain. But now it seems that they'd stayed and been arrested. *Why hadn't they left when they could*, he thought with a kind of belated anguish.

Francois finished his glass of wine and Tom poured him another. "I have been told, *M'sieur*, on 16 June 1942, a Tuesday, the French police began very early in the morning. It was called a *rafle*, a round-up, and it lasted two days. Thousands of Jews were put into the *Vélodrome d'Hiver*, the cycle track in the 15th arrondissement. Some say it was the biggest arrest of Jews in France. The French people saw the trains as they were leaving the *Gare de l'Est* station heading for Auschwitz. After that, we didn't know what happened to them."

Francois began to cry. Tom awkwardly patted his arm.

"You see, as another victim of persecution," Francois said. "I have only sympathy for them."

"You say the French police? Not the Germans?"

"No, French police."

"And your mother? What part did she play in that?"

"She pointed out where Jews were staying in this apartment and the one next door."

"So, the residents of this apartment were taken, all of them?"

"I don't know." Francois put his head down into his hands. "My mother mentioned just three, the couple and a child."

"A couple? Not three?"

"No, only a couple and a child. I only found out afterwards, when the Resistance people came and accused my mother. They took her outside and…. I am so sorry for her actions. Please, forgive me."

Tom swallowed hard. Madeleine had not been taken but the child had. But what about the letter?

"We can only be responsible for our own actions," he said, a silly superficial reply but his mind swirled with the image of Sophie being hustled out of the apartment with Emily and Aaron and never going back.

"Yes, but I have to live with the shame, Monsieur."

Tom could not 'forgive' this man for something he didn't do to someone he never knew. His mother would have to face her own judgement one day, that was all.

He thought for a moment, trying to imagine how fearful they must have been. How it had happened that Sophie had escaped being taken to the Velodrome, he couldn't possibly imagine. He'd find out in the morning, he was sure. There was a story that only Madame Durand could tell.

Francois said there was a couple and a child. Not three. If Madeleine had not been taken, where was she?

Chapter 12

The following morning, he woke to a state of almost euphoric bliss. Although it had snowed again during the night and the air around him was frigid, the world seemed flushed with warmth and sunlight. Today he would go to Antoinette Durand's dress shop and claim his child. He had evidence. Madeleine had mentioned the angel wings birthmark, and he would tell Mme Durand he could identify his child by looking at her back. Mme Durand would be gracious, would acknowledge that indeed Sophie was his child, mention perhaps how she had cared for Sophie and how good Sophie was. She would produce a little girl in the peak of health, clean and well-dressed.

Too excited to breakfast, he'd grabbed the last of the baguette and ate it running down the stairs.

But he should have known better.

The dress shop was empty and dark, just as it had been when he first arrived a week ago. He wanted to sink onto the cobbled pavement in despair. He'd built up his hopes and this darkened shop destroyed them. He knocked on the window, knocked again, cupped his face with his hands the better to see inside.

Behind him he heard a cautious cough. The bookseller stood quietly in the entrance to his shop. "*Bonjour, M'sieur* Blake," he said. "I believe Mme Durand's assistant is a teacher, so she'll only come later in the day, if at all. Perhaps you would like to come in here out of the cold. I have coffee prepared and you can wait in the warmth of my shop."

"*Merci, M'sieur.*" Tom rubbed his hands. "I am at a disadvantage. You know my name but…"

The book seller silently pointed to the window. In golden scroll copperplate he read,

Librairie des mythes et legends
G. Marat.

A Book Shop of Myths and Legends. *Nice,* thought Tom.

"Marat? No relation to Jean-Paul Marat of French Revolution infamy?"

"I believe I am, *M'sieur.* I have avoided all women in case I should meet the same fate as my illustrious predecessor."

Tom laughed. "Your predecessor was a revolutionary. You should be safe."

Marat raised an eyebrow. "You think so?"

"Ah." So perhaps the *Monsieur,* the unassuming book seller and descendent of a famed figure of the French Revolution who was allegedly murdered in his bathtub by a young woman, had been involved in the later 'revolution' against German occupation. France had become a country of secrets.

Marat placed a *demitasse* of coffee on a small table in the window of the shop and invited Tom to sit. He also placed a small plate with two halves of a *baguette.* "Please, I hope you will share my breakfast. We French still use the *baguette* as a symbol of our defiance and our cultural identity. The Germans prefer a big solid lump of bread. We on the other hand, are dedicated to the slender *baguette*. So, eat up and enjoy."

"Thank you, *Monsieur*, this is most welcome. Do you know *Mme* Durand?"

"Not well, and I haven't seen her for quite a while. But there's a younger woman who works in the dress shop. A niece, perhaps. I see her come and go but it's almost always in the late afternoon."

Tom sat inhaling the delicate aroma of the coffee. It seemed almost sacrilegious to drink it. "I must talk to her." He took a small sip. It was as good as its aroma.

"You have found something out about your wife?"

"Not about my wife, no, but about our child. Sophie."

"Ah, yes, the little one."

"Did you see them being arrested in '42 and taken to the Velodrome?"

"Yes, and to my shame I kept my door closed. I could have saved someone but, like most of the French people I stood by. It is our dishonour. You see, it is very hard to know what to do, the line between saying nothing or saying no. Most of us just stood and watched as the Germans took away the Jews in cattle trucks. Most have said nothing since, when none of those Jews have come back."

"The Jewish couple who lived with my wife were taken. Did you see a child with them?"

"It was so crowded. A mad, horrible maelstrom. All those people milling about, crying. There was a kind of anguished despair on the streets that day. It hung like an evil cloud. The French police were pushing people around. There was a great melee, you understand. I had seen her before, the child, I mean. *Madame* Blake used to take her out when it was warm. A blonde child. She never walked, bless her, that child. She always danced like a miniature ballerina. Tiny, tiny little thing. Always hopping and twirling and skipping as if to inner music. A handful for her Mama, I should imagine. But then it stopped. I thought *Mme* Blake might have moved on or found work and perhaps the carers could not take the child out for fear of arrest."

Tom sat silently drinking the excellent coffee and breaking off pieces from the *baguette*. It would have been easy for a Gentile to be swept up in the frenzy. But not Madeleine, please God, not her.

"But you never saw Madeleine in that crowd?"

"No. You see…"

There hung over them a past as brutal as any in the history of the world. Those Jews, their mechanised, industrialised murder, silenced and anonymous. 'Units' Hitler called them. Would it ever happen again? No, never. Surely not.

"What is it that you do, *M'sieur* Blake?"

Tom was startled from his brown study. "Do? Nothing at the moment. I am still part of the British war machine. In real life I was an art historian. My speciality was medieval manuscripts, and I'm trained as a restorer."

"You will find this work after the demobilisation?"

Tom laughed. "I very much doubt it."

Marat stood up.

"Perhaps while you wait for the dress shop to open, you might like to examine some of my books. I have some old treasures. My father and my grandfather and those before him were all collectors. So, I have a few rather interesting manuscripts."

"I would be honoured."

Tom wiped his hands on his handkerchief and followed the book seller into the back of the shop where there were several small rooms leading off a narrow passage. One larger room was obviously Marat's living quarters, for Tom spotted a small sofa, a table with chairs and an alcove covered by a curtain where the old man probably slept.

Marat led Tom to a small flight of stairs, hardly visible in the gloom. Marat stopped to switch on a faint light, the globe swinging in the fetid air. Downstairs another passageway and a room that must have been as big as the entire shop above. It was padlocked.

Marat took a key from his pocket and unlocked the door. It creaked open and he felt along the wall until he found the switch. The room was flooded with soft light and Tom stood in wonder. There were shelves down both sides of the room and there, when Tom examined them closely, were a large number of old manuscripts. As Tom allowed his fingers to lightly skim the titles, he was awestruck that such books should be in the possession of a single person. They should be in a vault somewhere. Or in a museum.

"*M'sieur* Marat, I believe you have a treasure trove here. More than any private collection."

Marat smiled. "I believe so. It has been a family tradition to collect old manuscripts. My family had connections as far back as the Knights Templar, I believe. That may be pure legend, but who knows. Perhaps you might like to examine one?" He handed Tom a pair of cotton gloves and Tom reverently took down one book and opened it. Gold lettering and handcrafted illustrations of fiery red dragons and silver unicorns glowed out at him. So much like the page he'd forged that his mind jumped back to the day. A twenty pound bet and his life in tatters.

"How did you manage to keep these from the Germans?"

Marat smiled. "What would they be doing to an old book seller in a small dusty old bookshop? All they cared about was that I held no Jewish books. I assured them I did not. I didn't add that they were all packed away down here in my cellar. But there you are. The Germans turned us all into liars."

Tom turned a luminous golden and red page and wanted to be swamped by the beauty of the medieval manuscript, but his heart's attention was drawn to the mass arrest of Jews that happened just outside the doors of the book shop. Emily and Aaron, his friends. And Madeleine.

He heard the cries. He felt the fear. He saw the buses pull away with their despairing cargo.

No, he didn't.

He couldn't.

Only those who were there that day would know, and they were all dead.

As Tom closed the book, *Monsieur* Marat dropped the bombshell.

"I remember now. I saw you wife later that day. It was after the buses had left with the Jews. She ran up the stairs and then came down again almost immediately. I could see she was distraught."

"Oh God. After the *rafle*? Are you sure?"

"I definitely saw her later that day. I remember she had a string bag with vegetables, so it was late in the afternoon. She dropped them on the stairs as she ran down, that concierge woman came and collected them. I remember that. But the child…?" *Monsieur* Marat gave an eloquent shrug. "Who can say?"

"There was a letter from *Mme* Durand, the dressmaker. I found it. Only one line. She wrote that she had the child."

Monsieur Marat smiled. "Well, it seems your search is over."

"Not until I have her, Monsieur. I was never privileged to know her, but I believe she has a distinctive birthmark. That's how I'll know she's my child."

"You never saw her?"

"No," Tom said. He didn't want to go into details about Sophie's conception. "I was away when she was born, and I never had the opportunity."

"But you'll know her by this birthmark? A romance, wouldn't you say? Shall we return to our vigil at the window. You won't want to miss the niece."

Reluctantly Tom placed the manuscript on the shelf where it had possibly lain for decades. One day perhaps he'd come back and the gold and red, the ochre and blue, the unicorns and bleeding figures on the crosses and the upside-down martyred martyrs would still be there for him to admire. Marat herded Tom out and locked the door. At the front of the shop Marat called out, "Oh, look, *M'sieur* Blake. The lights have come on in the dress shop. I think you had better go over there while you can. I wish you luck."

Tom ran across and banged on the window. "*Bonjour*," he called. "Hello? Is anybody there?"

A slight young woman emerged through racks of clothing. She waved her arms, mouthing 'we're not open'.

Tom pulled out the letter from his pocket. He pressed it against the dusty window.

"I must speak to you. Where is *Mme* Durand?"

The young woman peered at the letter and opened the shop door. She peered around the door frame like a frightened rabbit.

"I'm looking for Antoinette Durand. It is very important that I see her. Can you tell me where she is?"

"What is your business with her?"

"She sent this letter to my wife regarding our child. I've only just found it."

The woman read the single line, turned it over, re-read it and handed the letter back. "It's nearly four years old."

Tom could read *je t'accuse* in her eyes. "I understand, but I've only just found it lying on the carpet by the door. No one has lived there since that time, so it lay there undisturbed." Tom realised he was gabbling. "You see, my wife and child are missing, and this is the first opportunity I've had to find them. I've come from England to find them. Your aunt said in the letter that she had my daughter. Where is she? Can you tell me more?"

"Come in *M'sieur*, let me close the door and keep out the cold. It was a time of great torment, you understand. The French Police came and arrested the Jews and put them in the Velodrome. You know about that?"

Tom nodded.

"We saw it happening, from very early in the morning, all day. It was terrible. My aunt stood close by the window. She saw a man and a woman with a little child. She called to me, 'look it's the Jewish couple, the lawyers from upstairs.' They had helped her with advice when she had problems. Pro-bono. They were kind to her. When the police were looking elsewhere, the woman knocked on the window. 'Please take the child' she said when my aunt opened the door. 'Please get her back to her mother. Her name is Sophie. She is Madeleine Aubert's daughter."

"And then?"

"They pushed the little girl in through the door just as the police started herding them onto buses. After that we never saw them again."

"But Madeleine, the mother, came back?"

"I don't know, Monsieur. I didn't see her. We left this note at the apartment saying we had the child, but the mother never came for her. We thought that perhaps she'd been taken too."

"Where is *Mme* Durand now? Sophie is my daughter. I want to claim the child and take her home."

"I'm so sorry, but she is dead."

Tom's shoulders dropped. "The child?"

"No, my aunt. My aunt went to her hometown near Lyon. It's a small village, only a few hundred people. She went there to stay with her sister. There were several of her relatives living in the town. For all I know, your child may still be with one of them. If she isn't then someone will know where she is."

Despite the sense of relief that almost overwhelmed him, Tom was moved by this girl. She seemed so forlorn, so lost.

"*Mlle,* you worked for your aunt, but where did you live? With your parents?"

The girl's face clouded. "I am not a niece by law. I call her my aunt, but we are not related. I never knew any of her family, but she knew mine. Both my parents died a long time ago, *Monsieur.* When I was a child, my aunt who was a neighbour at the time, rescued me and I was brought up by her. She was a kind lady. You mustn't worry about your child. My aunt would have cared for her and so would her relatives in Lyon."

"Can you tell me more about her and the child she rescued?"

The girl's face softened. "My aunt was a creative, cheerful lady. You can see her handiwork in some of the dresses. We were successful in making dresses for the elite. They came to us and commissioned work. During the war it was difficult to get supplies, you understand, and even the elite stopped buying. So, work slowed down. Then suddenly we had another task. Looking after a little girl until her mother came to take her back. My aunt treated the little one well, *M'sieur.* When her mother didn't come, we took her home with us. She was with us for three weeks, perhaps longer. We cared for her, *M'sieur,* believe me. She was cherished." The girl laughed. "She never stopped, that one, like the ballerina on top of a music box, put some music on and she danced and waved her arms like a windmill. In the end we had to be careful at night when we wound up the gramophone, because she'd come down all sleepy-eyed and she'd dance. It was as if the music so enchanted her that she could not help herself."

"When you bathed her," Tom was almost afraid to ask lest the answer would confirm his worst fear, that this wasn't Madeleine's child. "Did you notice a birthmark?"

"Oh yes. Indeed. She had a birthmark on her back, like small wings. We called her Angela because of that."

Tom felt a profound sense of relief. At last, he had a solid lead. Sophie was safe, he was sure of that. But that didn't explain why Madeleine never came back.

"And so, Madeleine never came to collect her?"

"No, Monsieur."

"*Merci.*" He turned to leave.

"Another thing, Monsieur, she was still a young child and her talk was limited. But one thing she always said was, 'Papa Tom' She'd clap her hands and say 'Papa Tom'. Is that you?"

Tom nodded but her words had a strange effect on him. He suddenly felt weak, boneless. He held onto the door jamb; afraid he might fall over. His child knew him. Despite her never having met her father, she knew him. He felt a sudden onrush of love for this lost little girl. It flowed through his body, a visceral flood of emotion the like of which he had never felt before. If he were to do nothing else with his life, he would find the child.

Tom was almost angry that that this young woman had the temerity to have spent more time with his child than he had. For that matter, almost more than Madeleine, her own mother.

"Where do I go, *Mlle*? How do I find her?"

"Let me write the address down for you. And a short letter from me so that the family will know who you are."

His quest was not yet over. It seemed he was destined to go to Lyon after all.

Chapter 13

Lucien had said he would be in Paris in a fortnight, but here he was hammering on the door to the apartment just as Tom was trying to get to sleep. He hadn't expected to see his brother-in-law so soon and wondered if the man was checking up on him.

"What are you doing here? You said a fortnight."

"I have a meeting with a possible buyer, an American. So, I came early. I only have a day here and then I must go back. Have you found your forgery assistants?"

Tom had not yet traced any of his Resistance colleagues, but that seemed unnecessary now that he knew Sophie had been taken to Lyon. He'd thought of going to the chateau and confronting Lucien with the good news. It would have given him a great deal of pleasure to boast he'd made some progress. But here the man was on the doorstep, late at night when Tom had already gone to bed. But not to sleep. There was too much to digest and his thoughts were like squirrels, up one tree, down and up another. One thought chasing the other. So, when the knock on the door woke him from his semi-dream state, he presumed it would be Francois looking for something to eat.

Instead, it was Lucien, looking as cold as he had on Christmas Eve in Kent. "*Salut,*" Tom said, holding open the door. "I hadn't expected you."

125

"While I'm here I thought we could go into the city. I want you to meet some friends."

Tom looked at his watch. "It's after nine o'clock. Can't it wait?"

"*Non, mon ami*, the friends I want you to meet do not operate at housewives' hours. Come on, get dressed and we'll go."

"Before we go, I must tell you…"

"Come along, Tom. No time for chattering. It can wait. Put your trousers on."

"No, it can't wait. I have news of Sophie."

Lucien stopped. "What?"

"I think I know where Sophie is. In Lyon."

"*Mon Dieu*, Tom. That is indeed good news. All the more reason we go there at the first possible moment."

"There's more."

"Come along. We'll talk later. Now I have friends I want you to meet."

Tom stalled. "Wait, Lucien. There's a lot we need to discuss. About Madeleine. Why are you dragging me out at this time of night to meet some of your friends? For what purpose?"

"These men have the contacts we need. If you want to find your child, you need local knowledge. They have it."

Damn it, I know where Sophie is.

There was more he wanted to say. He was bubbling with the news, but Lucien gave him little room to talk, hurrying him along and out the door. Despite his frustration, he began to enjoy the walk. The sky was brilliantly clear, and he could see a whole mystery of brilliant stars almost to the horizon. The pavements were crisp and white, and the shuttered shops dozed under a cloak on new-laid snow. He felt like a schoolboy out of boarding school and suddenly free of all constraints. *A little dance might be appropriate*, he thought, doing a little one-step.

Lucien laughed. "You are full of *joie de vivre*."

"I am. Madeleine is alive."

Lucien stopped. "You're sure?"

"Almost sure."

"We'll talk later."

Lucien turned away and led the way to one small alley that turned off into another one, so narrow it felt like Tom could touch both walls at once.

"Where are we going?" he asked.

"Just a little way along here."

They came to a small dark bistro. Candles fluttered as they opened the door and quickly closed it again to keep out the wintry air. The place felt shadowed and dingy, the walls so dark Tom wasn't sure if they were painted or whether it was from years, no, decades of nicotine. On the walls were groups of paintings of a decadent Paris that looked like the art of Degas but couldn't possibly be. A faint aroma of grilled food caught at him. He suddenly realised he was very hungry. *Baguettes* and cheese were all fine but not as a constant diet.

As they stood just inside the door they were met with blank stares until one of the patrons recognised Lucien. There was a great shout of welcome as they walked through a warm haze of candle, chatter and cigarette smoke to a table surrounded by what Tom thought was a bunch of sinister rogues – until each face broke into a boyish grin of delight. Lucien went around the tight circle of men, grasping hands, kissing cheeks and hugging an old man with one arm. He introduced Tom to the men; an architect, a printer, an engineer, Jewish by his looks, a *passeur*, a fisherman far from his comfort zone, another who Lucien said was a big-time 'reliever of goods from those who did not deserve them'. Tom took that to mean he had relieved the Germans of stolen goods. One sat with his chair pushed back into the darkness. Lucien glossed over him with a short '*Salut, Jean-Luc*'.

Tom felt instantly at home. These were the sort of men he had worked with in the south. The *maquis* he'd lived with and fought alongside had been made up of just such an assortment of crazy, cranky, eccentric human beings, students, farmers, small business owners, teachers, housewives. Tom could almost predict which one had laid mines on train tracks, or who had pushed refugees through barbed wire and led them to safety, or who could dismantle a rifle in his sleep.

"Lucien has spoken of you," said one man, his unshaven face cracked into a grin. His hands shook as he leant forward. "He has only good things to say."

"That's very kind of him." Tom wondered if Lucien had mentioned his imprisonment. But the grins on the faces of the men assured him he was their kind of man. Prisoners, rogues, deserters, one-armed-one-eyed killers for France.

The *restaurateur* brought large tureens of grilled fish and rice, baguettes and flagons of wine. The food was almost unbelievably delicious, the conversation informed and interesting. Most wanted to know how England was, how had she survived? Much the same as Paris, Tom was able to reply. But more bombed buildings, one million homes destroyed, and 100,000 civilians killed in London alone.

The British government had made plans to contain panic and evacuate all of London, but Englishmen were not prone to panic and had stayed in their homes even as the bombs were falling. A dour stoic nation, not prone to scare tactics. Tom wasn't sure he should remark on that, remembering a quarter of the French population had fled ahead of the Germans. It would have been cruel to mention it to a group of men, most of whom had paid a high price.

The meal ended with a large ripe Brie and a perfect cognac. The meal would have been incredible pre-war but in the year after victory, Tom wondered how this was possible, and if he would ever have another such meal again.

As the men relaxed, the Gitanes appeared, and cigarette smoke spiralled to the ceiling adding to layers of nicotine. Soon the talk became desultory and there was at least one man whose eyelids could no longer bear the weight of the night. It was clearly time to break up the party and return home.

It was almost three in the morning when Lucien and Tom bade farewell and left the smoky bistro. As they walked away, Tom hazarded a question that had been on his mind all evening. He had been wondering why there were no women present. In his experience, women had been the backbone of the Resistance. Their delicate fingers, their guileless faces and their sheer bloody courage in the face of possible arrest and torture. He'd heard that women couriers only lasted six weeks before arrest and possible execution or transport to a concentration camp. So, why was there no representative at tonight's festivity?

"I wanted you to meet people who could help in our search," Lucien said. "Marc is an architect, as you heard. He was well acquainted with Jeanne Bonnet from the Arts Museum. He knows that she was arrested and that two of her assistants were also. One could have been Madeleine, he doesn't know."

"I see. And the others?"

"Marcel drives trains. At the moment he's on the Paris to Lyon run. He may find out something for us. The others drift around Paris, from bistro to bar and back again. Good at getting information. Jean-Luc runs a brothel down in Lyon and was able to winkle information out of his German clientele. You know, pillow talk. He has avenues of information we can only dream about. The fisherman handled boats ferrying agents coming across La Manche."

"Like I was, from an English submarine to a French fishing boat and onto a beach somewhere."

"Indeed. Which is why I wanted you to meet him. Maurice always wondered if any of the agents he ferried had survived. Now he is happy to know that at least one did."

Tom remembered the journey, feeling thoroughly seasick in the submarine and then being hauled onto a rocking fishing boat, so ill he didn't have time to feel fear. The other two men on the boat sat shivering, not from cold but from fright. As they approached the

130

coastline of France and saw the searchlights one man started cursing. He refused to get off and had to be manhandled back onboard the sub. Tom noticed handcuffs before a sailor shut the hatch.

He and the other man survived the rough handling by the fishermen and were silently rowed to shore. Once there, Tom and his colleague were hustled into a waiting truck. Who that man was and whether he had survived wasn't something Tom wished to dwell on.

"That Jean-Luc didn't seem to fit," Tom said.

"Ah, Jean-Luc. Yes. One of those men we could never be sure of. Was he a hero or a traitor?"

"Perhaps both, perhaps a double agent?"

Lucien shrugged, his jacket becoming damp with falling snow.

"I see." And Tom did see. There were men he'd come across who could have been both straight-up loyal or double agents or straight-out traitors. "But none have information for us?"

"Not yet. They know your story. They'll start digging for information. Marc has already suggested we go to Lyon and speak to Jeanne's brother. He'd seen her name on the Red Cross board of returned prisoners. So, she might very well be there."

"But not Madeleine?"

"Not Madeleine's name, although he wouldn't have known to look for her. He said he'd try again."

"About Madeleine…"

"Later, Tom. Why are you always in such a hurry?"

131

"Because…" Tom hesitated. Sooner or later he'd have to hold Lucien down and spoon-feed him the new information. "When do we go to Lyon?"

"When do **I** go," Lucien stopped, turned to Tom, a look on his face of such anguish and loss that Tom placed his hand over Lucien's. "Please, Tom, let me do this for you. Leave me to find Madeleine while you concentrate on the child."

"Very well."

It took all Tom had to agree to Lucien's proposal. He clearly couldn't do both, search for Sophie and Madeleine and Lucien had the connections as he clearly showed this evening.

There was clearly a guilt-thing going on here. What had Lucien done or not done for Madeleine? He thought of Lucien's parents lying dead in the family graveyard. Who else had Lucien lost? One can never gauge another's sorrow. Alright, let him find Madeleine.

"I must insist, I'll be going to Lyons with you. Come, let's get inside out of the cold, and I'll explain."

As they settled down in the apartment for a last glass of wine, Tom told him about the letter to Madeleine from the dressmaker.

"We thought she'd been arrested but obviously not. Not then, anyway."

Lucien put his head down and groaned. "When was it written? Have you been to ask? Where is she? Why did this damned woman not tell us? We could have had Sophie back years ago."

"There's no need to chastise yourself, Lucien. Even I walked over it. The thing is, Mme Durand wrote it to Madeleine in 1942."

"And it's been lying here all this time?"

Tom nodded. "We now know the child survived the round-up in 1942 and Madeleine also survived."

"We have been assuming she was arrested with her friends."

"The bookseller saw her later that day. She went to work for Jeanne Bonnet. That's our last contact with her. Now, in the light of this new information, we go to Lyon and speak to the Bonnets."

"First you must speak to the dressmaker's niece again. Find out all you can."

"She's given me all she can. I have a letter and an address to go to. Sophie must be there. Perhaps Madeleine will be there too. Why can't we just lock up the apartment and go to Lyon this minute?"

"Duty, my friend. Tomorrow I must return to the vines. They are gentle masters, but masters all the same. Perhaps, if you've finished here in Paris, you might join me. My place is halfway to Lyon anyway."

"What is this duty? What's more important than finding Madeleine and the child?"

"A great duty. We are busy pruning the vines. My next year's production and the year after that depends on a good pruning. After we've pruned during the day, we can spend the nights drinking good wine and planning. And I'd also like you to meet Adam Janssen. His mother thought very highly of you."

Tom laughed. "The housekeeper? She only met me once."

"Yes, but Madeleine loved you. For her that was enough."

Chapter 14

The next morning Tom woke with a crashing hangover. The 'midnight feast' plus the subsequent laying to rest of another bottle of wine in the *appartement* had come back to haunt him as his head pounded and his mouth tasted like jailbird's underwear. He lay for a while wondering if his head would ever feel normal again or, if he stood up too suddenly, it would fall off his shoulders. He got up very slowly testing the limits of his head, holding it onto his shoulders as he moved. Groaning he filled the bath and lay down in the steaming water with a cloth on his forehead. Time to assess. What next?

No. Too much brain-fog.

Lucien must have left very early, his breakfast cup and plate washed and draining on the sink. Had Lucien mentioned something about the vines last night? Something about pruning? Tom couldn't remember. Lucien had been in Paris for only one day. What was that about? Oh yes, the American buyer.

Late January and although much had been achieved, he wondered how much more he needed to do before he could leave. He now knew that Sophie had been cared for by strangers. Mme Durand, her niece – did he even know her name? – had done the best they could in an appalling situation. He wondered if the niece could tell him anything more than she already had. He had a name and an address. Surely, all there was left was to get on a train, go to Lyon and pick Sophie up. Simple. Why couldn't Lucien see that?

The nagging question was – why had Madeleine abandoned the child?

It had happened when the French police arrested Emily and Aaron. At first Tom and Lucien thought Madeleine might have been apprehended as well, but Monsieur Marat had seen her after the arrests.

Madeleine had come back from wherever she worked and found her friends gone and assumed Sophie had gone with them and had been sent off to Auschwitz. How truly awful. To imagine what she had gone through, imagining the child in a cattle truck and then in a camp. The gas chambers were not yet generally known in July 1942, the Wannsee convention had only been held in January of that year where the Final Solution of exterminating Jews had been decided. There were rumours aplenty, but no one could ever have imagined how brutal it was going to be. Not then, not even now.

How terrible to think that Madeleine believed her child lost forever. Such sorrow and all for nothing.

After he had found there was nothing to eat or drink in the kitchen, Tom moved slowly down the stairs, to the book shop and knocked on the door, his forehead pressed against the cold glass of the window.

"Ah, Mr Blake. Come in." Marat looked closely at Tom. "A heavy night last night?"

"I'm afraid so," Tom said. "I've just found my cupboards are empty. I was hoping for a cup of your real coffee. If you could spare a cup, that is."

He sat down and waited with his eyes closed until Marat had placed a demitasse in front of him.

"My apologies, *M'sieur Marat.* In Paris where coffee is almost unobtainable, I sit here and drink yours."

"It brings me great pleasure to share what I have, Mr Blake."

"How is it that you still have real coffee when no one in Paris seems to have any?"

Marat touched the side of his nose in the universal code of secrecy. "I have a contact, you could say. An Algerian Jew who spent some time hiding in my shop. He escaped and went to South America. His 'payment' is in parcels of coffee. So, you and young Aubert went out last night?"

"How do you know?"

"You made enough clatter to wake an army, *mon ami.*"

Tom laughed but the sound reverberated in his head, so he stopped. "I met some people last night. Friends of Lucien's."

"Ruffians, no doubt."

Tom smiled. "It would seem so. One who interested me was a man called Jean-Luc Renier, owner of a brothel in Lyon. Do you know the name?"

"Renier? From Lyon? Hmm," Marat rubbed his chin, a rasping noise and Tom realised that neither he nor the bookseller had shaved. "It's a fairly common name. Jean-Luc, you say. Hmm. The name rings no bells for me. Let me think."

Tom savoured the hot coffee. "No matter. It's not important. I'll be leaving in a day or two, *Monsieur.* My quest in Paris seems to be over. Is there anything I can do to help you before I go?"

Marat looked around his book shop and sighed. "Look at the place," he said. "It's dusty and old and full of books I have no chance of selling."

"There are the manuscripts…" Tom began.

"They were put aside by my forebears for what you call 'a rainy day'."

"Perhaps that day has come. I know someone at the Louvre. He, or someone, with knowledge, could come and give you an estimation of the value of your treasures. You don't have to sell them all. Just one or two perhaps. At least they would be in a safe place, at the Louvre. Anyway, I believe that if you sell all your books to a reputable museum, you could be a very, very wealthy man."

"Thank you. But what about you, Mr Blake? You asked what you personally could do to help me. You were here in Paris at the university, learning about such manuscripts. Are you not qualified to estimate the value of what I have here?"

"I could try." Tom wasn't sure he wanted to get into a task that could take days.

"I'm asking as a friend, Mr Blake. Tom. Will you tell me what you think the worth of my treasure is."

"Very well," Tom said, defeated by Marat's look of entreaty and his own gratitude for kindness offered. "We should still get hold of the experts."

After Tom finished his coffee, he took up the cotton gloves and a notebook pressed upon him by Marat and went into the old man's treasure house of old manuscripts. The air in the room felt dry but musty with the aroma of age and wisdom. A perfume that had enticed Tom to take up this work in the first place. He took one of Marat's manuscripts off the shelf and laid it on the small card table, drew up a chair. Slowly over the course of the day, he recorded twenty-eight large medieval antiquities full of colour and wonder, and their provenance, each worth a man's wages for a whole lifetime.

Late afternoon Marat knocked gently on the door. "I have a meal ready for you, Monsieur."

"Thank you. I've finished here. I was just sitting admiring this one. I can't estimate the value, unfortunately. I can only give you a vague figure. France's currency is in such a state of flux, as you know. But I do know that these manuscripts are extremely valuable. I have written down what I think each would fetch at auction. My God, man, you have a fortune sitting right here. Just selling one of these and you could retire and live in luxury. Look, I've been thinking. I know someone at the British Library in London, at least I did. There's the Victoria and Albert Museum in London. A Mr Freeman. There's the Sorbonne. There's also the *Bibliothèque Nationale de France* right here in Paris. Get someone out to have a look, Monsieur. Here's the name of the chap in London. I've written it down for you. I know this person. I've had dealings with him, and you won't regret it. He's honest."

He could hardly say that the 'dealings' were with an expert at the Victoria and Albert Museum, Cromwell Road in London who'd been instrumental in his arrest. Harold Freeman had spotted Tom's fraud before he'd had a chance to confess to the bet. The way Freeman had gone about it was to ask for provenance, which of course Tom couldn't provide. It gave officials at the V&A the opportunity to have Tom arrested. Still Freeman had come to see him in jail whereas Madeleine had not. It says something for a man who might have seen the good in Tom after all.

"The V&A in London would be my recommendation."

Marat took the piece of paper Tom held out to him with a deep sense of reluctance.

"My grandfather and then my father built up this small collection. They were never for sale. But," he said. "I have to eat and perhaps the time has come."

Tom laid a sympathetic hand on the old man's shoulder. "Nevertheless, they should be shared with everyone, not locked up here, out of sight."

"I know, I know."

When they stood at the door to the book shop, Tom felt reluctant to leave. Was there anything more he could learn in Paris or was it time to get on the train for Lyon? As he turned to leave Marat put up a hand.

"A moment, *M'sieur*. Jean-Luc Renier you said?"

"Yes, that is his name."

"There's been a thought idling at the back of my mind. Come. I think I might have something."

Marat shuffled down the passage between the bookshelves. In the room Tom had thought was his sleeping quarters, Marat opened a small cupboard and pulled out a roll of posters. He placed it on his table and slowly unrolled it all the while humming a slow stream of musical notes. "I was a theatre goer in those days. There was a time when I thought to place these posters on a wall in the shop. But time has caught up with me. Ah, here we are."

A large colourful poster announced a musical directed by Jean-Luc Renier. It had played in Paris before the war. Quite a family affair, with the Renier family active in most roles.

From a small drawer Marat took out what looked like a theatrical programme. "I believe it was disbanded when the men were conscripted. The old couple died in a car crash while driving from Paris to Lyon to escape the Germans. It was rumoured the younger Renier later put the female cast members to a less reputable career."

"What would that be?"

"Prostitution."

"That's him."

Chapter 15

Very early the following morning Tom left Paris by train and finally disembarked at the station that served the small village near Lucien's vineyard. He'd sent a telegram to Lucien notifying him but didn't really expect him to drop everything to meet him. So, he was pleasantly surprised when, on coming out of the station building, he saw Lucien leaning on the side of a horse-drawn cart. The horse, a roan, was young and sleek and twitchy, in need of a firm grip.

"And good day to you too, Lucien," Tom said as he was thoroughly hugged and had a kiss planted on each cheek. He wondered if he'd ever get used to the flamboyant way the French greeted each other. Compared to the spikey formal handshake of the Brits, this was pleasantly warm but still a little awkward.

"Come along, Tom. We need to get back. I have work to do."

"Something I can help you with?"

Lucien looked at Tom with a fair sprinkling of scorn. "You, a 'rosbif'? Hah. Well, I suppose so. I'm short of labourers. The French are slow in demobilising men from the army. And only a trickle of men coming home from German POW camps, so you'll have to do."

"So, what do you need help with?"

"I've told you. We're busy pruning the vines. We started last month but it's a long and arduous task.

Backbreaking. Exhausting. It could take a few more weeks and I can't go to Lyon until it's done. I can't leave Adam to do it alone, so the sooner we get done the sooner we can leave."

"Talking about Lyon, you'll be going with me?"

Lucien looked sharply at Tom. "Why not? I want to interview Jeanne Bonnet. She must know where Madeleine is."

"Of course."

*****

The horse was skittish, and Lucien concentrated on keeping her calm. They bowled along a road with tall snowbanks on either side. Beyond were fields of vines as far as the eye could trace, standing in regimented rows.

"All wine country?" Tom asked.

"Yes, these are the vines of a neighbour. You might remember Madeleine telling you, she was supposed to marry him."

"Ah, that one."

"Most of the vineyards in this region are small, so it makes sense to combine if possible. We've had a few bad years. 1939 and 1941 were bad. '39 was the weather and '41 the lack of manpower. Also, the Germans limited the amount of fertilizer and sulphates we needed to combat disease. On top of that, we were short of bottles."

"And the horse? I thought all horses were taken."

Lucien laughed. "My acreage is enormous, and the Germans were too lazy to search further than the main buildings. The stable is down in a gully, but I've brought her closer to the other structures now. No need to hide her. There are a few more secrets, Tom. Later I'll show you."

They drew up in front of the old chateau. Tom remembered the last time, a visit that had ended ingloriously when he was kicked out by Madeleine's parents.

"Here we are." Lucien jumped from the cart and put a hand up to help Tom out. "I'll call Adam to take the cart to the stables. Wait here, Tom." He loped off round the corner and Tom was left to look at the house from which he had been expelled almost ten years before.

He stood at the top of the driveway, with a late January sun pretending to be warm. The old stone house was much the same, its slanting slate-grey roof so bowed it looked like a Japanese temple, the image badly let down by two ridiculous turrets at either end. When he visited the first time, Tom had made some joke about those faintly ludicrous turrets. It had clearly annoyed Madeleine who was in a state of taut-wire tension. She was about to introduce her new boyfriend to her parents, her English boyfriend, and she had clearly anticipated the worst. He remembered a sheen of perspiration on her forehead and her hands trembling. She so wanted it to work that Tom almost felt sorry for her, knowing as he did that nothing about this wild joyous romance would meet with her parents' approval. He was, after all, an alien and a Protestant without much chance of a good job, who had come to rob them of their beautiful daughter.

"Come along, Tom," Lucien said, wrenching Tom out of his reverie. "Don't delay. We need a strong brandy and a good fire. Then we can start to plan."

"A brandy? This time of the day? Isn't it a bit early? We haven't had lunch yet."

"A good brandy at any time of the day. Especially if we're going to tour the vineyard. It'll be cold." He glanced at Tom. "You do want to take a look at my land, don't you?"

"Yes, of course. I'd also like to see where your parents are lying. Pay my respects, if I may."

"Thank you. That is comforting. But first, let's see if there's lunch. Come along, Tom, no delays."

He followed Lucien, trudging past an almost derelict fountain, up the stone steps and to the house.

The front door was as he remembered it. Heavy oak with a brass bell to the side. He recalled how it had slammed behind them, as they'd walked away on that last day. Now, Lucien put his shoulder to the door and it creaked open scraping on the tiled floor where the drip of water, snow and ice had, over years of neglect, changed its shape. The hallway was dark and a little dingy. No Janssen to take care of things, for she lay cold in the graveyard beside her employers. Tom shivered.

Lucien took off his coat and hung it on the deer antlers that substituted for a coat rack and invited Tom to do the same. Rubbing his hands, he made his way into the small living room where Madeleine's parents had once reigned supreme.

Nothing had changed in the years since he had been ignominiously bundled out; the black tiled floor worn smooth by generations of footsteps, the stone fireplace carved with fruit and leaves, the two armchairs on either side still bearing the imprint of bodies, the hefty table fit for a medieval banquet. Dark oak ceiling beams loomed above them, making the room feel gloomy and small. There was a tall mahogany armoire on one wall and several windows shrouded by dark green ivy clinging to the outside wall so the whole room was cast in a greenish tinge. Tom felt he was swimming underwater.

Lucien bent down and lit the fire.

He handed Tom the fire iron. "You tend the fire, and I'll go and find Marie, see if there's a meal ready for us."

Tom was left alone with a struggling fire and his equally struggling thoughts. Here he was, in France again when he thought he might at last find some peace in his little home in Kent. He wished with all his heart that this new pain, the loss of the little girl, would be taken from him. And that he could go back to Britain, back to the cottage and be at least content if not happy. He wasn't sure he could stand the agony of this extra burden. Not only was Madeleine lost to him but now his child. He tried to imagine what she would look like and failed. Blonde like Madeleine? Her blue eyes or his brown ones? No, of course he knew that. Blue eyes. Summer-sky eyes. All he knew of her was that she had a birthmark on her back that looked like angel's wings.

And of course he had seen her clothing, those small vests and socks. He had gone from total despair after visiting Philipe Moreau at the Louvre to trembling hope when he found Mme Durand's letter. Even so, he felt bound by a situation over which he had no control.

He couldn't go home, he knew that. He had to stay and find his daughter. How could he go back to the Kent cottage, never knowing if she was dead or alive? What if she were still alive and he abandoned her because he didn't have the courage or the strength to find her? He dug roughly into the fire and it flared up.

Lucien bustled in, rubbing his hands and smiling. "Good news, there is soup and bread. Also, our first butter made from our own milk. We can start with a brandy if you like or keep it for later. And of course, we must eat in here where it's warm."

The door opened and a young woman wheeled in an ancient tea trolley with a large tureen, two plates and a broad platter of buttered bread. She placed the food on the table and Lucien waved an invitation to sit. Tom didn't think he'd seen anything more inviting.

"Who is that?" He asked once the door closed, and he had a large plate of steaming soup in front of him.

"Marie, she lives in the town with her parents. She wants to learn the wine trade, but presently she is cooking for Adam and me and keeping house. Honestly, I don't think she'll be here too long. Housekeeping isn't what she wants and I'm not sure of her stamina to work on the vines. I think she would be better off going to Paris and learning to be a teacher or something."

After the meal, Tom and Lucien sat in the armchairs in front of the fire and fell into a contented silence. If he closed his eyes, Tom could almost imagine himself back in the Kent cottage with the forlorn little Christmas tree in the corner and a whisky in his hand.

Lucien's next request broke through his thoughts. "You have news?"

146

"Am I so obvious?"

"Yes, Tom. You came here today looking almost cheerful."

Suddenly Tom's depression lifted. Of course he would find Sophie. There were no ifs or buts about it. "Nothing new," he said. "It's just that I am so close to finding Sophie that I can almost touch her. She's in Lyon, I'm sure."

"So, Mme Durand went to Lyon? That's something definite," Lucien said settling back. "Tell me all."

"I've spent all this time running around Paris, coming up against brick walls. And all the while there was this letter in the apartment." Tom pulled it out of his inner pocket. "It was sealed, so evidently Madeleine had never read it."

"Well, what does it say?"

"Just a very simple message from *Mme* Durand saying she had the child. What's more important is the date, Friday 18th July 1942."

"After the big *rafle* in Paris."

"Yes. At first, I thought that perhaps Madeleine had been swept up in that. And Sophie. It seems fairly certain that Emily and Aaron were arrested and taken to the Velodrome. The son of the concierge told me his mother tipped the French police that there were two Jews in apartment number three."

"Madeleine could have been arrested as well."

"That was my first thought. As I told you, the bookseller downstairs saw Madeleine after that. So we now know she wasn't taken."

"Thank God. And the letter? May I read it?"

Lucien handled it as if it were an epistle from the archangel Michael. "A very short message. So, Sophie was rescued and taken to a place of safety by the dressmaker."

Lucien suddenly leant forward, put his hands to his face. Tom could see his shoulders shaking. "Forgive me. I'm overwhelmed. You know what this means? That they are both alive and somewhere in France."

"The niece said Mme Durand was old and tired and constantly hungry. So, she decided to close the shop and go to family in the country where she stayed until her death."

"Another dead end?"

"Not necessarily. It's still Lyon. And we have an address."

They sat in silence, watching the flames dance. The afternoon had come and gone as they ate, drank brandy and reminisced and now the country air that flowed through the tall windows was chilled. Lucien pulled the curtains closed and placed another log onto the fire. The flames were mesmerising, and Tom thought back to the flames in his small fireplace in the cottage in Kent. Whatever the result, he suspected his life would be changed forever. At the end, would he have a daughter and how would she fit into his solitary life? And what did it entail to bring up a little girl to womanhood? Would he always be alone, and would his child forever be motherless?

Lucien's hesitation was frustrating. Tom wanted to go and go now, right away.

"Lyon," Lucien said softly. "I was there when my parents were shot."

Tom placed his brandy glass carefully on the table. "Do you want to tell me?"

"A sorry tale. I was taking wine to the market. Throughout the war most of our wine was bought by people who worked for the Germans. But we had a few private clients. A restaurant here and there. I also had to pick up bottles from them which were hard to come by and so anyone buying wine had to present their empties. The restaurants were good, they always had their empty bottles ready in crates for me to pick up. They knew, of course, that the next delivery of wine depended on my having enough bottles. It so happens on that day I had company, two young men from England hidden in the back of the truck under some sacks. I had promised to get them into the city where there would be people to take them further. But I was unlucky that day. Or careless."

"You were arrested."

"Yes, my papers were checked. They were in order, but I had escapees under some sacks in the back of the truck, the two British airmen. I hesitate to even think what happened to them."

Tom stirred. "Generally, they were just returned to the POW camp."

"I hope so. I feel I let them down."

"Don't feel bad. I know the type; a prison camp would never have held them for long."

"Anyway, I was taken to prison."

"Were you there long?"

"Long enough. Two months. Maybe more. There was no way to calculate how much time had passed."

"Who was there with you?"

"Oh, the usual bunch of resisters of one sort or another. A wireless operator who was executed later, a bloke who was the local expert in blowing up trains although *le Boche* didn't know, he'd only been arrested for being drunk and disorderly. A couple of Basque fellows whose papers were suspect. They were out pretty quickly. There was also a snitch, put in there to report back on what we said. He didn't last long, had a nasty accident on the stairs and died. Dear me. How unfortunate. And there was me because I had British POWs in the back of my truck."

For a moment the men sat gazing at the dancing flames.

"They finally interrogated me and found me guilty. But I had already served a sentence of some months, so they released me. I was shocked. I hadn't thought I would be released. Of course, I played the drooling simpleton so they must have thought I was harmless."

"Even though you had two escapees with you?"

"I played the village idiot so successfully they assumed I hadn't known. Even through the times of torture. And the boys, bless them, assured the Germans I'd not realised they'd crept into the back." Lucien sipped his brandy. "It was hard, playing stupid for so many months. All the time, in case they were watching. And they were, through the snitch. Anyway, I returned to the vines. I remember coming home, walking over the hill and seeing the vines standing like soldiers in the fields and feeling content. I was in a sorry state, mind you, dragging my broken feet along the dusty road. Adam must have spotted me in the distance because, next thing there was the horse and Adam riding along furiously. He lifted me up and I rode back to the chateau in style."

"And the truck?"

"I got that back later, had to steal it from their depot. I can't remember much of that time, except the *weinführers* had been and Adam sold most of the wine we had."

"*Weinfuhrer?*"

"Hitler used men who knew the wine trade to buy up our stock. Most of them were good fellows. We knew them from before the war and now after the war I expect they'll be around again. Most were sensitive enough not to wear their uniforms when they came round. Their job was not a pleasant one. They were buying our wine for the Germans while still trying to give us a good price. A real tightrope. Anyway, when I'd been held in prison Adam managed to sell off a few hundred cases of wine. It wasn't a very good vintage, but it was all we had. At the time I was close to penniless. The vines were in a bad way as well. Adam hadn't been able to care for them on his own and so they had gone wild. Months of neglect and they were gangly, the stakes were collapsing and weeds everywhere. And no money to pay workers, not that there were any. I was going to have to put the vines to sleep, '*en sommeil*'. Or dig into our hidden stock of good wines and start selling them off. And that's where Madeleine comes in. She came down to the vineyard, saw I was in a bad place and went to the bank. She was now of age and so she could claim her inheritance. She spoke to our lawyer and with his help withdrew the whole amount, several million francs. And she gave it to me. So, you see, Tom, I have an obligation. She saved the vineyard."

Why wasn't Tom surprised? That was just so Madeleine, generous to a fault.

Added to Tom's vast source of nightmares was Violette Aubert. The insufferable, dreaded potential mother-in-law. The hag, the bag, the witch, the bitch. Not that he ever used such names in front of Madeleine, but he blamed her mother for everything. An embittered woman who didn't appreciate the worth of her only daughter and was prepared to use her as a pawn in a business deal. Damn it! Madeleine was worth more than that. Even he, as a total wash-out, had seen that.

He'd taken the measure of Madeleine's father that day. A kind gentle man who had suffered a mustard gas attack during the Great War, sickly and not in a position to oppose his wife. That was one fight too many for the old man.

Tom put old resentments behind him. Now wasn't the time…

Chapter 16

"I get the feeling that this whole thing, finding Madeleine and Sophie, is becoming blurred into one mission. Mine."

Lucien sat back with a sigh. "It is, Tom. I apologise. I was thoughtless."

"No, you're right. Two heads and all that. So, what did you have in mind?"

"Our first task is to find out who brought Madeleine's letter to me. It would give us some idea where Madeleine was when she wrote it. If the man who brought it was Resistance, then we assume she probably was too. Every bit of evidence builds up the whole picture. Do you remember Adam? No, perhaps not. I keep referring to him, but you've never met him. He's my right-hand man here on the farm. He's worked here since he and his mother escaped Belgium in the Great War. I have a suspicion he may know a little more about that letter than he's let on."

"You think he may know who delivered it?"

"It won't harm to ask."

Tom woke early, when a rooster crowed its welcome to the sun. His bleary eyes shunned the sharp light reflecting off the snow outside, and he turned over pulling the quilt up to his eyebrows.

He and Lucien had spent a convivial evening in front of the fire with a bottle or two of the vineyard's better wine. He'd finally staggered up to bed and had fallen into a deep and, for once, a dreamless asleep. Now in the early morning, he was paying the penalty. A sharp knock on the door and he burrowed down further into the bed.

"Wake up, Tom. Time to face the morning."

Tom groaned. *Doesn't Lucien know how I'm suffering?* He sounded far too cheerful. *Didn't he too have a pounding headache? No, probably not.*

"Go away, Lucien. I'm a cripple, an invalid. I am no good to man nor beast."

"I have coffee downstairs, and a good breakfast," Lucien wheedled. "Besides I want to show you the farm. The outside will clear your head in an instant."

Tom swallowed hard at the thought of a greasy English breakfast. But this was France, perhaps a *croissant* or two? Even that stirred his stomach unpleasantly. He staggered out of bed, dressed and made his way to the kitchen where he heard cheerful voices.

Lucien waved at Tom from beside the stove. "Ah, the survivor has arisen. Good morning, Tom. We have eggs for breakfast. A rare treat. Our chickens are laying at last."

A large, bearded man stood up. "We put them in a warm shed and they think it's summer. I am Adam."

Tom grunted, stretched out a hand to Adam who took it into his great gnarled paw.

"An honour, *M'sieur* Blake."

"Hardly an honour. Not this early in the morning. Please call me Tom. I'm part of the family."

"Yes, indeed."

When the eggs were ready, and the bread cut and buttered, they ate in silence and then put on their coats and scarves and stepped outside. Still cold but the air was crisp and invigorating.

"Come, Tom. You now get the full tour with a little wine tasting at the end."

Lucien led the way to the sheds. Inside, three huge grape presses stood dormant and covered by canvas dustcloths. Made of wooden staves circled by metal hoops they looked powerful enough to crush a man. Now they were silent and motionless.

"During *les vendanges*, the harvesting, they come alive," Lucien said. "These iron plates descend onto the grapes and press them. The liquid runs down into the underground vats. Come along, I'll show you."

Down a set of stairs and into a darkened cellar, vast and silent like a huge cathedral to the gods of wine, their feet echoed on the stone floor. Huge casks lay on their sides in rows, more than he could count. The air was clogged with the aroma of maturing wine.

"Here is where the juice ferments. The heart of the winery, Tom." Lucien gestured to the casks. "This wine will be ready to bottle in about three years. God willing."

"No secret stash?" Tom asked smiling.

He noticed a quick glance between Adam and Lucien.

"I'm sorry," Tom said. "In Bordeaux, I'd heard about wine growers hiding their stock from the Germans. Isn't there a story about one of the restaurants in Paris that was reputed to have the finest wine cellar in the world? They chose to wall in their best wines, including twenty thousand bottles of an 1867 vintage."

"That's right. *La Tour d'Argent*. The story goes that Herman Göring arrived and asked to see their famous cellars and taste the 1867 which he'd heard of. But it was all gone."

"That couldn't have gone down too well."

"No, Göring had his men take all the visible stock, about eighty thousand bottles. But it saved the restaurant because it was all there, the good stuff, when they finally opened again last year."

"So, did your father do the same thing?" Tom asked.

"Most *vignerons* did," Lucien said. "Our way of fighting the Germans, by withholding our best."

They were interrupted by the sound of hurrying footsteps on the stairs. Marie ran down smoothing her hair.

"*Monsieur* Lucien," she said breathlessly. "I've just heard. *Madame* Guillard is back."

Lucien's face darkened with anger. "Who told you?"

"Old man Duval, the man who delivers vegetables. He saw her at the train station waiting for a lift."

"Thank you, Marie." Lucien walked swiftly to a cupboard partly hidden by one of the large storage tanks.

Adam put a hand on Lucien's arm. "Wait, Lucien. We need to speak."

"I have nothing to say." Lucien shook Adam's hand away. "That woman was instrumental in the death of our parents. What can be said?"

156

"No, listen, Lucien…"

Lucien opened a drawer and pulled out a Luger. It was dull and menacing.

"Lucien," Tom shouted. "What the devil…"

Lucien pushed past them. "Stay here. I have business to discuss with Mme Guillard."

"No!" Adam tried to hold onto Lucien. As he turned, he struck Adam, his fist crashing into the man's chest.

Adam crumpled, gasping as Lucien ran out of the shed.

"Tom, stop him!"

Tom ran, his legs weak with shock.

He saw Lucien at the stables, leading an unsaddled roan out. Lucien jumped, held onto the roan's mane.

And then he was gone.

Adam sat on the floor of the shed, gasping and rubbing his chest. "Stupid. Stupid."

"I couldn't stop him."

Slowly Adam got to his feet. "Lucien will kill her."

"We have to stop him. Can we get there?"

"It's too late. We'll never catch him now."

Tom leaned against the wall of the shed, angry, shocked and helpless.

"The fool. The bloody fool. He's just jeopardised everything."

*****

The long bitterly cold afternoon sent Tom and Adam into the house to await Lucien. They huddled by

157

the fire in the living room, its dark greenly shaded interior making misery a familiar host. Tom tried to imagine what was going in at the neighbour's home. Adam had explained that she was the widow of another *vigneron*, the late René Guillard who had been a bitter rival of the Auberts.

"Should we have gone out there? Perhaps we could have stopped…"

"We don't have transport."

"What did the woman say that led to this?"

"If she said anything, it would have been as tattle, malicious gossip. Going back three or more generations, the rivalry was fierce. Who would produce the best wine of that season. Always with bitter words."

"Would she honestly have sent the Germans here? Hang on," Tom jumped up. "I thought I heard Lucien coming back."

The men ran out of the chateau and up to the stables. Lucien was there brushing down the roan which gleamed with sweat.

Adam looked at Lucien and waited.

"If you're asking if I shot the woman, the answer is no, I didn't. We had a very good talk instead. She offered to kill herself, feeling unworthy of living."

Adam took hold of Lucien and steered him out of the stable. "Did she admit anything?"

"Only of passing gossip onto the Germans."

"It resulted in the murder of three people." Adam's voice was mild.

"Yes, I did point that out. What she said next stopped a bullet entering her brain."

"Well?"

158

"Her stepson had brought Madeleine's letter to me. Rene Guillard's eldest."

"Didn't you recognise him?" Tom asked.

"No, he'd grown up when I was in Paris designing buildings."

"And did he say where he got the letter?"

"He wasn't there. He's apparently in Brittany at the moment, visiting a girlfriend. Mme Guillard said she'd send him over when he gets back. Or she'd send someone else."

Once again, after a meal the two men sat in front of the fire drinking a deep red burgundy from a neighbouring vineyard. "So, down to basics. When do we leave for Lyon?"

Lucien sat back. "I'm sorry, Tom, but not yet. There are things that I must do here. I've already wasted too many days; the pruning must continue."

"Come on, Lucien." Tom felt like a spoilt child, stamping his foot and yelling 'you promised'.

"Tom, I have a vineyard to run. Adam and I…"

"Adam and you…what?" Tom recognised the snarl in his voice. Time to calm down, he drank a gulp of wine. *Breathe, Tom, breathe deeply.*

"It's the time of the year when the sap is down so we prune the vines. It'll take us some time to finish what we've already started. When it's done, then we go to Lyon."

Tom felt a cold sort of frustration take hold of him. Prune the bloody vines? What the blazes was that all about? Couldn't it wait? What was more important, some bloody grape vines or Madeleine?

"Why the hell can't Adam do it?"

Lucien got up from the chair in a flash of anger. He grabbed Tom's collar and dragged him up, pushed him to the window. "Look out, Tom. Look at the vines. What do you see? Ten vines? Twenty? No, you see hundreds, thousands. We're waking the vines up, they've been *en sommeil* for too long. How long do you think it's going to take Adam and me to prune that lot? We've only managed about a third and the rest could take a month or more if we don't get some help. If I don't do it, I lose income for perhaps the next ten years. Everything depends on the pruning. It's the most important intervention of the year. It's my life out there, Tom."

"Are you saying it'll be months before we can get to Lyon? Look, if you can't go, I'll go by myself."

Lucien shook him. "Stop being churlish. You know as well as I do that together we can do the job in Lyon in less than half the time. Besides I'm the one with the contacts. All I'm asking for is a little patience."

"I can't wait that long, Lucien. I must go back to England, get a job."

"I'm asking for one month, two. Please, Tom."

Tom threw himself into the armchair and picked up his wine glass. "Very well. Then you'd better start showing me how to prune. The sooner we get it done, the better."

For the first time that day, Lucien smiled. "Good man," he said.

Tom longed for this journey over and done with. Perhaps they should just stop this charade, this search. It could not possibly bring any positive resolution. Lucien, the ever-optimist, would have to be convinced. But Lucien was speaking.

"Did Adam tell you we'd hidden our best wine?"

"Yes, he mentioned..."

Lucien pointed to an old armoire, heavy and dark. "We have to move that to get to it."

Tom stood up. "Well, let's do it."

"Now? It can wait, Tom."

"This is as good a time as any. Is there a room at the back of this?" Tom knocked on the armoire.

"A passage between the house and the sheds. It was built to allow us a dry walkway without having to go out in the snow."

"Did other *vignerons* have the same system?"

"The whole Burgundy region is built on limestone. So, there are labyrinths of caves underground, all available to the *vignerons* in the region. It started in the thirteenth century with monks keeping their wine cool. This hiding away of the best was our means of battling Hitler. That brute knew the value of French wine. Prestigious and profitable, he said. So he wanted it as much as he wanted our art works. So, we have tens of thousands of bottles down there that are worth a fortune."

Tom had a sudden image of Marat's manuscripts. The treasures of France, hidden away. "Aren't you interested in what's down there? The condition of the wine?"

"Yes, of course. Those bottles are our investment. I suppose it's time to check up on them."

Tom slid his hand down the back of the *armoire*. The piece of furniture sat very close to the wall. "I'm beginning to understand, or at least I think so. You are reluctant because you don't know what you'll find. Splendid wine that you can sell for millions or maderised bottles that you'll use to clean the toilets. So, if we must move heavy furniture around, let's do it. There are three of us. Besides, I'm interested to taste what you consider the best."

Lucien put his wine glass down. "My father and Adam did the hiding of the wine, so, I think Adam should be the one to bring them to light, don't you? I'll go and fetch him. He'll be in the kitchen with Marie."

Tom raised an enquiring eyebrow. Lucien grinned. "I think we may have a wedding in the not too distant future."

Tom cleared the area around the *armoire*. He rolled up the carpet and put it to one side. Then moved a small desk a few centuries old and he wondered when last it was moved. When the Auberts hid their wine? There were also glasses and knick-knacks to take from the armoire and, in one of the drawers some old tablecloths and napkins.

Lucien arrived with Adam and Marie. "Is there a torch anywhere?"

"In the kitchen," Marie said. "I'll get it."

Together they began to arduous task of moving the armoire. Slowly, groaning across the flagstones, it moved. By the light of Marie's torch, Tom could see an indent in the wall. If you looked close enough the new plaster was slightly whiter than the old. But so expertly hidden no one would notice it. Once the *armoire* was out of the way, Lucien took up a sturdy poker from the fireside and began to dig at the wall. It took a few minutes and some swearing and apologising to Marie but suddenly, one brick fell out and another and another. Soon there was a small pile of bricks and a large opening in the wall wide enough for them to climb in. The air was stale, and dust lay thick on the stone floor. Adam shone the torch into the *cave* and Tom could see racks of wine, dusty and cobwebby, stretching out as far as torchlight allowed.

"My God, Lucien. You have a lot of wine sitting here."

They stepped in over the pile of bricks and mortar, Marie grumbling about the amount of work she'd have cleaning up after 'her boys'. A short set of steps and they were into the passageway leading to the sheds where the wine was made.

"The Germans would have loved this. See here, Tom." Lucien picked up one bottle with a sort of reverence. "This was bottled by my great-grandfather. See the date? 1893. This bottle alone is worth a fortune."

"And there are hundreds of them."

Adam laughed. "More like thousands, Tom. This was our battle against the Germans, and we won."

Chapter 17

The three men were up before dawn the next morning and, after a hasty breakfast, they went to the sheds, blowing on icy fingers. There had been no snow during the night, but a slight haze hung over the vines and the grass between the rows was crisp with frost.

"Here we are in the midst of an important job, Tom," Lucien said. "You are going to learn the basics of being a good *vigneron*."

"Yes, 'Papa'," Tom said. "Let's just get on with it and stop being pompous."

Lucien rummaged in a cupboard and brought out leather gloves and secateurs.

"Come, 'Papa' will show you what to do," he said. "You're going to need a few lessons."

"I'll give it my best," Tom said, pushing his hands into the old leather gloves that were stiff with age and cold.

They walked the short distance to the first row of vines that seemed to stretch out into the far distance. Tom felt a sense of despair. There were miles of vines, thousands that needed pruning. There were only three of them. It was going to take forever. When would they get to Lyon and continue the search for Madeleine and Sophie?

"I thought you said you and Adam had already started."

"We did, down in the gully where it's a little warmer and the vines will bud earlier."

"There's a lot of them, Lucien," Tom said. "Are you sure we're going to get it all done and still have time to go to Lyons before old age overtakes us?"

Lucien laughed. "Later in the week we'll have a few more workers. They're busy on the Guillard place now. Come Thursday we'll be almost up to full strength."

"You think I'll last until Thursday?"

"You'd better. There's no one else." Lucien bent down and took hold of a vine. There was tenderness in his grasp, as if he were holding the fingers of a child. "See, Tom, the vine is basically a creeper. If we didn't prune it would be all over the place." Lucien pointed at the unruly vine. "See here? When we prune, we leave only two canes or arms, these two, and cut back this and this. Then, on each cane we leave eight or nine buds. Here, watch me."

He bent down and swiftly cut off some wildly growing tendrils, leaving two strong arms or canes. He counted from the bottom of the cane to eight small buds and snipped off the top ones. The others he touched tenderly. "See? These small buds are our hope and our future, our connection to the soil. From these small nodes will come the wine. By March they should start leafing."

"If we can get copper sulphate," Adam bellowed from the next row. He'd already cut a dozen vines and was well ahead.

"Adam's right. We mix copper sulphate with lime. It fights fungus and bacteria. Been used since 1880 and it's the most effective weapon against downy

165

mildew. Not available during the war so, in 1940, most Burgundies were decimated by rot and mildew. The wine was dull and maderised."

Tom bent over his first vine and snipped.

"That's right Tom. Just a little lower."

"How do I know if I've left the two best canes?"

"Just pick the strongest looking."

They cut and snipped in silence. After the first hour, Tom's hands were beginning to smart and tingle. He took off one glove and inspected his fingers. They were red, the palm a little swollen. *Not too bad*, he thought, slipping the glove back. *I can go on.*

By midday he was exhausted from the constant bending. His hands felt raw. He stripped off the leather gloves, exposing blistered and swollen fingers. Tomorrow he'd pull on a pair of woollen gloves under the leather ones and try to protect his hands. Otherwise, they wouldn't last until Thursday. For the time being, he'd have to try cutting with his left hand.

"That's enough for now," Lucien called. "We'll eat."

They made their way to a *cabotte* that stood in the middle of the vines, a small round building built of the local stone and capped with the tiled roof. In the centre was a fireplace made up of a circle of rocks where a fire had already taken hold. Marie stood nearby with a large hamper at her feet. She smiled as they approached.

Lucien called out, "Ah, Marie, what luxuries do you have for us today?"

The men sat as close as they could get to the fire and held out their frozen hands, rubbing them as icy fingers began to tingle back to life. Tom couldn't help

166

but notice both men were suffering sore hands. He felt a bit better knowing he wasn't the only one. They all needed extra gloves, woollen ones. He'd ask Lucien after they'd had lunch. Marie opened the hamper and took out four glasses and two bottles of wine. Also, a large loaf of bread, *un pain rond*, a bottle of pickles and cheese wrapped in paper.

"A feast," Tom said more than grateful for the break. "*Merci.*"

He nursed his aching hands as Lucien put a glass of wine on the bench near him.

"You did well, for a 'rosbif'," Lucien said smiling. Tom accepted the insult, knowing it was not intended to hurt. It was almost a brotherly gibe and bounced off him like a falling leaf.

Tom held up his hand. "Does this qualify as roast beef?"

Lucien looked concerned. "I apologise, Tom. I'm expecting too much from you."

"Not at all. I'll do what I can."

"We can give you some softer gloves to put on inside the leather ones. That should help."

Marie held the round loaf against her apron and cut huge thick slices of bread. They ate in silence. Bread, pickles and cheese washed down with a glass of Chateau d'Aubert's rich red burgundy. Tom compared the image of himself in a pub somewhere in pre-war London. Smokey, noisy, crowded. Men talking about football in loud brassy voices. Here it was quiet, a lone crow cawing nearby.

Tom suddenly felt nostalgic for his little home in Kent and his English life. And for a London he hadn't seen in a long while. It had all changed. He knew that. He had known London before Mr Hitler's Luftwaffe had flattened so much of it. Now it was full of bombsites. All that was left in many suburbs was a strange and barren landscape.

"Lucien," Adam called. "A visitor."

A small figure trudged through the vines. Hunched over with hands in pockets and head hidden beneath a large beret.

"It's the Guillard boy. *Bonjour*," Adam called out.

The boy was small, but there was a haunting slant to his posture that spoke of something more than his years. Tom could only think that he walked stealthily, as if afraid someone was watching him. His clothes were too big, which added to his Dickensian look. *He could easily pass for an Artful Dodger,* Tom thought.

The boy came up to the group and Marie sliced off a chunk of bread and, with a large piece of cheese, handed it to him. He grunted and sat down on the floor near the fire, grabbed at the food and stuffed as much of it into his mouth as he could, almost as if he was afraid it would be snatched back. Tom's heart ached. Poor little devil. War was hell on children. This one looked about fourteen but in reality, he could have been older.

After he'd finished the bread, the boy stood up and fumbled in his pocket. He brought out the Luger and the men held their breath and watched with wary eyes.

"Lucien," Tom said. "Watch out."

"No, no, it's fine," Lucien said, but his voice was a little shaky.

168

The boy held out the Luger, grasping it by the butt. "Here, Monsieur. With a message. She will not shoot herself. Not today, *M'sieur.*"

"Tomorrow?" Lucien asked, smiling.

"Not tomorrow, either. Not ever. She has me and my sister to care for."

Lucien took the Luger, pressed the magazine release button and slid the magazine out. "One round missing? Has it been fired?"

The boy took a bullet from a deep pocket, held it up and smiled. It was a grim effort at a smile, but the boy did his best. "It's mine, *M'sieur* Lucien. When she wants to gossip again, I'll take it out and show her."

"Good boy. Now I have a question for you. There was a letter. Someone brought me a letter and I think it might have been you."

The boy scratched his head and sat down again. Marie took the hint and gave him another piece of bread and some cheese.

"I think I remember. It was from your sister?"

Tom held his breath.

"*Oui*, my sister, Madeleine Aubert. Where did you get it?"

"Hmm, let me think."

Tom wanted to grab hold of him and shake him.

"Yes, I remember. *Mon oncle.*"

"Your uncle?" Tom asked. But Mme Guillard told Lucien it had been brought over by her stepson. What was going on here?

"A real uncle or just a visitor."

The boy was indignant. "Real, of course. She may have many failings, but she is not like that."

"I apologise. And where is your uncle now?"

The boy shrugged. "Dead?"

Tom let out a groan. Another lead gone. The boy stared at him. Tom shrugged, silently acknowledging both the boy and his dead uncle. "Where did your uncle get the letter?" He asked. "Who gave it to him?"

It was the boy's turn to smile. "Who else but the lady herself. The sister of *M'sieur* Lucien."

The men looked at each other. Would it be as simple as that? The next-door neighbour's brother?

Lucien stood up. "Come, now," he said. "We have to get back to work. You," he pointed to the boy. "Tell your mother I'll visit her this evening to find out the truth."

"Step."

"I beg your pardon?"

"Step. Stepmother. She is my father's second wife. I am the son of my father's first wife. My sister is the daughter of my father's second wife."

"Are you deliberately trying to make my life impossible?" Lucien said, but there was a hint of laughter in his voice. "Get along with you now. Tell your stepmother I'll be there tonight."

As the boy walked away, they went back to the vines. Tom could hear Lucien whistling. He looked across to Adam, raising an enquiring eyebrow.

"Crazy," Adam said. "He won't admit it, but Lucien has always admired Blanche Guillard. She is young and beautiful. A little, ah, shall we say light-headed and with it light-hearted. She has a gaiety that belongs only to the young. Not much use, in my opinion, for anything but *soirées*. Her husband was much older, one of those business arrangements, you understand, rather than a love match."

"And the husband?" Tom was almost certain Lucien would not go hunting in another man's patch.

"He died just before war started. A hunting accident, I'm told."

"So, the lady is free, and Lucien is going courting. A bit strange seeing he went out this morning to kill her."

"Our Lucien is a passionate man, Tom. He can love and hate in the same breath. But I don't believe his feelings for Blanche go deep. It would be more of a business arrangement than a love match. I'm sure they'll be married soon, and Lucien will have twice the land he has now. And a pretty wife on his arm."

"A good thing?"

"For Lucien? Yes. For you? Not so good. His mind will not be on the search. You may have to go to Lyon alone."

"But surely he wants to find his sister?"

Adam shrugged. "Perhaps. A man cannot know another man's head. His heart is easier to read."

"And you?"

Adam smiled. "I rather fancy my chances with Marie. She hates me or says she does. That gives me hope."

Tom shook his head. Relationships were complex.

Chapter 18

He felt strange sitting in Lucien's living room, beside Lucien's fireplace and drinking Lucien's wine, without Lucien in the room. Yet Tom felt his presence even though he had left an hour ago for the Guillard home.

"Lucien is an architect who is committed to the vines," he said, more as a statement than a question. "A strange combination."

Adam nodded. The two men had been silent since Marie had placed a large meal in front of them. Adam had invited her to eat with them. She had agreed, it was warmer here than in the big drafty kitchen. Now she sat with them close to the fire that blazed and spluttered. Each nursed a large glass of wine. The second or third, Tom had lost count.

He rubbed the wine glass against his right hand. The blisters had long ago burst and now there were several places that were bleeding. Earlier in the evening when they'd walked in from the vines, Marie had seen the blisters, and the places rubbed raw and bleeding. She had thrown up her hands in horror and told him to sit down and be quiet. Tom had obeyed, suitably cowed by the school-marmish instruction. Marie had fussed and muttered as she'd cleansed his hands. She'd plastered the wounds with something that was obnoxious smelling but strangely cool and comforting and bound them in clean strips of cloth. From the kitchen armoire she produced a pair of woollen gloves, exhorting him to wear them under the leather gloves when he went out pruning on the morrow. A layer of protection, she said. Although his bandaged hands made use of fork and knife a little clumsy and the holding of a wine glass an exercise in balance, they no longer throbbed, and Tom thought he would sleep well tonight.

Adam had sunk deep into the wing-backed chair, his wine glass resting on his stomach. "You must understand," he said. "The *vignerons* of France have survived revolution, two world wars and diseases like phylloxera. Lucien's father, his grandfather, the Aubert family from way back have been part of the soil, they have cared for the land and the vines for generations. They have made wine for more years than I can tell. Now that his father is dead, Lucien is beginning to feel his strong connection to the land and if he stays, one day his sons and his grandsons will be here to prune and harvest the vines."

He stopped, looking embarrassed. "Forgive me, I ramble. Life here in the vineyard hasn't changed much since the Middle Ages. Yes, we've changed from horse and cart to tractors. We no longer stamp the grapes with our feet but have a machine to press them. But we still prune and harvest and make wine much the same way as the monks did in the thirteenth century. Although we don't rely on reading the phases of the moon any longer. In the next five hundred years, nothing much will change. This land was here long before us and will be here long after we have left. It is the one constant."

"It's seductive," Tom said. "Even I, a rosbif, can feel it. There is always hope and optimism when you grow things."

"Making wine is *très ancienne*. Men like Lucien, their grandfathers and great-grandfathers all lived and worked in the same way. Days begin early and last until the work is done. It's hard but satisfying, full of hope for the new season and optimism that in time the grape will reveal itself."

"You too are committed," Tom said.

Adam grinned. "Yes, I am. You can't work here without feeling the pull of the soil. And wine has a peculiar and fascinating history. There are stories going back to the sixth century of great leaders ordering their troops to drink wine to prevent illness. In all his campaigns, Napoleon is reputed to have carried a vast amount of champagne for his troops. It is said the reason why he lost at Waterloo was because he didn't have time to pick up the wine and so his troops had to fight on Belgian beer only."

Tom laughed. "That doesn't say much for your beer, does it?"

"I wouldn't know. I've been in France so long I've forgotten Belgian beer."

"My father was in the trenches in the Great War," Marie said, her voice tentative as if she feared being ridiculed. "He said they were issued with cases of champagne when they would much rather have had ammunition."

"Your father was a brave man, fighting on with champagne instead of bullets. Did he throw the bottles at *les Allemands*?"

Marie looked at Adam. "Are you making fun of my father, sir?"

"No, never."

"I hate you, Adam."

"Yes, I know," said Adam setting back into the armchair with a grin on his face. "And it's lovely."

"Wasn't Lucien conscripted?" Tom asked.

"Yes, very early on in the war. Perhaps in 1940. He had some luck there," Adam said. "His company was called to the front just after the Germans crossed the Meuse River. Lucien was driving a truck when it had a flat tyre. He and another man stopped to repair it. By the time they'd fixed the truck they got the message their whole company had been ambushed and taken prisoner. So, he turned round and came home. With the truck."

"So, Lucien missed the war, all because of a flat tyre."

"It seems so. Of course, as you know, later he was arrested. He also played a small part in the defence of France although he doesn't speak much about it. We had several casks we used to carry weapons and sometimes Resistance men into and out of Lyon. There were checkpoints all along the road, but Lucien had a special look he put on whenever he came upon German soldiers. His imbecile look."

Tom smiled. "Ah, the drooling. Yes, he mentioned it."

After three large glasses of wine, he thought his smile would be benign, but he probably grimaced horribly, enough to frighten this rather nice young lady who sat so primly by the fire. He put his glass down and stood up.

"I am asleep on my feet," he said, stretching and yawning. "Would you forgive me if I left you and went to bed?"

Adam murmured something Tom didn't hear, Marie smiled shyly, and Tom retreated. He thought he had been very tactful. If Adam wanted to court Marie, now was a good time to start.

*****

By early March all the vines were finally pruned, and some were beginning to bud. Tom was frantic with impatience. A fair number of Lucien's workers had dribbled back to the vineyard and, as a result, the work had gone a lot faster. Tom's hands had acclimatised to the hard work, and he had gained strength and confidence. He worked side by side with the more experienced men and had thus earned their respect. He no longer heard taunts about the weak *Anglais* who looked like 'rosbif'. At those times he'd been tempted to remind them who had won the war for them but decided, in the cause of good Anglo-French relations, to keep his trap shut.

In the end, Tom looked at the rows of vines that they'd pruned and felt happy. He realised with a start that he'd been happier here than he had felt for a very long time. Happier than leaning over old manuscripts. Definitely happier than he'd felt at the bank. That was a horror he'd sooner forget. The horrors of prison were off the scale. But here, close to the soil he had found almost a soul-stirring joy that he couldn't explain, not to Lucien anyway. But Lucien would know what contact with the land could do to a man.

What had he been doing in those war years when Lucien had been growing grapes? He'd been in the south of France blowing up trains and making sure members of the *maquis* were getting supplies of weapons from Britain. And killing people. They were careful not to kill too many Germans, the result of which would normally be vicious reprisals against innocent Frenchmen and women. And children. He'd seen that happen all too often. It hit hard, especially seeing the dead children. He had seen some of the burnt-out buildings where Germans had herded people and set the building alight. Had come across atrocities he would neither speak of nor forget.

As a gesture of gratitude, at the end of the pruning Lucien had organised a large party for the workers and their families. These men had come home from whatever hellhole they'd been in and immediately picked up shears and gone to work. They had pruned and cut from early morning until late afternoon when the twilight and the cold had stopped them. Now there was a whole lamb on a spit, with bread, cheese, some home-grown tomatoes and a great many bottles of wine. They'd earned it. They and their steadfast women and their children who had waited for their return.

Lucien stood next to Tom as they watched the workers file past the long tables forking meat and potatoes onto their plates and having their glasses topped up with Chateau d'Aubert wine.

"By the end of the week we must be in Lyon," he said.

"I was beginning to think you'd forgotten," Tom said.

"Never. It's time to find Madeleine and the child. Did I tell you I spoke to Blanche…"

"Blanche?"

Tom could have sworn Lucien blushed. "Ah, Mme Guillard. About where that letter came from. Remember the young Guillard boy said it was his uncle who brought it to me."

"Of course, I hadn't forgotten. What did she say?"

"Her brother was in Paris, working at the museum where Jeanne Bonnet worked."

Tom whistled. "So, it was a brother and not a son. The pieces fall into place. Where is he now?"

Lucien shrugged. "I believe he may be dead. But now, we need to go to Lyon to see *Professeur* Bonnet. She holds the key to Madeleine."

Chapter 19

The March morning dawned cold with a late frost that crackled underfoot. Tom wrapped warmly, blowing on his hands as Lucien led him through the vines. They tramped down towards a gully about two kilometres from the chateau and hidden by a small stand of trees. First a set of empty stables and Tom remembered the roan had been hidden away down here. It seemed there was more to the structures than he first thought, for around the back of the sheds was a large barn. The door was padlocked, and Lucien fingered a bunch of keys until he found the right one. He unlocked and pulled the door open.

"*Voila,* Tom." He pulled at a tarpaulin and there was a large Army vehicle, solid, square, painted the ubiquitous khaki with a small French flag on the side.

"What the…?"

"A Citroën U23. I 'borrowed' it from the French Army. They've not yet missed it so I can safely say it's mine. We don't use it too often as it's petrol-driven and fuel is almost impossible to come by. I have a contact who is in the black market. We do an exchange, wine for petrol but I can't do that too often."

Tom ran his hand along the grille. "Are we using it today?"

Lucien nodded. "We have orders to deliver. Last night Adam and I loaded up 100 cases of wine for our

Lyon clients and then parked her back here. We'll deliver the wine and pick up empty bottles. Also, we'll have a quicker ride than on the train."

Tom climbed in and shut the door. "Adam mentioned you came home after your battalion had been ambushed. Is this the truck that saved your life?"

Lucien grated through the gears and patted the steering wheel. "Yes. A treasured family heirloom now."

Remnants of snow lay like tattered flags on the fields. Black crows swooped and cawed as they drove by. Tom marvelled at Lucien's ingenuity. This must have been in the barn when the Germans came looking for wine, when they shot his parents. How did he manage to keep it from them?

As if he could read Tom's thoughts, Lucien said, "They weren't looking for vehicles, although if it had been full of weapons I fear the worst. It was down in the gully and they were too fixated on wine to think about searching further."

"So they left the truck."

"They didn't find it nor the petrol. That was in a cellar off the *cabotte*. Nor did they find the casks we used to transport men or weapons."

Tom laughed. "Another hiding place?"

Lucien nodded. "I'm afraid unless I can find some petrol, this could be our last ride in her."

"Have you tried the Brits? They'll help."

"I shall, if nothing else works."

"Every day there's something that amazes or amuses me about you and your country."

"Good, then you've had a good time."

180

And, amazed, Tom found himself agreeing. It had been a good time. There had been hard back-breaking work and long cold days. Followed by convivial evenings full of good conversation and better wine. But here had also been other rewards. First, the long rows of vines cut back into obedience. A wonderful sight, knowing they would be yielding the best harvest in the summer. As important, while working on the land he had not once had a nightmare. The corpses, eyes pleading, skeletal hands reaching out had left him alone. His sleep had been uninterrupted.

Soon they were in the outskirts of Lyon, the roads were packed with stranger vehicles than the Citroën U23. Tom noticed a Continental version of a tuk-tuk or rickshaw he'd once seen in the Orient. A cyclist pedalling away with a covered seat on the back for two passengers both of whom looked cold and uncomfortable. Another version had a small charcoal burner attached to the back. He'd seen them in the south, a *gazogène* which used charcoal and turned it into gas as fuel for an internal combustion engine. Several of them followed the truck, puffing away as they moved slowly through the streets. Lucien glanced over to Tom.

"We had to be ingenuous, Tom."

"I see that. No petrol."

"No petrol, unless you knew someone in the Gestapo. Ah, here we are." Lucien drove through a small archway and into the back of a building that leant over towards its neighbours. Tall, at least three stories with steps going down to a small basement. The stonework was grey and streaked. The windows streamed, green with mould, and a downpipe leaned over, on the verge of collapse.

"Where are we?"

"This, my friend, is The Owl."

"Not very high-class," Tom said jumping out.

"Wait 'til you've been inside, and you've tasted the food."

They began offloading as a young man came out of the doorway, a cigarette hanging from his lower lip.

"*Bonjour*, Armand," Lucien shouted. "Come and help us."

The boy spat out the stump of his cigarette, squeezed off the glowing stump and loped over to the Citroën. He mumbled something to Lucien who laughed. Together the three men off-loaded the cases of wine and shouldered them down the stairs and into a dark basement.

"Is the boss around, Armand?"

Another mumble which seemed vitriolic in content.

"Alright, please get Madame Clouthier to give me the money while my friend here and I load up the empty bottles."

The young man lit the cigarette, shoved his hands in his pockets and strolled into the kitchen.

"We'll be staying here tonight," Lucien said as he hauled out crates of bottles.

"What is this place?"

"A basement which, in the past, hid stolen armaments and also our wine. There's a kitchen and restaurant on the ground floor. Above that is a *maison de tolerance*, and above that are rooms to rent."

"A brothel? We're going to spend the night in a brothel?"

"Only if you want to."

No, Tom did not want to. Tom Blake did not do brothels.

They pulled the tarpaulin tight over the crates of empty bottles and went inside. The kitchen was warm and steamy with the mixed aromas of food being prepared and cooked, Lucien gave a great shouted greeting to the chef, a small, thin man with the drooping moustache of a walrus.

"Usually I would say, never trust a thin chef, but this one's fine." Lucien grabbed the man and giving him a bear hug.

The man choked out a greeting and asked, "Did you bring me my wine?"

"Of course. Where is Madame?"

"Sleeping. Where do you think. She must work tonight. It is only the kitchen staff who work morning, noon and night. We don't get to lie on our backs like Madame and her girls. Lazy, they are. Just lazy."

"Just see I get my money."

Lucien swept through the kitchen shouting out greetings. They walked down a short passage and into the restaurant where Tom stopped, amazed. It was small with intricately carved wood panelling. Intimate tables were covered with white tablecloths, silver cutlery and linen napkins. Wine glasses at the ready. From above a fireplace the head of an antlered stag stared down at them, glassy-eyed. A dusty chandelier spoke of more affluent times. And a few mirrors glinted hazily from a by-gone era.

183

"You're looking at one of the most popular restaurants in Lyon. Popular among the Germans too, unfortunately. Small but with food to savour." Lucien kissed his fingers. "We'll dine here tonight. Come on, let's settle in upstairs."

The next two floors were obviously where the brothel operated. Crimson velvet curtains, chandeliers with most of the bulbs missing so that the light was dim and almost welcoming, deep piled red carpet underfoot. Mirrors made the hallway look much larger than it was. All spoke of a debauched kind of luxury and Tom instantly hated it.

They started up towards the stairs leading to the rooms when Lucien stopped, as if frozen.

A young woman, a girl really, walked through the crimson curtains. She'd obviously just woken for she yawned and ran her hands through her short dark curls.

Lucien looked as if he had been struck.

The girl looked up. Stared at Lucien. "*Bonjour,*" she said, her voice husky with sleep.

"Lucien," Tom said, touching him. "Lucien. Come now."

Lucien nodded at the girl and dragged his feet up the stairs. "Tom, what has just happened?"

"You saw a prostitute."

Lucien turned a savage face to him. "No, something else. There was something hovering between us. Did you not see it. Like a ball of lightning. Go to the room. Wait for me."

He shoved his bag at Tom and raced down the stairs. Tom called after him, "Come on, Lucien, we have no time for this."

Two empty bedrooms and Tom chose one. Two beds, a basin for washing and a small cupboard posing as an armoire. He lay down on a surprisingly comfortable bed and fell into an uneasy sleep. It was some hours before Lucien returned and threw himself down on the bed. "I've bought her for the night."

"I'm sure you'll enjoy her, but not in here."

A swift movement and Lucien towered over him. "Not what you think, *mon ami*. The only way I could keep her from lying on her back for other men. Tomorrow..."

"Are you going to buy her tomorrow night as well? This is stupid, Lucien. You can't change this."

"Will you take a bet on that? Do you know who owns this brothel?"

Tom sat up. "Who?"

"You met him in Paris. Jean-Luc Renier. This girl is his daughter."

"What? I don't believe it. His daughter? He is prostituting his own daughter?"

Lucien looked grim. "She wants out."

Tom shook his head in disbelief. "I found out a little about Renier when I was in Paris. The owner of the bookshop showed me an old theatre programme. Renier's parents owned a theatrical company before the war."

"Madame Clouthier explained all this to me. There was a company of thirty, men and women. Some married couples, one or two with children. A big family, really, led by Renier senior, the director. Actors, actresses, lighting, stagehands, all the activities of a successful theatre company. Then the war came, and the men were conscripted. That left Renier senior with a theatrical company but no actors or electricians, only a lot of actresses. So, he had another idea. He turned the company headquarters into a bordello, with a restaurant below so that it would seem respectable and a few tastefully decorated rooms above for guests like us. They all worked as prostitutes. Except the children like Manon. But later, she was absorbed into the business. Renier insisted she 'pay her way'."

"His own child? Didn't her mother protest?"

"Her mother is no longer with us."

"So, the girl is, what, nineteen?"

Lucien nodded. "She'd have been thirteen or fourteen when she started. Too young. Too damned young. She needs a chance, Tom."

"We all made sacrifices, Lucien. You lost your business. I lost…" Tom couldn't go on. His voice stuck. A wife and a child.

"Tomorrow she will have a choice," Lucien said. "Either to stay here and work for Renier or to come home with me."

"And what about Madame Guillard?"

Lucien flicked away the question as if flicking at a bothersome fly. "Merely a business deal. This is as real as it gets. Go to sleep, Tom. Tomorrow changes everything."

"I've no intention of going to sleep until I've had the good meal as you promised."

"Ah, of course. Come on. This will make your heart break into many pieces. To think those bastards, *le Boche*, ate so well here…"

186

In the panelled dining room, they sat at a small table set for two. There was no menu or wine list. Instead, the head waiter came to them with a bottle, still encased in dust and cobwebs. Lucien looked at the label.

"Ah, perfect. *Merci*."

It was opened and poured. Lucien picked up his glass. "A toast, I think. To new beginnings."

He swirled the glass and drew in the aroma. "There is a technique for tasting wine. First you look at the colour and the wine legs…"

Tom laughed. "Wine legs?"

"The viscosity. Take this seriously, Tom. It's important. Move the glass so. And so. Can you see the oily viscosity? Then the nose. You smell it, thus. You draw it in as if you're in a dark forest. In the reds like this, the fruits, black, blue berries are all in the aroma. Only then the taste and texture or high alcohol level. A small sip to begin with."

"I'm used to drinking beer in a pub, Lucien. If it foamed it was good."

"Infidel!"

"So, a new beginning. They are always exciting," Tom said. "But I agree. Tomorrow, you find Jeanne Bonnet or at least her brother. And I'll go to the address given to me by Mme Durand's niece."

Lucien took a small sip and put his glass down. "About that…"

"You're not backing out now, Lucien."

"We shall see."

"We have an address. Two, in fact. We have a vehicle that will take us there. There are the both of us."

Lucien held up his hand. "Tonight, we dine in princely splendour. Tomorrow will take care of itself."

"No menu," Tom said, looking around.

"No need. They make one meal and that's it."

A plate of soup was placed in front of Tom. The classic onion soup but the aroma indicated this was not some ordinary onion soup. A touch of cognac, perhaps? On top were two thick slices of baguette coated in grilled cheese. He pushed them aside and took a sip. "I'm in paradise, Lucien," he said.

"Just wait, there is more paradise to come."

There was. Duck and sausage *cassoulet* followed by a dessert of blueberry *millefeuille*. They ate as if it were their last meal, slowly, with reverence as one does when tasting the creation of a master chef.

Tom sat back with a satisfied sigh. "The chef has been sent by God to remind me what Heaven's going to be like."

Lucien pushed his chair back. "I have business to discuss with Jean-Luc Renier. Will you forgive me? There is coffee, which I would heartily recommend, but you will have to drink it on your own."

It was only after the coffee had been served that Tom heard raised voices. Lucien and someone else. Renier? He half-pushed his chair back, then decided Lucien was quite able of sorting out his own life and settled back to enjoy the coffee.

The voices slowed, and Tom heard a scuffle. A glass breaking, a door slamming. Shouting. A scream of pain. This time Tom left the restaurant. Lucien obviously needed his help.

Tom ran up the stairs to the brothel. There in the red hallway Lucien and Jean-Luc stood, toe-to-toe, fists clenched. Like dogs, snarling. Circling. Looking for the vulnerable spot.

Then one threw a punch. A melee of shouting, shoving and, finally Jean-Luc let rip with a knotted fist straight into Lucien's face. He fell, rolled and was up in one swift movement. Blood sprayed onto the red walls, red on red. Lucien, fists ready. He jabbed. Jean-Luc fell. Then up. And ready.

The noise had attracted two muscled bouncers who roughly peeled the men off each other. A flurry, Tom yelling, getting into the middle of it. There were bodies and fists and noise.

"*Arrêt! Merde*, Lucien! Stop, you idiot! Jean-Luc! *Arrêt!*"

And in the melee, in the shouting and shoving, Tom ordering Lucien to stop immediately which he disobeyed and continued punching. Blows landing everywhere. Blood and snot and voices. Tom found himself pummelled from both sides when a sudden and lethal blow from someone's fist sent him flying. He fell, hitting a small table with his head, feeling it shatter beneath him.

And then blackness.

Chapter 20

Later, all he remembered was being flung across broad shoulders and taken upstairs, his head banging on a hard male rump. Perhaps this was to be expected in a brothel, he thought rather vaguely and through a head swimming with pain – but not in your average hotel or restaurant.

He was thrown onto his bed, and he lay there with the taste of blood in his mouth. For a long time, he slipped in and out of a dazed sleep. In his waking moments, he looked at the ceiling, at the unusual ceiling pattern, half there, half not, wondering why the fresco just disappeared behind a wall. Someone had come in and lit the fire and the room was cosy enough for Tom to come partially back to his senses.

He realised the room had formerly been part of a larger room. Sometime in the history of this establishment, someone must have thought it a good idea to turn one good-sized bedroom into two smaller ones with a flimsy wooden structure pretending to be a wall dividing the two. Lucien and the girl were next door and Tom realised he was going to hear every small sound. It would be an uncomfortable night.

Not that the sounds he heard were in any way compatible with his brother-in-law and a prostitute. When Lucien had said he'd 'bought' the girl for the night, Tom had expected to be awake most of the time by sounds of sex and cries of orgasmic jubilation. But that was not what he heard. Instead, there was *thluck* of a wine cork being drawn from a bottle, the occasional clink of wine glasses, but mostly the low murmur of two voices. It went on, a low comforting susurration, well into the early hours until finally Tom turned over, putting aside his puzzlement and his sore head and finally fell asleep.

*****

The knock on the door that woke him did nothing to allay his fears. Lucien stood there, looking battered. His shirt was torn, one eye was black and his lip had been bleeding. Tom saw that his knuckles were raw.

"You've either had the worst in a fight or the best sex of your life," Tom said holding the door open for Lucien.

"No sex, I assure you." Lucien sat on the end of Tom's bed. "You don't look too good yourself."

As Tom stood over the wash basin, even the mirror grimaced. This was not the usual Tom Blake who stared at him in the cracked mirror. This was some ogre with a large bruise on his cheek, a nose that looked out of kilter and a swollen black eye.

He glared at Lucien. "Do you want to tell me what that was all about and why I seem to have been at the end of someone's fist, not once but several times?"

Lucien sighed. "All rather complicated," he said. "But the bottom line, you must go to see Hugo and Jeanne Bonnet on your own while I take the truck back to the chateau."

"Why?"

"As I said, it's complicated. I need to get Manon Renier out of here as soon as possible."

"Jean-Luc will kill you. Or his goons. He will say this is a family matter and you have no right to interfere. And he'd be right."

"As I said, it's complicated."

"Look, I have to agree, the man's a bastard, turning his own daughter into a horizontal collaborator. But it's not up to you…"

"Enough, Tom!" Lucien roared. "Enough! I know it's not for me, but she needs me."

"What the hell. Are you now a knight in shining armour? Are you, Lucien? Have you forgotten why we're here? Have you forgotten your own sister in your lust for this girl?"

Lucien got up slowly, and grabbed for Tom, clutched loosely at his chest and winced. "I can't even give you the smacking you deserve, Tom. I'm too sore so I'll forget you ever said that. I know, I know. It's all so strange. My life has fallen into several parts. There's my love of the grape, there's my need to look for Madeleine. And now there's this, as you say, this 'knight-in-shining-armour' Lucien who seems to think that by rescuing one prostitute from a life of sin he can save the world."

"And what about Blanche?"

Lucien tried to shake his head. Decided against it. "She's not for me, Tom. She's the next-door neighbour's widow whose loose lips destroyed my family. I could never forgive that."

Tom thought back to the day Lucien grabbed a Luger and went to kill Blanche.

"Just give me time to sort my head out. Go to Bonnet, find out what you can, and come back to the chateau."

He left, the door swinging closed behind him.

Lucien had obviously gone mad. He was going to smuggle one of Jean-Luc's prostitutes out of the building. And Renier's daughter, to boot! Did this constitute a kidnapping? Tom washed his face tenderly, changed from his blood-stained shirt – not his blood he decided after a quick search – and left the room to go downstairs for breakfast.

The chef bent over his pots, not looking at Tom. "He's gone, *M'sieur* Blake. Left in a great hurry."

Tom ran to the back door. The truck was gone. The Phantom Kidnapper had already struck. Tom shook his head in despair.

In the kitchen he found the chef stirring something in a pot and muttering what sounded like evil incantations. Frowning. Scowling. Gesticulating. The chef was not a happy man.

"*Bonjour, Monsieur le-grand-chef.*" Tom tried to inject a little lightness into the gloom, assuming the *contretemps* between Lucien and the brothel-cum-restaurant owner was at the back of the chef's malaise.

"A good day for some, I suppose, but not for others."

Tom sat down. "May I ask why?"

"Your friend, the *vigneron*, has put my boss in the hospital. That's why."

Tom tried for a look of surprise. "Renier in hospital? What happened?"

The chef placed his wooden spoon down and turned to Tom, his face a palette of misery. "You should know. By the damage to your face – you were there. Don't argue. Look at you."

"I may have a few bruises, but I was trying to stop whatever was going on. So, what did you hear?"

The chef shrugged, the usual signal of French indifference, an extravagant lifting of the one shoulder. "Something about a woman. Always about a woman. From beyond history men have fought over women."

"Do you know who the woman is?"

"Just one of the prostitutes."

"No one special?"

Tom was trying to find out more about Manon but clearly the chef knew less than he did. "Is there any possibility I can get some breakfast?"

At the suggestion of food, the chef brightened. "Of course, *M'sieur* Blake. *Croissant* and coffee?"

"Perfect. Splendid. *Merci*."

"I apologise," the chef said moments later. "Wartime and all we can serve our customers is this."

"War's over, my friend," Tom said, gazing into the black depths of what appeared to be coffee. "This is The Owl. It has a reputation for excellence. I'm sure you can do better than this. Just remember what is at stake, your supply of good wine which I will be delivering next month. Or maybe not."

"Blackmail," the chef sighed. "I always knew we shouldn't trust the *Anglais*."

The chef took the offending cup away and brought another one that Tom could smell was the real deal. The croissant was also superb, crusty, buttery and fragrant. There was a small pot of strawberry conserve and Tom used it liberally. A simple meal but one to set him up for the day.

First thing this morning was to find Hugo and Jeanne Bonnet, somewhere in Lyon. He turned to the chef with a query.

"I know the street, *M'sieur* Blake," the chef said. "It will take you about an hour to walk there. Here, let me show you." And on the back of an old receipt, he drew a map for Tom. "You turn here and then here you go right. Along here is a *boulangerie* and just after that the market. And then down here is the street you're looking for."

Tom tucked the map in his pocket and bounded out the back door. It had been raining during the night, but now the sky had cleared, and the morning spread out like a rich clean carpet. Even the cobblestones glittered in the morning air.

The house was halfway down a quiet cobbled street, narrow with rain dripping from the eaves and the mush of fallen leaves underneath a solitary tree making the stones slippery. He stood in front of a tall thin house with blue shutters and a large brass fish for a door knocker. Tom banged it. When there was no reply, he banged the fish again.

"Come on, come on."

Tom thought he heard shuffling as slippered feet approached to the door.

The man who opened it was either old or life had drained his youth away. His hair, while still thick, was grey and his skin pale. He had on a knitted cardigan in faded green. The slippers were old, once a bright tartan,

195

now just a muddle of colours. A bright red bow tie was the only incongruous item. Otherwise, he looked just as Tom thought all French academics should look.

"Yes?"

"Are you Hugo Bonnet?"

"Who is asking?"

"My name is Thomas Blake. From England. I believe your sister Jeanne knew my wife in the war. Is your sister here? If so, may I speak with her?"

The man opened the door a little wider. "She is here. I can't tell you anything, but you can talk to Jeanne. She's taken up residence in the conservatory with a glass of wine and a cigarette. Follow me. Mind the cats."

Bonnet led him through the house and to the back to a dark conservatory filled with green plants and heavy furniture. Three cats, their eyes filled with curiosity, had followed them in, twining their sleek bodies around Tom's legs. They jumped up on a sofa, curled and went to sleep, their bodies around each other in a mixture of fur, white, grey and tabby, looking like a multi-coloured pillow.

"We spend our days here," Bonnet said. "It's warm and the plants help us to imagine living in sunnier climes like the Caribbean. Of course, the cats prefer it too. Here is my sister. Jeanne, you have a visitor."

A tall thin woman stood up from a deep rattan chair that would have looked more at home in India. She had a cigarette in a long ivory holder in one hand and a glass of wine in the other. Her eyes were deep-set and her face pallid, a paleness Tom associated with prison. Perhaps she had been in a camp somewhere. The janitor at the museum had mentioned this woman had been arrested.

"Who are you and what do you want with me?"

"*Professeur* Bonnet, I am looking for Madeleine Aubert," Tom said. "I am her husband."

"Tom?" Jeanne asked. "Tom Blake?"

Tom was startled. "Yes, *Professeur*. I am Tom Blake."

"Ah." She sat down again, the beams of sunlight a halo round her head. Tom could not help noticing her hair was thin and ragged. "Sit down. We can talk. Be careful. Don't sit on the cats. They're Hugo's pets. Personally, I loathe them."

"You do not," Hugo said from the doorway. "Whose bed do they sleep on?"

She ignored his protestations and looked again at her visitor. "My God, you look a mess. What have you been up to?"

"A quarrel at a brothel."

"I beg your pardon?"

"My apologies, *Professeur* Bonnet…"

"For heaven's sake let's stop fussing about titles. Call me Jeanne. It's so much easier. Now, Tom, what is this about a brothel?"

"A long story, Jeanne," Tom said, trying out her Christian name for the first time.

"I have time." She settled back into the rattan chair, looking like an ancient and ravaged Indian rani.

"Well, you see, my brother-in-law and I are staying at The Owl. There was a scuffle between him and the owner."

She held up an emaciated hand. "Ah, no need to continue. He refused to pay for poor service."

"Not exactly. He has just kidnapped one of the girls and I fear it will not turn out well."

"Hmm. You better tell me the story to its conclusion. I don't like spending time wondering. They have rooms to let as well, don't they. At the Owl. I am prepared to give you the benefit of the doubt. You were staying in a rented room and not visiting the brothel."

"You are correct. We had just delivered a hundred bottles of wine."

"We?"

"Lucien Aubert, my brother-in-law who runs a vineyard."

"Madeleine's brother. Yes, she told me her family owned a vineyard."

"May I offer you a glass of wine?" Hugo asked as if the word 'wine' had ignited his hospitality.

"A little early but that would be a pleasure, *Monsieur*."

"How about I make mulled wine. We have cloves and it will be warm, just right for the day, I think."

"Wonderful. Perhaps I may sit here and talk to your sister?"

"I don't know why he has to mess up the wine," Jeanne said as Hugo left the conservatory. "I like my wine straight out of the bottle. There's no stopping him when he gets a bee in his bonnet."

Tom could hear Hugo in the kitchen, rummaging about, when Jeanne suddenly stood up.

"Come here. Stand in front of me," she commanded. Tom did as he was told. Jeanne Bonnet took hold of his nose. There was a small cracking sound. He yelped with pain and leapt backwards, almost fainting. Tears ran down his cheeks. He staggered back, fell into the chair. "For God's sake, woman..." he said gasping.

"There you are. Your nose was not broken, merely out of alignment. Dislocated. Now it is straight. Just don't get into another fight for the next couple of weeks. So," she said sitting down again and picking up her cigarette holder. "You want to know where your wife is? Well, I can't tell you because I don't know."

Chapter 21

Tom felt dizzy with pain, not sure what he was going to ask Jeanne Bonnet or why he was even there. Something about Madeleine. Oh, yes, Madeleine. Although the image of Madeleine was suffused by a hazy blur of pure agony.

"You were arrested together?" His voice was clogged. He felt as if his nose had been ripped off his face. "Were you sent to a camp?"

"No. Yes, of course we were in a camp. Leave your nose alone. And don't touch it or you'll mess up all my good work."

Hugo returned and Tom caught the perfume of spices. So, he could actually breathe, his nose was still in place despite the torture he'd just been through. Hugo held out a glass and Tom took the proffered wine. Gulped. Hoping to would dissipate the pain in his face. Dabbed at his upper lip, expecting blood. "This is most pleasant, Monsieur. The base is a good white. From Alsace perhaps?"

"You know about wine?"

"I'm learning. My brother-in-law is a *vigneron* in Burgundy. I've been helping with the pruning and in the evenings, Lucien has been teaching me about wine." Tom turned to Jeanne. "To go to the beginning. You also served in the war. And Madeleine with you."

"Yes. I should have kept her out of it. She was so vulnerable. You know about the baby, I presume?"

"I know a child was born while I was in England."

"And the rest?" Jeanne asked.

"That's where it becomes complicated."

Tom could see she was waiting to find out how much he knew.

"How exactly did you serve?" Tom asked again.

"Playing at being heroes. We were so naive. Never thought our messing about printing an illegal newspaper would have such dire consequences."

"I hear the men in your team were executed. I'm so sorry."

"Thank you. We just didn't know what we were doing. Writing tracts, writing columns for an illegal newspaper. We felt so heroic. But we were innocent to the dangers. What did we know? We traipsed around thinking we were Jeanne de Arc when all the time they knew exactly who we were, and they could pick us up at any time. We were like mice with the cat watching us all the time."

"After they arrested you, where were you sent?"

"Madeleine and I were sent to work in Germany, in one of the ammunition factories. Dangerous work and we women prisoners were expendable. Fortunately, we managed not to blow ourselves up and survived the war. We were in a camp, of course, but we went to work every day. When the allies came, they put us on trains to France and then in hospital. It was at that stage I lost contact with your wife. She had been with me all those years," Jeanne said, suddenly bitter. "I'd looked after her, protected her. Right at the end I lost sight of her. She was still alive then. Now, I don't know."

"Were you liberated by the Russians?"

"Good God, no. I wouldn't be sitting here if that were the case. I'd be in some Gulag. No, it was the Yankees. All *bonhomie* and innocence. Clean. God, so clean, and there we were in our filth with lice and sores, so thin you could play music on our ribs."

"Where would Madeleine have been taken? A hospital?"

"I can only imagine so. We'd been working with chemicals that damaged us. Our skin went yellow, and our hair fell out. We were a mess, physically, mentally and spiritually." She pulled at her short hair. "See, it's only growing back now. And it's gone grey. Damn it! I used to be quite a looker…"

"You were never a looker, Jeanne," said Hugo.

"Shut up, Hugo. You go too far."

"This is my house, and I can say what I like." He got up and pranced out of the room.

"You're a pompous old ass!" Jeanne called after him. "Do you have siblings, Tom? No? Hugo and I squabble but we're really on the best of terms. Old goat, he has a lot to put up with. I drink too much, I smoke too much and I have nightmares that wake him up in the middle of the night. And he still he allows me to recuperate in his home. It'll smell like an ashtray when I go." Jeanne lit another cigarette. "Now, back to Madeleine. She would have been treated for the same poisoning we all endured. She was also showing signs of tuberculosis so perhaps they sent her to the mountains."

"Where?"

Jeanne sighed. "Switzerland, I suppose. Or here in our own mountains. Have you asked the Red Cross?"

"Her brother is in contact." After a while Tom found the courage. "There was also the child who is now lost," Tom said.

There was a pause, and Tom heard a clock ticking loudly. Outside a boy ran down the street laughing. "Yes, she spoke of a child," Jeanne said. "Madeleine believed she had died."

"I am happy to tell you that Sophie isn't dead. Just lost."

"You have lost two family members," Jeanne said raising an eyebrow. "You sound a little like your Oscar Wilde. To paraphrase him: 'to lose one family member may be regarded as a misfortune; to lose two looks like carelessness'."

Tom smiled, a thin slit of the mouth, not allowing any humour to pass. He'd always rather liked Wilde, now he wasn't so sure. Too close to the bone. "Indeed, Madame, I have lost both. But not through carelessness. Through the horrors of war."

"Hugo, what are you doing? Looking for something?" She sighed. "Well, stop looking and come here."

Again, Hugo mumbled something from the next room.

"Well, find it, will you and come and sit down and have your wine." She turned to Tom. "While Hugo dithers, let me tell the story. I worked at the *Musée des Arts et Traditions Populaires*. You're nodding so I expect you've been there. Looking for me? Ah, more likely looking for Madeleine. Anyway, museum is a rather fancy name for a collection of all sorts of local antiquities and oddities that fit nowhere else. We did have an enormous library, and I was in charge of the architectural side of things. I had books and architectural plans and models. One day your wife came to the library. I remember her standing rather shyly in the doorway asking for a job. A small but lovely girl. I took to her immediately. She reminded me of me as a young girl. Once I heard her story, of being married to an Englishman, I thought more of her. My mother was English, so I felt a natural affinity. And there I was at the museum, almost at the end of my tether, packing up everything I could, dragging crates to the basement, thinking they'd be safe from the Germans. So, I employed her. I was exhausted, not ready to admit I couldn't do it on my own, but Madeleine was just what I needed. And, of course, she had a particular interest in my section. She said her brother was an architect. I believe we had two of his prize winning plans on display."

Jeanne paused long enough to empty her wine glass as if she were drinking water.

"We were invaded eight months after the declaration of war. We all believed the Maginot Line would hold them, but of course it didn't. The first we knew of the invasion was the oil depots north of Paris being blown up. You cannot imagine the fear and hysteria that went with the sound of those explosions and the dark oily clouds in the sky. Everyone believed the Germans would kill us all. And so they ran. A quarter of the population ran, can you believe it? To my shame, I also ran. All of us fleeing the Germans, not knowing where we were going, except that we were trying to get beyond the reach of those savages. It's so easy to get swept up by other people's hysteria, Tom. To my shame I got caught up in it. That's when I came down here to my brother."

"And Madeleine?"

"I don't think she ran. To her credit. She had obligations, I believe."

Tom nodded, remembering Aaron and Emily. "But you came back?"

"Yes, I got back before the Germans closed the border between occupied and Vichy France. So many refugees, especially of the Jewish persuasion, were trapped in the south and couldn't get home. Whatever happened to them, I don't know."

"Bad times."

"Paris had changed in the few weeks I'd been away. Unnaturally calm and eerily quiet. No pigeons. Even the birds had deserted us. But you could hear the drone of planes overhead, hundreds of them. The Seine like a bright ribbon of light guiding them into the heart of Paris. And the shrieking of the sirens warning people. The Metro was no hiding place, too shallow, so people went into basements and cellars. The time for false optimism was over.

"Anyway, when I got back to the museum from my mad scramble, there were notices stating entrance for German troops was free. All others had to pay. French people had to pay to see their own heritage." She clicked her tongue in annoyance and handed her glass to Hugo for a re-fill. "I'll have some of that wine you ruined, thanks, Hugo. Hot wine, I ask you. What would your brother-in-law say? Anyway, by the time I got back, my library had changed. We'd managed to pack up all the Jewish material and that was safe, but the Russian ones were left. They were ripped up and in their place were books by German authors. Mediocre, of course. Stupid German soldiers, too young to know anything, tramping around trying to look like they actually knew what it was all about. Stupid *putain*!"

Jeanne flicked out the cigarette stub from the holder and fitted another one in its place. Tom looked for matches. On a small table nearby lay a finely wrought silver lighter, resting on an untidy heap of books. He took it and lit Jeanne's cigarette.

She nodded her thanks. "When next I saw Madeleine, she was pregnant. I apologise if that offends you…"

"Not at all. I am the father."

"Hmm, I wondered about that. She spoke of you, but as you were a convicted criminal of the worst possible kind, according to her. She wasn't happy with you."

"I was in prison for attempted fraud." There, he'd said it and it didn't feel like the shame it used to be. Most people in Europe had some idea of capture and prison.

Jeanne peered at him. "You don't look like a criminal. But then, who knows what a criminal looks like? Anyway, she must have forgiven you. Madeleine didn't seem the sort to sleep around. So, the child was born, and Madeleine had people looking after her while she worked at the museum."

"It seems so."

"Strange. She spoke of you but not the child. So, what happened? Madeleine wouldn't say, but she came back here one day looking quite dreadful. White, wild, hysterical."

"That would have been in July 1942?"

"Yes. How do you know?"

"The friends who were looking after Sophie were arrested." Tom stopped, trying to catch his breath, trying not to imagine.

"With the child?"

Tom hesitated. "I believe Madeleine thought so."

"That explains why she was so distraught. She never said. *Mon Dieu*, what was going through her mind? Did she try to find the child?"

"I don't know. I've imagined her rushing to the Velodrome where the Jews were kept until transport, screaming for her child. But I really don't know. You see, I found out only in the past few days, the Jewish friends managed to pass Sophie on to someone else before they were taken away. To a Parisian dressmaker who had family here in Lyon. The person responsible has since passed on, but her family is still here. I'm hoping that Sophie is with them."

"Now that is very interesting. There is a woman here in Lyon who was part of a group hiding Jewish children. Hugo knows her. Don't you, Hugo." Jeanne shouted into the next room and Hugo replied. Something, but Tom wasn't sure what.

"Sophie wasn't – isn't Jewish," he said.

"Nevertheless, you may want to find her and ask."

Tom nodded. "Her name?"

207

"Hugo," Jeanne called. "That woman, the one, you know."

"And Madeleine?" he asked, anxious not to lose sight of Madeleine. "I must find her. Do you know where she is now? Some hints, some clues?"

"I have no idea. In a hospital somewhere, I imagine."

Tom got up, began to pace. "Which hospital? Where? That is what I need to know, Jeanne. Precisely, where is she?" His voice was loud, too loud. Jeanne looked at him with mild impatience.

"I'm trying to help," she said. "If I can't help with your wife, perhaps I can help with your child. Oh, for heaven's sake, man, sit down. You're making me feel nervous."

Tom slumped in a rotting rattan chair, felt it give way slightly beneath him, and grabbed for his glass of mulled wine.

"Look, go and find this family," Jeanne said. "If your daughter is with them, then we can cross one task off our list. After that we concentrate on finding your wife."

Tom nodded It was time to leave. He still had to find the Durand family.

He swallowed of the last of his wine and left Hugo and Jeanne in their humid conservatory with their cats and plants.

Chapter 22

Tom decided to go back to The Owl. He had an address for the Durand family in some tucked-away corner of Lyon. He needed a map. Or better still, a taxi. He should have asked the Bonnet siblings for help, but it was too late now. And so, he trudged back to The Owl.

The moment he arrived he saw that all was not well.

His suitcase was lying on the cobblestones of the back yard.

Renier had returned from the hospital where, according to the chef, he had only been kept in for a few hours' observation. On his return, he had ranted and foamed about Lucien taking away his property. Renier was now in consultation with Madame Clouthier, the fat madam of the brothel, working out a plan to get Manon back. Losing Manon was a financial loss Renier could not and would not tolerate.

The chef looked nervous. "*M'sieur* Blake, you had better leave as soon as possible. Jean-Luc is on the warpath. If he sees you there will be blood spilt."

"More than last night? Come on, I'm an innocent bystander. What did I do?" Tom heard in his voice that of a whiny child.

"You are Lucien's brother-in-law."

"Yes, well…"

"Then you better go."

"But I've nowhere to stay."

The chef shrugged. "Not my problem."

As Tom turned away to pick up his luggage from the cobblestones, the chef called after him. "Don't forget my order. I want the wine here next month."

You'll be lucky, my friend. Tom found himself uncharacteristically giving the man the finger, hoping Lucien never sets foot there again. *That'll teach them.*

But he was without a place to stay, his face was still hurting and he hadn't finished what he'd set out to do. There was no alternative, he'd have to go back to Hugo Bonnet and throw himself on their mercy. Like all vulnerable people, Tom Blake loathed asking for help. But there was no alternative.

Hugo was delighted at the thought of having an academic, as he called Tom, to stay. He showed Tom to a small room off the kitchen where he could sleep. It was warm and the bed large, comfortable and covered in a faded quilt of wonderful summer colours.

"Jeanne will be so pleased," Hugo said settling into the only chair as Tom unpacked his small supply of clothes. "She's sleeping now so I can talk honestly to you. She treated your wife as the daughter she never had. After whatever happened with losing the child, Jeanne found out that Madeleine hadn't been home for weeks. The cleaning staff at the museum told her that there was a young woman haunting the museum after hours, walking the corridors, walking, walking, talking to herself, gesticulating, acting mad. Not much later Jeanne found that Madeleine had made a small nest for herself in one of the basements and she was sleeping there on a pile of canvas." Hugo sighed. "Jeanne took her home to her apartment, fed her up. Tried to find out why she wouldn't go home to her apartment. All the girl said was that she had lost 'Tom's daughter'."

Hugo must have noticed Tom's shock. "That's what she said. At first, Jeanne didn't understand what she meant but it came out eventually, about the arrest of her two Jewish friends. Madeleine believed the Germans had taken them and Sophie to a concentration camp and eventual death."

Tom wanted to sit down and try to imagine what Madeleine had gone through, believing Sophie was dead. Such agony of mind and soul. And it was all so avoidable, had she found Mme Durand's letter. He was filled to the brim with her anguish.

"Jeanne is full of guilt that, at the end, they were separated by the Allies who rescued them," he said. "Don't tell her I said that. She likes to think she's as tough as old leather. But she isn't."

"I'll keep it in mind, thank you."

"Come to the conservatory when you're ready. We can have a glass of wine before I begin supper."

In the conservatory the cats had not moved. Each one opened a sleepy eye, gazed at him and slept again. He sat there for a moment in the humid air surrounded by fronds of strange plants and was comforted by the thought that in Jeanne, Madeleine had found the adoring, comforting mother she'd never had.

The following day Hugo gave Tom instructions on how to get to the home of Mme Durand's sister. It was out of the city and the walk was long and cold. Tom

211

almost relished the icy wind, the pain in his face from the infrequent wind-borne sleet and then pain in his feet from the icy cobblestones. Finally, a small group of houses drifted out of the softly falling snow. Although a suburb of Lyon, it looked like a quintessential French village clustered around the grey stone church, like a group of frightened children hiding in the apron folds of their mother.

Someone pointed out the house of the old lady. "She's old and not all there," the stranger said. Tom thanked her and moved on.

Finally, he was there, outside the small house, no bigger than his cottage in Kent and tried to imagine Sophie inside. Again, he saw her as happy and well-fed even though no children in France looked nourished. His imagination shielded him from the awful image of an emaciated daughter, with rickets and dried-out skin and hair. Instead, he saw her as he wished, running eagerly to him shouting 'Papa Tom'.

He began to shake. Was she here? Had his quest finally come to an end? Would he now be free to take her home to Kent? And then? What would he do? To a small cottage in the middle of nowhere in England. A French child who spoke no English? She would be like a fish out of water. And what did he know about girls? He needed a job to be able to support a child. And what would Lucien demand of him? Adoption of the child? Was a farmhouse surrounded by grape vines in the middle of France a better place for a child? Was he being premature in wondering where and how he would manage? Find the child first and then worry, a voice sounding much like his mother's filtered through his mind.

Find the child.

The front door opened. An old woman stood there. Not too clean, a little too fat, staring at him.

"Yes," she said in a harsh voice full of suspicion.

"My name is Thomas…"

"*Anglais?*" The suspicion grew.

"*Oui,* madam." He wondered what there was about him that shouted English? His French was impeccable, so it wasn't that. Or was there some small hint in his vocab or his accent? His name was a common one. French even.

"I cannot buy anything from you. I have no money." She started to close the door.

He put his hand out, anxious. "*Non,* madame. I'm not here to sell anything. I need to know about the child, the one that your sister Antoinette brought from Paris."

She stared at him again and, after a small hesitation, opened the door and walked down the passage and into the kitchen. He assumed he should follow and found himself in a large untidy room that served as kitchen, dining and living room. The sink was full of unwashed dishes, the kitchen table weighed down by cutlery, newspapers and the debris of living.

She sat down and drew the chair towards the table with a shriek of wood on stone.

"Sit down and tell me what you want from me."

Tom tailored the story into a short narrative of how his wife and the child had become separated, of how Antoinette Durand looked after her until her health became bad.

"Your sister-in-law came here to recuperate?"

The woman nodded. "She was dying although we didn't know it at the time. She brought the child. A nuisance, really. As my sister-in-law became weaker the duty of caring for the three year-old fell to me. Forgive me, Monsieur, but I never had children of my own, so it was like trying to sweep without a broom."

"Where is the child now?"

"Well, that I can't tell you. They came for her, that's all I know. You see, when Antoinette died, I was at a loss. The child was growing and needed extra food, which I didn't have. She'd already outgrown her shoes, I'd cut the fronts off so she'd get a few more months out of them. Then her dress. Beyond saving." The old woman sighed. "I found an old blouse in the back of a cupboard. I put it on her. Green velvet, a bit of lace around the throat. I did wish at the time that the blouse had been blue. And clean." She looked sharply at Tom. "You know of course that in France it's pink for a boy and blue for a girl. The colour of the Blessed Mary's robe. Anyway, all I had was an old green blouse with sweat marks. I tied a leather belt around her waist because the blouse was far too big. I'd cut the sleeves off and hemmed them. I'm no seamstress like Antoinette, but I managed. And you should have seen her. You'd have thought I'd dressed her in satin and lace. Like a proper duchess. She was that delighted. There she was, dancing around the kitchen, her arms high and a smile as big as the ocean on her little face. And there was her hair. So blonde it was almost white. And so curly. With those blue eyes she would have been a target for any wandering Germans wanting to adopt a child. They took our children to Germany, those they thought would fit in with the Aryan race theory. So, I dyed her hair black. She was safer that way."

"I've heard that, yes." Tom's throat tightened. The image of the child dressed in someone's cast-off blouse scoured him, stone on skin, raw and bleeding.

"I need to know if she was my child. When you dressed her, did you see a birthmark on her back?"

"Oh yes, my sister-in-law pointed it out to me. Like angels' wings."

Was it about the birthmark that did it for Tom Blake? The angel wings or the image of his daughter dancing around that filthy kitchen, wearing the discarded green velvet blouse of this unkempt old woman. He began to feel his spine give way, as if the vision was too much for him to bear. The agony of seeing his daughter, Madeleine's child in this environment, he wanted to get rid of it by retching it out. He stood up about to make his way to the front door. But the old woman wasn't done with him.

"It cost me a lot to feed that child. She was always hungry, you know."

Tom fumbled in his pocket, pulled out his wallet, found a few hundred franc notes and put them on the table.

The woman grabbed them and thrust them deep between her breasts.

"Where is she now?" He managed to croak out.

"The childcare people came for her. They took her away to the mountains."

His voice was harsh. "Precisely where did they take her?"

The old woman shrugged. "To some place of safety, I should imagine. They never said, but then no one talked. It was the war, you see."

Tom walked away from the old woman in a haze of wretchedness. It was a nightmare, one in which you walk through molasses in a maze that has corners and turning points that go on and on. You bang your head on unseen projectiles, blood runs down your face and still you turn corner after corner, slam into blank walls and still go on.

He felt empty. Depleted.

Tom managed to find his way back to Hugo's house. They were waiting for him. Hugo saw his face and immediately poured a glass of wine.

"You found her?" Jeanne asked. "Your daughter?"

Tom dropped into the rattan chair, careless that it creaked and groaned under his weight. "She was there and now she's gone. The woman said the childcare people came and took her to the mountains. I don't know where. I don't think I'll ever find her."

"It looks as if you need some nourishment. Come and sit and have some soup. Hugo makes a very good chicken soup with the carcase of a chicken that never had any flesh on it in the first place. And we have bread."

Tom had no appetite. He tried, he really tried to appreciate the kindness shown to him, the food, the wine, the warm bed. But all he could see in his mind's eye was a little girl in a green velvet blouse, dancing with joy.

Was this his girl? Where was she? Would he ever find her? And what if it came to the point where he was facing just such a child, how would he know she was Sophie Aubert? What if he picked the wrong girl who also had some sort of a birthmark and he misinterpreted it, thinking it looked like angel wings. What if he went home with her and left his own child lost in France forever?

And that was what it all boiled down to. Picking the wrong girl and leaving his own behind.

It was all too much to bear. In the silent hours well before dawn, well before the time when nightmares usually kicked in, he got up, dressed, grabbed his suitcase and tiptoed into the kitchen where he tore out a page from his notebook and wrote – I need to go home. *Merci beaucoup.*

He wanted to write – I'll be back, but knew it wasn't true.

He tiptoed out of the house and ran to the railway station as if the hounds of hell were after him. There was no one in the ticket office but he sat on the platform praying for a train. The first one through was a goods train, slow enough for him to run alongside yelling for a ride. The stoker saw him, grabbed his suitcase as Tom jumped onto the ladder leading to the cab and hoisted himself up.

For once he was in luck. A train just when he needed it.

And luck again played a part. Or bad luck, whichever way he looked at it.

The engine driver was Marcel, the man he'd met in Paris at the dinner he and Lucien had attended. Lucien had mentioned that Marcel was on the Paris-Lyon run. Tom hoped the man would not want to question him.

What could he say? I'm running away. I'm chickening out. I've lost my nerve.

To meet one of Lucien's friends like this was unfortunate. Word would get back and Lucien would know that Tom had failed.

"What the hell are you doing on the platform in the middle of the night?" Marcel said. "I didn't expect to see you again. But in such circumstances…"

"To be honest, I'm not sure myself why I'm here."

"You're going to Paris?"

"I'm going home. To England."

"Does Lucien know?"

Tom shook his head.

Marcel said nothing more.

And Tom was like a wounded animal limping towards its lair. To Kent and away from the vision of his daughter dressed in that green monstrosity.

Could he explain it to Jeanne and Hugo? To Lucien? What words could he use?

Sometimes it was the smallest of things that break the dam. Along this journey there'd been signs pointing the way. Hopeful signs. And then dead ends. Then there had been more hope and then even more hopelessness. And suddenly, in the midst of hope and optimism and the challenge of finding the child, something had broken. Some small thing inside of Tom Blake that had given way, some inner cog in his psyche had broken.

It had been the thought of his child in that soiled green blouse.

That had done for him. That filthy bloody green blouse.

He needed to go home and hide from it, from Madeleine's accusing eyes, from the pity of Jeanne and Hugo, from the contempt of Lucien Aubert, from his own failure.

He had to hide from himself.

He needed to go home.

Chapter 23

The train Marcel had driven from Lyon to Paris stopped on a side track close to the city. Tom walked blindly, towards Paris, found his way to the nearest train station and bought a ticket to Calais.

He had thanked Marcel and his stoker profusely, but it did nothing to subdue the look in Marcel's eyes.

Tom Blake had been found wanting.

The train to Calais was slow. Several times it had stopped completely on a side line, somewhere in the countryside. There seemed no reason for the hour's delay, until a goods train huffed past. And then they were off again amid the choking smoke and the rumble and shaking of the old train. Outside, the remnants of snow lay like tattered flags on the fields. Once or twice, they passed a wrecked train and there would be a work gang of locals working industriously with a few British Army engineers overseeing the task. If Tom was close to anything like a positive emotion, he would have been grateful that at least some trains were running and inwardly thanked the troops who volunteered to come back to help France get back on its feet. Truth to tell, he felt nothing. It was the only way he could deal with what he had just done.

Soon they were in Calais, near the wrecked harbour. Not much had been gained in the way of recovery since last he was here with Lucien. Tom realised it'd only been a few months ago. It just seemed a century. There were the same dock workers leaning on shovels or tying cables or pushing wheelbarrows. The same faces at the ticket office and the same ferry he and Lucien had travelled on at the beginning of January. Last chance to go back and take up the quest. Last chance to save his integrity and his pride. But he couldn't. He was tired, more tired than he had ever been. It wasn't a physical tiredness although it manifested in aching muscles, and a head full of rusted nails rattling and piercing. It seemed as if something else within him was dying. All the things he'd seen, all that he'd done, all that he had to do weighed like a rock, and he was mentally, physically and spiritually on his knees.

And then the thought of Sophie dancing with pleasure at being clothed in a sweat-stained green velvet blouse.

It was unbearable.

The trip to England was uneventful. From the deck, Tom stood aft watching the cold grey sea spread out from the ferry like old women's grey hair. Soon Dover appeared with the pompous castle towering above the harbour. Then he had the onerous duty of confronting his friends who had stored the Austin. Tried to explain that it was government business in order to obviate the necessity of telling them that he had tried to find his wife and child and had failed. The car needed to be cranked but it took him dutifully if slowly home.

The snow around the cottage had melted, leaving a cold brown muddy sludge. The living room was cold, and the Christmas tree had shed its needles onto the carpet where they lay brown and crisp.

Tomorrow, he thought, I'll get rid of it. Visit the Masons and get some food.

But in the meantime, he was so cold and so tired and so grief stricken, all he wanted to do was fall into bed.

He lay there, his overcoat wrapped around him, unable to sleep and thought of his first night in Paris, in Madeleine's bed, with the aroma of his wife settling all around him. He remembered holding onto the small blouse of his child. Did he cry? Probably. Could he cry now. Probably not.

How had he come to this point in his life where he had lost all courage and integrity and had basically run away?

Because that's what it was. Trying to escape reality. Trying to hide from his duty to Madeleine, to his child. Trying to protect himself from the pain and joy that love always brings with it as inevitable companions. Just when there was hope that he'd find her, he ran away. His daughter was braver than he. Madeleine even braver. She had endured losing Sophie, thinking her dead and she had still gone on to work with the group at the museum, printing an illegal newspaper. Until she was caught. Just to have survived in a German concentration camp would have needed a level of courage he no longer had.

What must Lucien think of him? Jeanne and her nice portly brother. Such good people, and here he was wallowing in grief and guilt.

Eventually he fell asleep, but his dreams became nightmares, riddled with images of a dancing girl in a green velvet blouse.

In the morning, he put on an old pair of Wellingtons and walked over to the Masons. John Mason took one look at him and gave him a one-armed hug. Patting him awkwardly on the back.

"I need to work," Tom said.

"Layin' ghosts, are ye?"

Tom nodded. He didn't need to know what he looked like; it showed in Mason's face that the person before him was a haunted caricature of a man.

"Well, nobbut more peaceful than milking a few cows, I'd say. Come on, let's get you started."

And so it proved. Just as the pruning of the vines in France had brought joy to Tom, so the gentleness of the large-eyed cows soothed him. As did driving the tractor and the lifting of heavy bales of hay. Each day throughout the spring and into summer, he went to Mason's farm and worked, his back straining, muscles broadening and gaining in strength. His hands grew harder and more calloused. His sleep less fraught and his mind more at rest.

The solace of nature, he thought. The soothing of memory. There was an infinite restfulness in working with the soil. One felt connected with the universe. He was not so alone when he was surrounded by the cows; these tender animals with their all-knowing eyes were a comfort. Beetle, the farm dog, had taken a liking to Tom and followed him around. Tom found that lying on the cool ground with Beetle close by had a soporific effect

223

on him and there were days when he and Beetle lazed in the sun instead of going to work. He would lie there with the sun on his face and the sound of birds high up and the smell of dog close by. And closer, the bees searching for nectar. Once he thought he'd seen a deer. When he mentioned it to John Mason, the old man laughed. Not likely, he said. But perhaps he had. Nothing was impossible.

Mason mentioned a badger sett and one evening they sat very still and watched as the badger family came out and ate the small snacks, peanuts and sunflower seeds, the farmer had left for them. Then they trundled away to do whatever it was that badgers did. Long after they had snuffled off, Tom and John Mason lay there in the quiet night, their backs against the cooling earth.

"Lookit the sky, Tommy-lad," Mason said. "Lookit them stars. So close together ye c'n hardly see the dark between them. My goodness-gracious, if that isn' the face of God in all Its glory. 'Tis the Divine Plan all laid out for us like a book."

Later Tom went to bed, his head full of badgers and his heart full of stars.

The Masons were also teaching him a silent lesson. Their unspoken devotion to each other proved that love could endure. When, if, he found Madeleine, he promised himself this couple would be the gold standard.

He worked hard and found a certain contentment shovelling cow manure or digging posts. Until a letter came from Lucien, terse, almost unfriendly. Lucien had traced Madeleine to a hospital for tuberculosis patients high in the mountains lying between France and Switzerland. He'd gone there. Yes, he'd been told,

224

Madeleine Aubert was a patient. Or had been. She had stayed for a while then booked herself out. No, they didn't know where she had gone.

I believe she may be making her way to Paris, Lucien said in his letter, to the apartment or back here to the vines. The final line – come if you want – and Tom knew that somehow, he had to redeem himself not only in Lucien's eyes but in his own.

He sat down, read the letter again and found his hands were shaking. Madeleine was not dead in some stinking concentration camp or in the ash from the gas chambers. She was alive, albeit lost somewhere in France, but alive.

It was time to return to France.

Not to Lucien, but to Jeanne and Hugo. He made a promise to himself, to Madeleine. To Lucien. He would not see Lucien Aubert again until he had found Sophie.

Chapter 24

"We wondered when you'd be back," Jeanne said. "You left in rather a hurry."

"I apologise," Tom said, sinking into a well-remembered rattan chair and settling gingerly. "I lost my bottle."

"Bottle? Bottle? What is this?"

He didn't realise he'd fallen into the instinctive habit of speaking English. He changed to French. "I lost my nerve. I ran away."

"Ah," Jeanne said. "That I can understand. Remember I told you how I also ran in 1940 when the Germans arrived? An instinctive reaction."

Tom felt the reprimand and the subtle pardon.

"Hugo! More wine. We have a visitor."

Hugo Bonnet shuffled into the conservatory. He had a small notebook in one hand and a bottle of wine in the other. His glasses were perched on his nose, not close enough to his eyes to be of any use. Tom noticed the bottle was a pale blue-green and not the usual brownish green the Burgundians called *feuilles mortes* or dead leaves. This was wine from the war.

"I'm delighted. This gives me an excuse to bring out the better wine. I give Jeanne the rubbish to drink, you know."

"No, you don't."

"Yes, I do."

And Tom instantly felt at home among this bickering pair.

Hugo scrabbled in a cupboard and found three glasses. "Your wine, Jeanne, and make it your last, my dear."

"Stop trying to be my mother," Jeanne said sipping the golden liquid. "Yes, you've chosen well."

"Only the best to welcome Tom back."

"I have news for you," Tom said accepting a glass. "I had a letter from Lucien, Madeleine's brother."

"And..." Jeanne leaned forward. "What? Come on. Don't leave us in suspense."

Hugo held up a restraining hand. "If you stop talking perhaps Tom will tell us."

"Lucien said he'd found out that Madeleine was in a hospital for tubercular patients, a preventorium of sorts high up in the mountains. At a time when she was deemed well enough to leave, she discharged herself. The hospital staff didn't record where she was going but Lucien feels certain she's on her way back to the chateau."

Jeanne lay back in her chair. Her eyes closed but Tom thought he saw a trace of tears on her lashes. "She's alive?"

"It seems so."

"Perhaps she'll go to the apartment in Paris."

"I doubt it," Tom said. "The apartment would have too many bad memories for her."

"She may go back to the museum," Jeanne said, suddenly standing. "I must get back to Paris. She may be looking for me."

"Jeanne, please be sensible," Hugo said. "She would go home to her family before looking for you. You need only return to Paris when you're well enough and certain enough that Madeleine is there."

Jeanne sat back in her chair and sighed. "You have a point. I was not more important than her family. Of course, she'd go back to her childhood home. Are her parents still alive?"

"No. Sadly they were shot by the Germans. But as it seems now that Madeleine is still alive and is on her way home, I have a duty," Tom said. "I must do what I can to find our child. Can you help me?"

Hugo stood up. "I will concoct something for dinner while you sit here and drink my excellent wine. Afterwards I will tell you how we can help, and we can devise a plan."

Tom lay back in the rattan chair and felt that this was the right decision. Not going to Lucien before he had redeemed himself, but to people who didn't care that he was a flawed human, only that he needed their help.

They put aside their worries and enjoyed a quiet meal. Hugo had found a neighbour who knew someone who knew someone who went fishing. He'd been able to buy some small pike and had turned out a very good fish stew.

"*Pôchouse*," Hugo said, ladling a portion onto Tom's plate. "Sometimes called the *bouillabaisse* of Burgundy, fish poached in white wine and flavoured with garlic or bay leaves. Bacon if you have it, which we don't. Here," he picked up a round loaf of bread and a sharp knife, held the bread to his chest and sawed thick

228

slices. Tom breathed in the aroma of fresh bread. "Dip it into the sauce, Tom. Makes it go further."

"This is magnificent, Hugo," Tom said. "You should start up a restaurant."

"Don't put ideas into his head, Tom," Jeanne said. "He has enough to do looking after me."

"And how long do you think you are going to sponge off me?" Hugo's words were mild.

Jeanne turned to Tom. "He used to be a great cook, but he got lazy."

"I got old. I'm past the time when I can stand at a stove for eight hours cooking for an ungrateful sister."

"I was never ungrateful."

"Always dieting or something so she couldn't eat this or that."

"That was a long time ago. Now I eat everything we can lay our hands on. I do draw the line on rats. I never ate those."

They raised their glasses to the one-time cook turned physics teacher at the university.

"And so, you're back in France with renewed vigour," Jeanne said. "It looks as if you have been in the sun."

"I worked for a time on a neighbour's farm. I was in contact with the soil, and I think there is a great healing in that."

"Digging ditches, were you?"

Tom laughed. "That and milking cows and shovelling dung."

"Set you up for dealing with French officialdom," Jeanne said.

"A humbling experience, no doubt," said Hugo. "Now let's see what we can do to find Sophie." He pushed the dishes to one side, refilled the wine glasses and pulled out a shabby notebook.

"Now, who can we contact? I remember you thought she had been taken by some child welfare group."

"So the old woman told me."

"Here we are." Hugo sat down, still paging through the notebook. "During the war there were several groups."

"Yes, yes, Hugo," Jeanne said, sipping her wine. "Let's get onto the kernel of it all. Tom, there were many saved by the Huguenots who live up on the Plateau of the Vivarais-Lignon. A whole congregation of them up in the hills who apparently took in refugees, fed them, hid them and got a lot of them over the border into Switzerland. Not only a whole town but a whole region. This is one of the least-known tales of true French heroism. We should be trumpeting it from the roof tops."

"Jeanne, we don't yet know the full story, only the rumours," Hugo said. "The history of the Huguenots in France is one that we Catholics should be ashamed of. The way they were persecuted. You've heard of the St Bartholomew's Day Massacres in 1572?"

"Oh, come on, Hugo. Tom isn't interested in history. Let's get on with it."

"He must know why that part of France, le Chambon and other villages, are called '*pays de grand silence*'."

"The land of great silence? Why?"

"Because they were Huguenots, a persecuted people who were used to keeping their mouths shut and their Protestant beliefs to themselves. They were used to silence; many still worship in silence. No hymns, no genuflections, no confession, no wild-eyed martyrs, no sleepy-eyed virgins. None of the entrapments of our religion. So, when Jewish refugees came to them, they were not only sympathetic but secretively active. They were carrying out their Christian imperative, love thy neighbour. They translated that into helping Jews and others escape."

Hugo smoothed out the page of his notebook. "From what I know of them, they are dour, plucky and moral, highly intelligent with a clear love of knowledge and education. The children who landed up there got very good schooling. They're also well aware of the Jewish roots of Christianity, which is why they took to saving Jews."

"Of course they're also a gloomy bunch. Living so high up and being snow bound for half the year when all they can do is make lace and carve birds. Probably makes them depressed. But more to the point, there were several organisations involved," Jeanne said. "At that time Lyon was full of Jews. We're a large industrial centre, the second-largest city in France. We had resident Jews and refugee Jews. Then there was a big clean-up, and captured Jews were placed in an old disused military camp, waiting for transport to the concentration camps."

"How did this affect Sophie? She wasn't transported out, was she?"

"There were several priests and social workers trying to save the dispossessed from the internment camp at Vénissieux," Hugo said. "Mostly the children."

"He's being modest, Tom. Come now, Hugo, no need to be secretive any longer. Tom, Hugo was part of that group. He's just too shy to tell you."

Hugo's cheeks reddened. "I take no honour for myself, you understand, Tom. I was a very small cog in a very large organisation. Our task was to save as many children as we could. Jews and non-Jews. We Catholics left it far too late to help. Catholics tend to be obedient and the Church never set the example of saving Jews. So, we languished behind the Protestants who took individual action."

"What Catholics tend to forget, Tom, is that Jesus was a Jew. They like to pretend otherwise. Anyway, Hugo and I spoke of it when you were gone, Tom. We think Sophie may have been one of the children taken by the organisation and placed in a children's home in a town called Le Chambon. That's where a lot of children were being hidden."

"As a Gentile, would she have qualified for their attention?"

"You told us she was blonde and blue-eyed. That made her a target for the Germans."

"So, you think she's in Le Chambon?"

"There, or nearby."

Tom stood up. "How do I get there?"

"Sit down, Tom. So impulsive, like a teenager," Jeanne said. "Go on, Hugo."

"A sort of pattern was established, Tom. A group of children would be gathered from wherever they were hiding. Sometimes from a camp like Gurs or Rivesaltes. Or, as the old Durand woman said, from individuals who could no longer care for a child. We would take them up to Le Chambon. There's a jolly little train that goes up there once a day. We'd walk them down the hill to Hôtel May and to the café there. We'd sit and wait. And farmers or the villagers would come in and say, 'I will take two boys' or "I'll take a girl'. And so it went until all were chosen. The children would pick up their belongings and leave. That's how all the children found a home."

"And you think Sophie was one of those children? Why?"

"Be patient, Tom. Hugo is slow these days. He has to be warmed up to get to the kernel of the story."

"Why do I think Sophie was one of them? Because I remember her. It's the green velvet blouse I remember. Tied around the waist with an old leather belt. Strange how things come back. She was different. Her hair had been dyed, inexpertly because I could see blonde roots. But such blue eyes. And she wasn't like the Jewish children who were always wary, always ready to run. Always listening. She was merry. I got the impression she thought life was an adventure that had to be savoured."

"And you think she's up there, in the mountains?"

"I believe so."

"So, I am to go to this village called Le Chambon and pick up my daughter. On a toy train?"

"By train," Hugo said smiling. "But I need to go with you."

233

Tom shook his head. "You must understand, Hugo. This is my journey. I must do this on my own."

Hugo nodded. "I see the need for redemption. The ancient archetypes are working. The hero's quest and all that. All very fine. I admire your resolve, Tom, but there is more at play here. You are a stranger. You are British. We as a nation have become suspicious of strangers. I fear you will not fare well on your own."

"Nevertheless…"

Jeanne stubbed out her cigarette. "Stop being *stupide*, Tom. You go up there and I guarantee you'll never find her. What are you going to say if anyone asks you what you're doing? You'll say, 'I'm looking for a little girl' and they'll immediately assume you're some sort of manic paedophile."

"Oh, come on, Jeanne. If I tell the truth…"

"Won't help you, my friend. Hugo's right. You need a nursemaid."

"Thank you, but no. I do it my way." It was the word 'nursemaid' that riled Tom the most. It made him more determined than ever to go to Le Chambon and find Sophie by himself.

Jeanne poured more wine into their glasses. "So, you really think you can do this on your own?"

"I'd like to try. The hero in all the quest stories I've read does it alone."

"Don Quixote had Sancho Panza."

"Nevertheless…"

"We both wish you well. And when you come back with your tail between your legs, we'll do it our way."

"I can't explain it very well," Tom said. "I'm not a man of words but let me try. I left here in a bit of a state. My demons got the better of me and I ran. Since then, I have found something inside, some inner peace or courage, whatever you want to call it. And it's brought me back. But I need to prove myself. I need to test that what I found within myself is real. I can see it in your faces you don't believe me. I worked for the Resistance, and I killed men who would have killed me or my *maquis* mates. I did things that no ordinary man would do. Ugly things. When you're together in a group it's easier to be brave. It's when you're on your own that the real man emerges. This man is here before you. But this man also needs to prove he is a real man not the manikin I was before. I'm sorry, I haven't been clear."

"Oh, yes, you have," Jeanne said. "But I repeat, when you come back, as you will because you don't know those people, we'll do it our way."

"Will you at least let me try?"

Chapter 25

Very early the next morning Tom walked to the railway station and asked for a ticket to Le Chambon.

"On the le Tortillard," the ticket office clerk said as he handed over the ticket. "Only once a day, once there and once back."

"Am I in luck?"

"Indeed you are, sir. Train leaves in half an hour."

Tom stood on the platform blowing into his hands. Mid-September and it was already getting cold. He shrank into his coat and scarf and watched as the train arrived. Definitely a toy train, the smallest engine possible, three wooden carriages with wooden benches. Some indignant puffs of smoke from the stack.

A few women, laden with parcels and string bags, climbed in ahead of him. As soon as they had settled, the train chuffed away from the station. It steamed and grumbled its zigzag way up the escarpment, one thousand metres up into the mountains of the northern Cèvennes, a place of dense forests and open pastures surrounded by volcanic peaks. The train creaked and groaned, puffing as if to catch its breath.

They rode through open pastures and dense forests of pine trees relieved occasionally by oaks, straight-backed birches and chestnut trees. And a few isolated farmhouses with smoking chimneys beside fallow fields.

Politeness forced Tom to smile and nod his head and answer questions. He was circumspect, allowing the old ladies the assumption of a sick child for whom he was on a reconnoitre. A place to heal, he said.

"It's lovely in summer, but you've come at the wrong time," one said.

Another nodded. "One of the coldest places in France."

"Winters last from October through to April. Wrong time of year to go looking for a warm place." Another chuckled at Tom's innocence. "Winter coming soon with snow drifts so high you can't get out."

"Is there a place I can stay?"

"Nine hotels to choose from."

"Go to *Le Panelier*. It's in the middle of town."

Tom was beginning to despair at keeping up the pretence when eventually the train arrived in Le Chambon, the grey stone two-storey ticket office a little foretaste of what was to come.

The hotel was bleak but empty, the owner welcoming. One customer was better than none. Tom was shown to a small bedroom up two flights of stairs. He placed his small case on the bed and sat down. The mattress was thin and hard, covered by a brightly crocheted woollen blanket. The walls were wallpapered in a brown textured paper with large twists of elongated flowers in purple and red, joined by what looked like snakes but was probably supposed to be tendrils. Tom wondered how he would sleep with that stridently visual cacophony.

Downstairs the hotelier assured his visitor they had a generator, so there would be hot water for a bath and a hot meal. But first Tom wanted to walk around, to feel the energy of the town. Was it going to be welcoming or not?

The houses around the square were all built of grey stone, basalt or granite. Two, three or four-storeyed under black tiles, silent and forbidding, all crouched close together as if for protection. Heated by wood burning stoves, the chimneys were tall and crooked, breathing smoke like tiny upright dragons. Through the small windows Tom detected oil lamps, so no electricity. He could see cows stabled next door, probably for added warmth. No outdoor work this late in the year. He wondered what the residents did during those long icy winter months. Jeanne had said lacemaking and wood carving. He'd go mad.

He walked round the square once and then again. He had a strange feeling of expectation as if he would look down a side street or through a window and see a little blonde dancing girl.

Back at the hotel Tom settled at a table in the dining room. The food was plentiful if solid. Heavy soup, a small slice of beef and a few vegetables. A small glass of cognac ended the meal. Tom went to his room. There was nothing else to do but go to sleep.

But sleep was a long time coming. He thought of those simple narrow streets he'd walked along, bordered by stern grey buildings that towered over him, and wondered if one of those was home to his little girl. Even if it turned out to be so, would he ever persuade her carers that he was her legitimate father? He had no birth certificate, no photos of Madeleine and Sophie. Nothing to prove his case. All he could say was she danced a lot. Oh, and the birthmark.

In the early hours of the morning, he fell asleep.

After breakfast he began again to search the streets. This one and this one he remembered, he'd been there before, recognised the sunflowers in a wooden box, their bright faces bravely facing the encroaching winter. Le Chambon was small, one main street and a few side streets. What was he hoping for? To see a little blonde girl going to the local school or to play at the river? He was walking in circles, getting more and more agitated and despondent. Beating his hands on his thighs, he began to chant. "Sophie. Sophie." As if an incantation would force her to emerge from a doorway.

The hand on his shoulder was startling. It felt heavy and unfriendly.

"Who are you and what are you doing here?"

He turned, tried on the old charm. "*Bonjour, monsieur.* A visitor to your charming town, that's all."

Anglais?"

"*Oui,*" he said. "But a friend."

"You are not welcome here."

"Oh, come now. I'm not the enemy. Those days are over."

"We don't know that. Come with me. I'll take you to someone who will know what to do with you."

The man grabbed hold of Tom's arm and pulled him along like towing a reluctant boat along the Seine. They came to a shed, an annex to a house, and the man thrust Tom through a rough doorway. Inside was smoke-filled with several men sitting around a small table. Tom could see a game of cards was underway. Cards in a purely Protestant village? They were hiding and men who hid things were always dangerous.

"I found him wandering around peering into windows."

A general murmur, suspicious.

"What are you doing here?"

Tom realised bleakly that Hugo and Jeanne had been right. If he said to these men he was looking for a blonde child, they would cut his throat. He had to skate as close to the truth as he could.

"My child was lost in the war. I've been told she may have been brought here."

"Are you sure?"

"No, but she's lost somewhere in France, and I want her back with me."

"France is a huge country, *M'sieur*."

"But not any with the big heart of this place. I've heard…"

"What have you heard?"

"That Le Chambon was the centre of an operation to save children. I've followed a trail, and I think my daughter is here."

"Many people have lost not only children but whole families. What proof do you have that your child is here?"

"None. Just a tug of the heart."

"Not enough. Pierre, escort this man to the railway station and see that he gets on the train."

The man, Pierre, grabbed hold of Tom. "Give me at least an opportunity…"

"When the Germans came in 1942, we had to hide our children. We knew what they would do to them. We heard stories of the gas chambers where little children were led, unsuspecting. We've heard of the scratch marks on the walls. High up for the men, then the women's hands scratching on the wall. And below, the hands of the children. How do we know you are not Gestapo?"

"Damn it, man. That's over."

"You are lucky we are only getting rid of you by putting you back on the train. A year ago, and we would have shot you."

No time to pick up his case from the hotel. As much as he protested, he was marched to the station. It looked bleaker than when he'd arrived. This time there were no old women with cracked-tooth smiles. Only this hostile man whose breath indicated that tooth-brushes were in short supply in Le Chambon.

As the train idled in the station, the man opened a door and shoved Tom in.

"As a matter of interest, *Anglais*. What is the name of your daughter?"

"Sophie," Tom said dully. "Her name is Sophie Aubert."

The man was silent as the train pulled away.

"So?"

Jeanne sat among the green fronds of the conservatory with the usual glass of wine in her hand. Tom threw himself into a chair and sighed.

"You were right," he said. "I was hustled out of le Chambon as if I were peddling pornography."

"I hope you haven't spoilt your chances of finding her."

"She probably isn't even there. I understood from the hotelier that Le Chambon wasn't the only village hiding the persecuted. There were several. Where is Hugo, by the way? Is he here or do I have to pour my own wine."

"He's gone to the market. He saw you through the window and went to get enough food for a meal. We live hand to mouth, Tom. We all do."

"I'm sorry. I'm a burden, I know."

"Nonsense. We'd do anything for Madeleine. Now, go and pour yourself some wine, I hate drinking on my own. It makes me look like an alcoholic."

Later, Hugo apologised for the meal. "A hodgepodge of whatever I could find at the market," he said as they spooned down a hearty soup. "Now, Tom. What is next?"

"I should have listened to you. I was bustled out of Le Chambon in a rather undignified manner," Tom said. "I wasn't given a chance to speak to anyone there who might know. The pastors of the various churches, the owners of the *pensions* of which there are several. Even the hotelier of *le Panelier* where I stayed and where my clothes are still. I didn't have time to speak to him either. I've failed, once again."

"Now, really, Tom. You speak like a character in a Shakespeare play, all drama and tears. The Japanese have a saying, 'fall down seven times, stand up eight.' The real test for you will come later when you have the child and you have to look after her, bring her up to be a good human being and not a tribal savage."

Tom felt the warmth behind Jeanne's chastisement.

"Hugo has been busy while you were away making a fool of yourself," she said.

Hugo nodded. "I went to see a friend who worked with in the OSE, the *Organisation de Secours aux Enfants* in Rue Montée des Carmelites," he said. "We didn't always know other workers and tended to keep to our own little group. But there were others like us also busy rescuing children from the camps and taking them to Le Chambon and other sanctuaries. Those poor children all suffering in some way, physically, mentally, all enduring the psychosis of terror. A big job, Tom. A big job looking after such children. I met with someone there the other day with whom I had worked, and she promised a letter of introduction for us."

"Us?"

"Yes, us. We cannot allow you to go back there bumbling around, making enemies. If Sophie is there, we need to make friends not foes."

"Duly reprimanded," Tom said. "Did this person hold out any hope?"

"Only that they took in any child who was at risk. When I explained that Sophie was blonde and blue-eyed, they immediately understood the position."

"So? You have the letter?"

"No. She will only issue it once she has spoken to you. I'll take you there tomorrow. First thing. The next day we go to Le Chambon."

"Hugo, I am very grateful for all the help, for all the wonderful meals and the roof over my head. This is how I see it." Tom hesitated.

"I suspect you are going to open a vein and expect us to feel sorry for you," Jeanne said. "Don't bother. It's obvious how your brain works. I remember your saying you didn't believe that your wife and child were still alive. So negative. I should imagine having all this hope thrust upon you is making you feel vulnerable at a time when you would prefer to remain in a tiny capsule of self-pity. Am I right?"

"You're very insightful," Tom said. "It's an uncomfortable but true synopsis of me and my failings as a man."

"I have no doubt that during the war you were a man of great bravery," Jeanne said. "You couldn't be a Brit in France, with the *maquis,* and not be courageous. But like most men, you are unacquainted with your emotions."

"Spoken like a woman who has had no husband and so can't compare," Hugo said.

"Jeanne's right, Hugo. You know these people and I don't, so I must concede. Will you at least allow me to go up there on my own once again and face those men who threw me out? Then you could follow if you wish."

"Of course, if you want to tilt at windmills." Hugo's sigh was of resignation. "Now, tomorrow I'll take you to meet my ally at the OSE and then you go up to Le Chambon and get the wheels rolling. We'll follow the next day. It will give me time to get in someone to care for the cats."

"You can't possibly imagine that Hugo and I will sit here, spending the time wondering if you've found her. We're going to be there for the moment when you first set eyes on your little one. And I'm willing to bet she'll look just like Madeleine." Jeanne upended the bottle of wine over her glass. "I've made myself a promise, Tom. You too, Hugo, you should hear this. The moment I set eyes on the child I am going to return to Paris and begin work again. I've had enough of this lying around. No, don't argue, Hugo. I've been a burden. I'm well enough to begin work again and I miss my museum. But I want to see the child first."

The letter safely in his pocket, Tom clambered onto le Tortillard, the puffy little train that would take him back to Le Chambon. It looked as if the same old women were there again, with their heavy baskets. This time, a small goat tied to one woman's basket bleated its bewilderment.

"Not for eating, *Monsieur*. This one will give us milk through the winter. Look at her, she's beautiful. We'll have many goats from her. But in the meantime, it's her milk we want."

And winter was fast approaching. Tom could feel the cold creeping closer. The first snows blanketed the higher reaches of forest and fields. The chimneys of outlying houses belched smoke, and a few cattle stood in the fields ready to take up their residence as the local heating system for the houses.

Le Chambon was once again drab and silent. Where, Tom wondered, were the artists, the singers and musicians that would enliven the town? Who made beauty for the people?

As he walked along the main street to the hotel, his question was answered. A loud joyous chorus of voices burst from the school as a crowd of children, big, small, some only toddlers, ran into the street. They were the children of the village, all dressed in grey overalls, shabby, some with coats reaching to their knees with rolled up sleeves. Each one had a smile a yard wide.

This is what makes the village beautiful, Tom thought. *The children.*

He wondered which one in this flood of happy faces was his child. If she was here at all.

The hotelier recognised Tom. "Ah, *M'sieur* Blake, you have returned. Is it just to pick up your luggage or do you wish to continue your stay here?"

"I would like to stay for a few more days, if you still have my room."

"This time of the year we don't have too many visitors eager for accommodation," the hotelier smiled. He handed Tom a key, indicated where the room was with a jerk of his head.

As the turned to go up the stairs Tom glanced back. The hotelier was on the phone.

Tom's small suitcase was still in the room. He took out his shaving kit and placed it on the wash basin. On the train he'd tried to map out a course of action in his mind. He now had a letter that virtually authorised his queries but thought that perhaps the pastor of the nearest church would be his first option. He thought of the hotelier's phone call, it would probably be to the man called Pierre who had bundled him out of Le Chambon two weeks ago. Well, he thought. It wasn't going to happen again. This time he'd meet Pierre face-on.

He fully understood why Pierre had taken offence. He had looked in the windows of private homes. He certainly wouldn't be doing that again.

Chapter 26

This time Tom avoided windows and side streets. He looked instead for the largest Protestant church. Temple, he reminded himself. Protestant temple. Not church.

The air had taken on an icy aspect. Early frost clung on in the shadows of houses. It crunched as he stepped on it and made the cobblestones treacherous. He walked down the main street, occasionally peering down a side street, hoping to spot a church, any church. Just a little way down the main street Tom noticed a stern and solid brick façade with a door at the centre and a bell tower above. This had all the aspects of a temple with none of the fancy facades of Catholic churches. This was uncompromising, a no-nonsense place of worship.

He pushed open the door and stood looking at the interior. Stark, no icons, no swinging lights, no aroma of incense. No bloodied dying Christ on a Cross. A long line of graceful pillars held up a rounded domed ceiling. The temple felt strangely empty but, at the same time filled with reverence floating in the air above him. Tom sat in the nearest pew and allowed the stillness to penetrate. But not for long. He had a job of work to so.

"*Bonjour,*" he called, but there was no reply. Clearly standing in an empty church wasn't going to be of much help. As he turned to leave a small figure rose out of the gloom. Tom reached out a hand. It was shaken but the pastor was wary, a stranger asking about a child. He shook his head.

The next church, then the next and the one after. No answers. A pastor suggested the doctor. A long wait in the reception area among fidgeting patients proved fruitless. The doctor couldn't or wouldn't tell him anything.

"But surely you know of a little blonde girl here? Sophie Aubert?"

The doctor shook his head. No one of that name. She must be healthy, he said.

It was getting colder, and Tom rubbed his hands together, wishing he'd thought of wearing his woollen gloves. Clearly winter was almost upon the plateau and time was running out.

The hotel seemed no busier than when he'd left for his walk. The foyer, dark and gloomy, was lit by two oil lamps that threw shadows on the panelled walls. Tom thought a good long talk to the hotelier would be useful. He waited by the reception desk for a while, pressing the small bell on the counter, hoping someone would arrive. But no one emerged from the staff door, so Tom decided on an early supper, when the hotelier would inevitably appear to hear praises for his lowly meal. He thought of the grand dinner he'd had with Lucien in Paris, surrounded by raucous, happy friends. And the meal at The Owl before he was unceremon-iously bundled out. Being bundled out of places was becoming familiar. Not again, he vowed as the waiter came to take his order.

He took his notebook out and began to write.
Pastor No. 1. No dancing girls in Le Chambon. Dancing not allowed.

Pastor No. 2. No, let me see...ah...five years' old...hm...I can't be sure...

Pastor No. 3. You had best ask Madame Bloch, she runs the children's side of things.

Pastor No. 4. Who are you and why do you want to know?

Pastor No 5. Dancing? Go and ask the doctor. He runs the theatrical events. He may know.

Le docteur: I cannot say.

Tom bowed his head in despair. Working on his own it would likely take him a decade to find Sophie. He needed Hugo and Jeanne. At least it would cut the decade to five years.

He didn't have long to wait before the waiter brought him a plate of soup with toasted garlic bread. He finished the soup, indulged in a hearty plate of vegetables with a small slice of beef, still keeping an eye out for the owner, who arrived with the dessert, a sort of a crème brûlée in a very small dish which he handed to Tom with a sense of pride.

"Milk from our own goats for your enjoyment," he said. "Now please excuse me. There are other guests who have just arrived."

As if in answer to a prayer, Tom heard the booming voice of Jeanne Bonnet.

"So, there you are, Tom. Sitting slurping your food when you should be out looking for Sophie."

Tom felt a sudden surge of relief. The cavalry had arrived. Hugo and Jeanne sat down at his table. "What's the food like?" Hugo asked.

"Presentable," Tom said. "You could teach them a thing or two, Hugo."

Jeanne took a sip of his wine. "This is good. Where is the wine waiter? Yes, I know, you wanted time to test yourself. Sorry but I got tired of Hugo marching up and down never sitting down, always on the go, always worried about what was happening here."

"Not so," Hugo said. "It's your fault, Jeanne. Drinking too much, smoking too much."

"I beg your pardon…"

"Is so."

"Isn't so."

"Is."

"Children, children," Tom said holding up a hand. "Contrary to what I said I am truly pleased you're here. This is too big a job for one person."

"So, what have you done so far?"

"Seen a lot of church leaders who haven't been helpful, plus one doctor, ditto."

"Thought of going to the school?"

The Bonnets settled down at his table and the hotelier bustled up with a bottle of wine and two glasses. "*M'sieur et Madame.* Welcome to *Le Panelier.* I hope you stay will be enjoyable." He poured two glasses full to the brim but as he looked up, his face changed from smiling connoisseur to wary. He stepped away from the table still clutching the bottle. Tom looked back. A group of men stood in the doorway of the dining hall, their arms folded, their faces grim.

"I think I may be in trouble," Tom said. "Best I eat this delicious dessert before they come and kill me."

One of the men walked to the table. He picked up a chair turned it round and straddled it. It was the man

251

called Pierre, the one who needed a toothbrush. Jeanne and Hugo sat very still.

"You are persistent, *M'sieur*," Pierre said.

"There is much at stake," Tom said, digging into his dessert and trying to stay calm although his heart was hammering. "My daughter."

He'd been in similar situations before, in France, where his identity or authority had been questioned by rival *maquis* or by Gestapo agents. He'd found it essential to maintain an outward calm, a quiet assembling of his inner strength.

"I believe I told you to stay away from Le Chambon. We don't like people like you here."

"What exactly are 'people like me'? You don't know me."

Pierre stood up, pushed away the chair and went to grab at Tom. Something from the past kicked in and Tom stood, caught hold of Pierre, twisted the bigger man and threw him onto the floor. Pierre struggled, managed to turn over grunting, shocked. Tom shoved his arm across the man's throat. Straddled him, knees on the man's arms, pushing hard with his forearm over the neck and two fingers of his left hand ready to gouge at the man's eyes. Pierre struggled, but there was no letting go. Tom knew when to stop, just the moment before the man's lips turned blue. Pierre was close but not that close.

The other men moved closer. "Tell your men to move back or else you die," Tom hissed.

Pierre spoke weakly. The men took a step back and then another.

Hugo began yelling. "Stop! Tom, let him go! He's not worth it."

"Tell me *M'sieur* Pierre, exactly what sort of a man am I?" Tom gritted out.

The man's breath became ragged. He tried to reach at the arm against his windpipe, but there was too much at stake for Tom to let go. "Tell me." Tom added a little pressure.

"Alright, alright," he croaked. "You are a very angry man. Let me speak."

Tom waited, watching the men, then pulled Pierre upright, pretended to dust him down. The man was unarmed. Tom allowed him to right his chair and squeeze in between Jeanne and Hugo. As he sat down the three men in the background began to mutter in low voices. Tom watched them warily and changed the position of his chair so that they were in full sight.

"*M'sieur le Panelier,*" Pierre croaked to the hotelier who stood rivetted. "Coffee and cognac for all." He turned to Tom. "You fight like a man who knows how to defend himself. So, what is at stake exactly?"

"I'm here to find my daughter. Five years old, blonde, who loves to dance. Her name is Sophie Aubert."

At the door there was a sudden stirring as one man pointed at Tom. In the soft murmurings Tom thought he heard the word '*l'Arabe*' but he couldn't be sure. What had he heard? It was just a whisper, nothing more. *l'Arabe*. The Arab. It had been his nom de plume with the *maquis*, chosen by SOE because of his first names – Thomas Edward.

Like his own father, someone in SOE had been an admirer of the great Thomas Edward Lawrence.

Lawrence of Arabia, who, during World War I, had tried and failed to unite the Arab's undisciplined nomads roaming the deserts of the Middle East. And now, here in this remote corner of France, someone was using his *maquis* name. This was either very good or very, very bad.

"Birth certificate?"

Tom shook his head.

"If you find a child you think is yours, what proof do you have? Photos of a happy family? Birthmarks? Her running to you shouting, 'Papa'?"

"Birthmark," Tom said, relieved that his brain had started working again. "Also, she calls me 'Papa Tom'. Her mother taught her…" He stopped filled with an awful longing for Madeleine. If she were here now it would be so much easier.

Even now

I know my princess was happy

Pierre stood up, walked over to his colleagues, friends, gang members, whatever. Tom didn't know how to classify them. They huddled, spoke in urgent whispers, all the while pointing at Tom.

"What is it," Tom called.

Pierre returned to their table sat down again. "What did you do in France in the war, *M'sieur*?"

Tom looked down at the now empty dessert plate. Oaths binding him to secrecy still prevailed, even though the fighting was over.

"My friend here tells me you are *maquisard*. You fought with our people. He says he recognises you from the *Maquis du Vercors*."

Still Tom said nothing.

The hotelier stood by with a tray of coffee and glasses. They rattled slightly. "Is this true, sir? Then, for God's sake tell them. Your life may depend on it."

Tom looked up at the hotelier his eyes full of sadness. "You don't understand, *M'sieur le hotelier*. These people could be my enemies or my friends. I don't know yet. If friends, they will help me find Sophie. If they're enemies then I can expect a bullet behind the ear sometime tonight."

"*Non, non*. They are not like that."

"How do I know which side they fought on? There were so many collaborators."

"On my mother's grave," the hotelier said. "There were no informers here in Le Chambon, no denunciations, no collaborators. These are good men. Christians."

"Where did you learn to speak such good French?" Pierre persisted.

This was an easy question to answer. "I went to a university in Paris. A post degree. I lived among French people. I spoke French for four years. I'm married to a French lady."

"Post degree? What is that?"

"It means that I had qualified in London but came to Paris for further education."

One of the silent ones at the door spoke up. "It's him, *mon ami*. No doubt. I heard he was an educated man. An academic."

"You are *maquisard*," Pierre said flatly. "That makes a difference."

"In what way?"

"On what you did or didn't do in the war."

Chapter 27

Pierre sat for a long moment steadily watching Tom. Then he said, "We are simple men, you understand. We rely on the Word of God to inspire us to make the right decisions. I am usually good at judging men. With you, I cannot decide. Are you a good man looking for his daughter in the aftermath of war? Or are you a chancer? However, if you are *maquisard* as my colleague asserts, then I am content. We'll see, huh? So," he said slapping the table. "Here's the plan. The men and I will do everything in our power to help you find this child. If you put one step off the line, I will kill you. Do you understand?"

"Yes, I understand. Now, could you and your men sit down like civilised human beings and drink some cognac and coffee?"

Pierre signalled to his men who crowded round, pushed two tables up together, and sat down with a sense of relief. Tom looked at Hugo and Jeanne and saw only a new respect. This was no longer the old Tom, haunted and afraid. This was the new man he said had arrived as he worked in the fields of England

"First, perhaps you should introduce me to your friends," Pierre turned to Jeanne and Hugo. "I think you are brother and sister, although perhaps by different fathers?"

Hugo nodded.

"I see a faint likeness."

"No, you don't. I'm the pretty one." Jeanne took a cigarette out of a silver case, tapped it on the table. One of the men stood up and lit it for her with a Lucifer. She smiled her thanks.

"I am Professor Jeanne Bonnet of the *Musée National des Arts* in Paris, and this is my brother Dr Hugo Bonnet who teaches physics at the Lyon Catholic Institute. We are here to help our friend Thomas Blake find his daughter. And who are you now that your tail feathers have been clipped?"

Pierre croaked out a laugh. "I am Pierre, a farmer, and you could say I am the unofficial policeman of the area."

Jeanne nodded. "Now, we'll eat while you men have coffee."

"Not so much of the coffee," Pierre said. "Our friend the hotelier still uses chicory and acorns. But the cognac, we'd like that and, as we drink, we can discuss with you what to do about the child."

Tom explained how he had discovered the route his child had been taken on from Antoinette Durand in Paris to her sister in Lyon, to someone in OSE who very possibly transported Sophie to Le Chambon. He held out the letter as proof. Pierre glanced at it, gave it back. Tom wasn't sure if it had had the desired effect. Or any effect at all.

He told of finding the old woman who had dressed Sophie in a sweat-stained green velvet blouse. He didn't say that it was the green blouse that had undone him and that he'd turned tail and retreated to England.

"We know of such children, orphaned or given to the social workers rather than have them accompany their parents to the death camps," Pierre said. "Or, in the case of Sophie, an old woman who could no longer care for a stranger's child. They found refuge here in Le Chambon and in the vicinity."

"She loves to dance," Tom said forlornly. "She just loves to dance."

"So, we look for a dancing girl who is blonde?" Pierre said.

"Yes," Tom said, ignoring the sarcasm in Pierre's voice.

One of the men put down his glass. "Where is her mother? There must be a mother."

Tom wanted to speak but his voice seemed to have been caught up in the back of his throat. "I...we...don't...know. We are still looking for her. She was sent to work in an ammunition factory in Germany. We believe she has returned. We think she may have been in a hospital," Tom said. "Perhaps near here."

The thought that Madeleine could have been this close to her child broke Tom. He put his head down, rubbing his eyes to stem the threatened tears. Hugo awkwardly patted his shoulder like a child in need of comfort.

"So," Pierre said. "Who have you spoken to so far?"

Tom took out his notebook, read out the names.

"You spoke as a stranger. No wonder you got nowhere. I have a plan," Pierre said. "First, we need to speak to every pastor, yes, even those you've spoken to. We must ask them to announce at the next church meeting, the search for Sophie. You two, that's your task." Two men nodded. "There are also a number of *pensions* that were converted to housing for refugee families and for single children. You can also ignore the ones that were for boys only. And also those for young men escaping STO, Service du Travail Obligatoire." He turned to Tom. "When the Germans demanded forced labour a lot of young men fled. They came up here for safety. In that way the Germans made a mistake. It sent hundreds of thousands of young men into the Resistance. I think we can discount the scout groups, she's too young. I know for a fact that hundreds of children came through here. We were able to smuggle a large number into Switzerland."

Tom knew of the STO and knew a number of young men who preferred the forests to deportation to German factories. They had proved to be good fighters. The thought Sophie might have been taken to Switzerland was dispiriting. Would he ever get her back?

"You think my child may be in Switzerland?"

The man who thought he recognised Tom put down his glass. "We don't know, so we look here first. There are two places in my village, I'll call on them. Are you sure your child would have retained her own name?"

"I don't know. I should imagine so," Tom said, suddenly doubtful. "The pastors are a good start. They would all know that was happening in their own parish."

"Yes, a good first step."

"You'll need more people on the ground, my man," Jeanne said. "My brother has some useful connections."

Hugo explained his connection to OSE. The men nodded.

"We wait. If we find nothing in a week, we'll bring them in."

"Well, what are you waiting for?" Jeanne asked. "Get going. You have work to do."

Tom finished the last of his wine. "Do you think we could sleep first and start tomorrow morning?"

"I can see this is going to be like herding cats," Pierre said. "Allow me to lead my own men."

"We'll do whatever you say," Jeanne said. "We're the strangers here."

"Very well, we each have our tasks. Tomorrow night we gather here with information."

"What would you like my sister and me to do?" Hugo asked.

"There are two homes right here in Le Chambon. You go and see the ladies who run them."

The men left as quietly as they had arrived. Hugo and Jeanne were served a late meal while Tom finished his coffee and cognac. They went up the stairs to bed, each with their own doubts and fears. Who, after all, were these men and could they be relied on to help?

Tom lay on his bed with a mixture of gratitude and frustration. Despite his explaining to Jeanne and Hugo that this was his own quest, they had understood better than he that he needed help. And there were the men of Le Chambon. Brigands by their looks. Rough men of the fields or helpers?

He decided he was being childish. Every extra pair of eyes meant finding Sophie before the winter set in. It was now a race against time and the weather.

I can't do it on my own, Tom thought. *I can't visit every pension, each house in all the villages. I can't speak to every pastor. I must have help. And accept it gracefully.*

But it still rankled. What was supposed to be his quest, had turned out to be a search by a rabble of miscreants.

What would Madeleine say? Probably that he'd found his place in the hierarchy of things. He was at home with troublemakers. She had known him well.

He lay thinking about her and the words of the eleventh century Sanskrit poem came back to haunt him:

Even now
When all my heavy heart is broken up
I seem to see my prison walls breaking
And then a light, and in that light a girl

They had their first break at the school. After three days of nothing, even one clue was welcome. And this clue came in the form of a large English lady, Miss Mable Jepson, who ran a tight ship, as she called it. Marching into class, silent until spoken to, no smacking, of course, but detention for infractions.

"Discipline gives children boundaries," she said, her large bosom like the prow of a ship. "They know where they are with discipline. We don't do insurrection. There's enough of that in the world today. They all look the same when they come to school. It's the grey overall that does the trick. A uniform is a great leveller, don't you think? Saw it in the army. Most wear second-hand

262

clothes and that way we can keep the shame and humiliation down to a manageable size," she said. "Now, what can I do for you, Mr Blake?"

Tom explained that he was looking for his daughter, Sophie Aubert. Aged five. Blonde. Blue eyes.

Miss Jepson settled her large frame into a small chair. It squeaked in protest. "Five years' old? Hmm, she'd be in my class then."

"And she loves to dance."

"Ah well, why didn't you say so before? That would be about right. I think that's her. A little imp," Miss Jepson said fondly. "Can't keep her feet to herself. Always pirouetting. Hears music in her head and she's off. Nice little girl, for all that." She looked at Tom keenly. "So, you claim to be her father."

"I am the father of a five-year-old girl called Sophie Aubert who loves to dance," he said stubbornly, offering the only proof he had.

"They're not here today. On a field trip before the snows come. We have a gymnast boarding here, a good man. He takes the children for a day at a time and teaches them how to do all sort of twisty things with their bodies. She lives at either Beau Soleil or Tante Solly. Beau Soleil is run by crazy missionaries just returned from Africa. Who would want to go out to Africa with all that sun and dust and lions and men carrying assegais? I ask you. But there you are. The good Lord makes us all different. The one who runs the Beau is as deaf as a doorpost. She plays BBC London so loud Hitler could hear it in Berlin. It's a wonder the Vichy haven't been up here to take her away. Still, they're kind people. They take in all sorts. Like liquorice, every ethnicity, every religion." Miss Jepson gave a barking laugh which gave time for Tom to interrupt

"Yes, Miss Jepson, thank you. So, you think Sophie lives there."

"No. Come to think of it, probably not. The missionaries at the Beau normally take in families. She was on her own?"

Tom nodded.

"I would say you should start at Tante Solly, right here in the centre of Le Chambon. It's that tall thin house directly onto the street. Just like the owner, Solange, tall and thin. Not that we aren't all thin here. Never enough food and what we have goes to the children. She cooks well, I hear, that Solange. Good husband too, Jewish but I suppose you can't have it all, can you."

"Thank you." Tom began to walk away.

"Tell me, Mr Blake," she called. "How is England?"

Tom smiled. "Still standing, Miss Jepson, still standing."

Chapter 28

On the way to Tante Solly, they met up with Pierre and explained where they were heading. His face lit up. He knew them, he said, good people.

He tagged along and Tom began to feel like the Pied Piper. Hugo. Janne. Pierre. It was an uncomfortable sensation. He wished with all his heart that he could be he alone to say, yes, this is my child. Or no. What if he wasn't sure? He had never seen Sophie. All he knew she was blonde with blue eyes and had a birthmark. But what if that wasn't enough? What if this so-called birthmark had changed over time and no longer looked like angel wings? How would he handle rejecting a child in front of all these well-wishers? They all wanted a happy ending, even the formidable Pierre. What if he couldn't supply it? Did he have the right to pick up any child, thinking it was Sophie and only later find out that Sophie was still somewhere in France? The idea that he would of necessity have to choose made small beads of sweat stand out on his forehead.

If only he could do this alone then, if it became necessary, he could slip out without anyone knowing. Go back to England and return to his solitary life.

Tante Solly's *pension* was indeed tall and thin. At least four storeys with a front door painted blue and another door opening onto a lower level at the back leading to a flagstone terrace. Tom thought it an ideal place if someone had to disappear quickly. Always good to know another way out. In case.

Solange was also tall, as Miss Jepson had said, but her eyes sparkled, and her smile was wide. She invited them in.

"I heard there was an Englishman in Le Chambon looking for his daughter," she said. "And you think she may be here?"

"We're looking everywhere, *Madame*," Tom said. "Miss Jepson at the school suggested we try here."

"So, explain to me how you came to be here in Le Chambon and who is it you are looking for."

They settled into soft armchairs near a feeble fire and Tom told his story again. Jeanne added her explanations of Madeleine and how she had been arrested and taken to Germany to work in an ammunition factory, until liberty. Hugo added that Madeleine was somewhere in France, they were sure. In his mind Tom thanked him as those were always the words he struggled with. How to explain Madeleine when he wasn't sure she was still alive.

Pierre stood silently, arms folded, a forbidding pillar behind them. Madame Solange seemed to know him and his presence was obviously a tick of approval.

"Sophie? Yes, we have a child by that name. About the right age. It's hard to know, malnourishment tends to slow normal growth. So, she's small for her age. Now, Mr Blake, there is a question of legitimacy. How do we know she's your child? What evidence do you have?"

"None."

"No evidence? No birth certificate? Photos?"

266

"It's what I said to him, Madame Solange." The granite pillar by the door spoke.

"And do you believe him to be the father?"

"Yes." One word, a throaty growl. "He nearly killed me."

"And that's a recommendation?"

"He's *maquis*. I believe him."

Solange turned back to Tom. "Tell me what you know about your child."

"Five years old. Born on December 24, 1940. Blonde, blue eyes. Everyone I've spoken to says she loves dancing."

"A dancing girl? That isn't much. Anything else?"

Tom felt in his pocket and drew out Madeleine's letter, the last one she wrote to him that told of Sophie's birth. And of the birthmark on her back. He handed the letter to Solange. By now it was tatty; it had been fondled and kissed more times than Tom could remember. So, the corners had become bent, and the folds frayed. Solange opened it carefully.

"A birthmark," she said." Like angel's wings. I believe I may have a child who might fit, Mr. Blake. She is not here right now. A day out at school I believe. When she returns you can see her. But you must understand, you will say nothing to raise her hopes. We will speak in English so she cannot understand what we say. A precaution in case this child isn't yours."

Tom nodded wordlessly. In a short while he would be face to face with his daughter. His and Madeleine's, the child they had created out of their love. All that was left of their love. All else was gone.

"Before you meet her, please be aware that all these children are damaged. They have been through things we as adults can't even begin to imagine. They have been separated from all those they love, from a home that was familiar and from pets they loved. They have seen death and they have been impoverished in ways we can only surmise. Their problems are very complex and very likely life-long. Are you prepared? This child you speak of, Sophie, on the surface she is cheerful, but I suspect underneath she is very lonely and feels isolated. You will have a long journey ahead of you, Mr Blake, filling in the gaps in her life."

In the face of Solange's warning, Tom felt inadequate. And afraid.

Solange stood up. "In the meantime, please come and see where we eat and play and where the children sleep. Pierre, please go to the kitchen and see if my husband has something for us to drink while we wait."

The dining room was big with a long trestle table down the middle and bench seating on either side. Through the windows Tom could see the surrounding volcanic peaks already covered with snow. The room felt bleak, although Solange had pasted up drawings by the children. Tom tried to imagine his little girl sitting in among a throng of others.

Tom saw there was the other exit that led to the terrace outside. He went up to the door, tried it. It was open.

"The children feel safer when there's another way out," Solange said. "They come here terrified, always listening for the march of feet, the sound of trucks arriving. We want them to know they can always get out."

"It's hardest on the children, isn't it," Jeanne said.

"A judgement by ordeal for all of us, but for them especially. Occupation showed what each man and woman was capable of. Who they were in their core. The persona they will show when they finally must face their God. Did you stand up to be counted or did you stand back? Not many stood up and the ones who suffered the most were the children."

Solange took them to the dormitory where the girls slept. Another long room, impersonal, with small beds covered either by a blanket or a faded quilt.

Tom stared aghast. Yes, it was probably wonderful for children who had been traumatised and felt lost and confused. But his child? No.

"Which bed is hers?" He asked.

Solange walked down the row. "This one. Oh dear, she hasn't made her bed again." She straightened a tumble of bedding.

"Does she have a doll or anything to cuddle?"

"No, Mr Blake. She has nothing."

They sat again in what passed for a guest lounge and waited, assured by Solange that the children would soon be home.

"Our first two years of occupation were calm," Solange said. "We had numbers we could handle. We'd started a secondary school with a few Jewish University professors who were in exile. But in 1942 everything changed. Then it was all about saving the Jews who were arriving in droves. Loyalty to Petain was waning as he cooperated with the enemy. People in the region absorbed as many people into their households as they could afford to feed."

Solange stood up. "Forgive me, I must attend to the lunch. You will stay and eat with us, won't you?"

Tom shook his head. "Thank you but we are booked into the hotel."

An hour later, after both Jeanne and Hugo began to express some impatience, they finally heard the stomp of little feet in wooden clogs and the shrill laughter of excited children.

"They're back."

Jeanne turned to Tom.

"You must be brave, Tom," she said. "If this child isn't yours, you must say so. You can't take up another child as a substitute."

"I know, I know." His voice was harsh.

Solange returned. With her was a small girl. Tom looked at her with a sinking heart. This couldn't possibly be Sophie. He looked at her tiny frame, her thin legs, the socks hanging down onto her clogs, knees grubby. And then the dress. Too large and it fell from her thin shoulders. It took a while for him to find the courage to look at her face. There were a pair of blue eyes, slightly sunken above thin cheeks, and the hair. Blonde, as he had expected, with thin curls covering her ears.

Tom cleared his throat. "Madame, may I see her back?"

Solange took Sophie's cardigan off, turned her around and unbuttoned her dress. And there it was. High up, close to her shoulders was a small pair of wings, like the tattoo of an angel.

Tom sat very still. He saw the birthmark but for a moment his mind went blank. All the sorrow, the fear of failure, of never finding his girl, and here it was, the moment. No words came.

He nodded.

"Yes?" Solange buttoned the child's dress and replaced her cardigan. She spoke in English, as planned. "So, Tom Blake, is this your child?"

A little voice broke the atmosphere. "I spik Ingliss..."

"Pardon?"

"I spik Ingliss. Miss Jepson, she say Ingliss for me."

Jeanne laughed. "There goes your cover, Tom."

The child stepped forward. "Tom?" she asked. "Papa Tom?"

In that strange cold lounge, with Jeanne and Hugo and the silent Pierre, with Solange her face full of anguish for the child, Tom could only sit frozen, his hands whitely clutching the arms of the chair.

Slowly the child walked forward and in a strange submissive gesture, she placed her forehead on his sleeve.

A tableau. A silence so profound it was a church, a confessional, a forest, a silent sea.

Then the child looked up. "I remember now," she said. "Maman told me you would come."

After that it was hazy. Tom remembered only flashes. Yes, this was his child. And, yes, he would take her now. They would first go to Lyon, to the home of Hugo Bonnet and stay for a while. After that to England.

And, yes, he remembered snatches of the train ride, its jollity as it rumbled puffing down the hill. And Sophie's delight at riding in the 'toy train' again. And, yes, there were the three or more weeks of snowstorms and wind lashing at the windows and Hugo going out to buy food dressed as if for the Arctic. The trip to the *boulangerie* for baguettes and the round loaves called *un pain rond* that Hugo brought back and sliced against his chest. His trips to *le boucher* for what little meat they could get, and the *cremerie* for milk and the few vegetables still in the market that he could find. All for Sophie, of course.

"We must build up your strength," he said as he placed a small potato on her plate.

And, yes, Tom tore up bread and put the pieces into Sophie's soup, as sailing boats, just as his mother had done for him.

And, yes, he remembered Sophie sitting close to Jeanne being read to and Sophie's delight when she recognised a word.

And, yes, he remembered Sophie's timidity when first faced with three sleepy cats. Encouraged to touch them softly, she'd said, "But they are so soft. So beautiful." After that she and the cats were inseparable.

"Grand-mère Jeanne, what are their names?"

"I don't know. You'd better ask Hugo, they're his cats."

Hugo waved a soup ladle around. "This one is *le chat numéro un*. This one is *chat numéro deux* and this one is *chat numéro trois*."

"But you can't call cats those names."

"So, what should we call them then?"

"This one is Lulu, this one is Aubergine and this one is Cassandra."

"*Mon Dieu,*" Jeanne said. "We have a tom cat called Cassandra."

And, yes, the cats curled around Sophie in a profusion of warmth and love. Because she attracted love.

And, yes, the time Hugo found an old piano roll with its tinny scratchy sound that Sophie danced to, her skirt whirling and the blue ribbon in her hair bouncing and her eyes full of joy.

And the feel of a snowball in his hands and a snowman, its beady eyes following them as they ran inside for a cup of warm milk with a piece of chocolate floating, a dark ship marooned in a white sea. Until the chocolate melted and they drank the sweetened milk through straws.

And finally, on the last night as Tom lay in bed, a small figure climbed up, placed her cold feet against his warm body and they had fallen asleep, his arms around her, contented like the cats that joined them.

And, yes, he thought. It's going to be alright.

Chapter 29

Before England, Tom decided he would go and see Lucien. He was family and deserved to meet his niece. Also, although Tom hesitated to acknowledge such a puerile thought, he wanted to show Lucien that he had kept to the plan. He had found Sophie.

He'd sent a telegram without mentioning Sophie. All he said was, 'I've found her.' He thought afterwards he should have written, 'I've found Sophie', so that Lucien wouldn't think it was Madeleine he'd found. It was too late now. They were already on the train.

He was pleasantly surprised that Lucien was waiting at the station. Tom held onto Sophie's hand as they clambered down the train's steps. Lucien walked towards him, hesitated, ran, held out his arms. "Tom! *Mon Dieu*! Who is this?"

"Lucien, meet your niece, Sophie Aubert." He turned to Sophie. "Sophie, this is your uncle Lucien, your Maman's brother."

Sophie very politely put her hand out. "*Bonjour, oncle* Lucien. *Je m'appelle* Sophie."

"Sophie? *Un miracle*." Lucien threw his arms around Tom and gave him the traditional kiss, first left then right. "Tom, this is beyond words. You found her. I can see Madeleine in her. So beautiful. But where have you been? I've been writing to you, letters, so many letters. And urgent telegrams." His words all tumbled together in a rush of joy. "Come, come, let's go home."

In the dying light of a late November evening when the sky was liberated from its blue canopy and had become streaked with orange and pink, Tom noticed Lucien had brought the French Army truck, instead of the horse and cart. He was thankful that, on this chilly afternoon, they would not have to freeze slowly. Instead, they would freeze quickly, he thought with a certain amount of cynicism. The truck had no windows and only a canvas covering over the driver. Never mind, it would be over soon, and they would be inside the chateau, in front of a fire with Marie serving plates of soup and *baguettes* torn up ready to dunk. His mouth watered. Meals with Jeanne and Hugo had been wonderful, but it was always the camaraderie that made them so. Frugal meals could be eaten with relish accompanied by Hugo's repartee, Jeanne's acerbic tongue and, in later weeks, Sophie's crystal laughter.

He lifted Sophie into the cab of the truck and followed sitting close so that he spared her the worst of the winter rushing in the truck. Lucien threw their luggage into the back and clambered into the driver's seat.

Lucien slipped the truck into gear. "So, where have you been?" he asked.

"I've been up in the mountains." Tom had no desire to explain. It was merely enough that he had found Sophie and was taking her home to his little cottage in Kent. He'd started to plan. First a visit to the Masons, to show Sophie where milk came from. Not from a glass bottle but from a living breathing cow with calm eyes and the smell of sweet grass on her breath. And the hens. In spring the Masons would have chickens. That would please Sophie.

Lucien pulled away from the station and they began to slow climb to the vineyard.

"Is all well at home?" Tom asked.

"More than well. For one thing, I think we'll have a wedding in spring?"

"Yours?"

Lucien's face grew sad in the fading light. "*Non,* Adam and Marie."

Tom tried to be hearty. "Well, that's good. And Manon? Is she still with you?"

"Manon returned to her father. He wanted to have me arrested for kidnap. So, she decided the best thing was to go back. To protect me."

"To the brothel?"

"She said not. She said she would work in the kitchen, learn how to cook." Lucien shrugged. "So, I don't know."

"But she'll be back, won't she?"

"We'll see. I hope so. But you tell me your news. How did you find this little one?"

Their voices were low. Sophie's head had begun to nod, and she leant against Tom with a small, contented snicker of sleep.

"It's a long story, Lucien. To be told with a glass of wine."

They rode on towards the chateau. Each time Lucien looked down at the sleeping child, wonderment on his face.

Yes, there she is right beside me, Tom thought. Our child, Madeleine's and mine.

He thought back to the early days of his courtship of Madeleine Aubert. There had been the same look of innocent bravado on her mother's face. He tried to imagine Madeleine and Sophie together. Two blonde heads bending over a story or playing tag in the garden. Their laughter. How joyful Maddie would have been to see her child again, the one she thought was dead.

But it wasn't going to happen. Lucien had failed. If he'd found Madeleine, surely he would have said so? He'd said nothing. And so the search had been futile. Maddie must have died in the camps. Or perhaps at the hospital Jeanne Bonnet had spoken of.

He remembered snatches of their life together. Going to the south of France where they'd hoped to find the Holy Grail and instead only found their love for each other. Better than any Grail. Their wedding had been a crazy spontaneous affair with a group of students, with flowers in their hair, bacchanal style, dancing around them in a park in Paris. And then that frantic blissful weekend when Sophie had been conceived.

In a rush of agony Tom accepted that Sophie would never know her mother, he would never hold Maddie again. He wondered how would they live the rest of their lives without her.

He thought of the old poem from the book he'd stolen from prison. A black marigold, symbol of sorrow.

Even now

I know that I have savoured the hot taste of life

Lifting green cups and gold at the great feast.

277

Just for a small and forgotten time
I have had full in my eyes from off my girl
The whitest pouring of eternal light.

Thinking of Madeleine and of all the joy and sorrow of their lives together, had undone him and he was glad that Sophie couldn't see him. But Lucien noticed.

"You miss her, *mon ami?*"

"As if half my heart has been carved away."

"And the other half is here beside you?"

Tom looked down at the sleeping child, frowned with amazement that in so short a time this wisp of humanity had captured him. He thought of her journey, from the home where three adults had cared for her and kept her safe: Emily, Aaron and Madeleine. All dead. All dead. How mysteriously that life had disappeared, and she was in Lyon with Madame Durand and her old sister. And later that changed, and she was with strangers shuttling back and forth, dyeing her hair, shoving her onto a train. And finally, some sort of stability with Solange in the Tante Solly *pension*. All before her sixth birthday.

Other children had had it worse. Tom remembered Lucien telling him of the French children sent to the camps, none of whom came home.

At least Sophie Aubert had come home.

Lucien, sat in his purloined truck, humming the national anthem.

Allons enfants de la patrie,
Le jour de gloire est arrivé

278

"And what glory has arrived?" Tom shouted above the roar of the truck.

"Well, let us count our blessings. We had a good harvest, Adam is in love, so it is a winter full of hope for the future. We have our small princess here. What more?"

"Will Manon come back?"

"Perhaps."

"I'm sorry," Tom said.

"No, don't be. I have a plan to offer Blanche Guillard something she can't resist."

"Marriage?"

Lucien laughed. "No. Money. I want to buy her vineyard."

"And she'll sell?"

"Yes, I believe so. I hear tell she wants to live in Paris and enjoy society life. Buying her out will double my acreage."

"You'll need another manager."

Lucien looked at Tom. "Yes," he said.

A small voice interrupted their conversation. "Will we stay for here for *Noël*?"

"Yes," Lucien said. "Most definitely."

"Will Grand-mère Jeanne and Hugo be with us?"

Lucien looked questioningly at Tom. "Why not, if your uncle will invite them," Tom said.

"I miss them," she said in a small voice.

Tom looked down at the anxious face. "Who do you miss? Jeanne and Hugo?"

"No, silly. The cats. Can we have a cat, Papa Tom?"

"Yes, why not?"

"Can we have two cats?"

"Two? Well, I suppose so."

"They would get lonely with only two. So, I think we should have three."

"Three?"

"Like Jeanne and Hugo. They have three cats."

"We'll have to see about that, *ma chérie*."

Sophie settled back as Lucien chuckled. "I see some person already has you tightly wrapped around her little finger."

They drew up outside the chateau.

"Go into the living room," Lucien said. "I'm sure Marie has a fire going. I'll just garage the old girl and join you."

"Lucien," Tom said. "Before you go. You didn't say. Why all the letters to me in England? Why the telegrams? What was so important that you had to send telegrams?"

Lucien grabbed hold of Tom's arm. "*Mon ami*, Life could not be better. There is so much joy, so much to be thankful for. Take the little one and go inside and then we'll talk." Tom jumped out and took Sophie in his arms as Lucien changed gears, before he slammed the passenger side door Lucien said, "Pour us some wine, will you, Tom. We'll celebrate."

"Celebrate?" Tom called after him, his words spun away in the cold grasp of the wind. "Celebrate what?"

"You're in time to help with the pruning, what else?" Lucien shouted. And the French Army truck that had saved Lucien's life rumbled off to the shed.

Pruning? Damn it. Tom hadn't forgotten the back-breaking, hand crushing toil of pruning thousands of grape vines. Not if I can help it, he thought. And yet there was something alluring about it…

In the evening light the old building with its ridiculous turrets looked quite romantic. The fountain in the courtyard had been cleaned and filled, although the water had a thin shield of ice over it now.

"See, Sophie, a castle," Tom said.

Sophie began to jump. "Yes, I see. I see! It's just like the story Grand-mère Jeanne read to me. Is there a fairy princess inside?"

"Let's go in and see, shall we?"

Marie would have to substitute for a fairy princess. There were no fairy princesses in our story. If only…If only…

They hung their coats on the deer antler coat rack and walked to the living room. Tom pushed the door open. It had the same creak he remembered. The feel of Madeleine's hand as they faced her parents. So long ago but it still hurt.

There was someone sitting in one of the chairs drawn up to the fire and covered by a blanket. He could see it was a young woman, excruciatingly thin with hair a thin fuzz.

"Bonjour," Tom called cautiously. "I hope we're not disturbing you?"

She stirred and turned round, looked at him with eyes dark-ringed, at the child and gave a small shriek.

"Tom?"

She got up, held onto the chair with an emaciated hand. Half staggered towards him.

"Madeleine? Oh, God. Maddie."

She ran.

"Maddie!"

Tom Blake gave a great whoop of joy and surprise and grief.

He held out his arms and gathered his two girls and held them.

ABOUT LE CHAMBON

Le Chambon-sur-Lignon is a small town high up in the mountains of south-central France.

At the time of this story, the villagers were mostly Huguenot or Protestant, having been chased into the mountains by Catholic intolerance over the centuries. During World War II they made the area a haven for Jews and others fleeing from the Nazis. Many refugees were taken into Switzerland and to freedom by the villagers. Other stayed with farmers until the end of the war.

In 1990 Le Chambon was honoured as the Righteous Among the Nations by Yad Vashem in Israel for saving Jews in German-occupied Europe. Only one of two villages thus honoured.

ACKNOWLEDGEMENTS

If you read the Acknowledgements in other books, you'll note many authors state a book is not the sole creation of one person. Each book is birthed by a number of interested and talented people. This book is no exception. Vicky Adin, writer, friend and beta-reader extraordinaire, must be the first to be mentioned. Her keen eye, her honesty and her encouragement gave me courage to plough on despite many medical issues, both personal and family. Bev Robitai, as usual, proved her artistic talent by producing a brilliant cover and a professional interior. I am so grateful for having friends like these.

I also have a wonderful writing group who read through most of the book, pointed out incongruities and typos (many and often, and any that still lurk, that's my fault not theirs), and who saw me through to the end. Gill, Lyn, Joan, Cosmica, Raewyn, Ron, thank you.

Last but not least, Howard, my husband. Thank you for giving me the space and encouragement I needed.

ABOUT THE AUTHOR

Jenny Harrison has been writing for thirty years. Her first book, **Debbie's Story,** was published in South Africa in 1997, to great acclaim.

She now lives in New Zealand with her husband and their cat, Anzac.

Since the publishing of her first book Jenny has continued to write. This novel is the fourteenth. Her other books are available on Amazon in both print book and e-book format or directly from the author. They are:

Debbie's Story
A New Life in New Zealand
To the Child Unborn
The Lives of Alice Pothron
Out of Poland
The Ninth Candle

The Falling of Shadows
Accidental Hero
The Indigo Kid
Rusty & Slasher's Guide to Crime
Rusty & Slasher and the Circus from Hell
Dead Before Curfew
Death of a Countess
Death and the Dancing Girl

You can contact Jenny via her website
www.jennyharrison-author.com
or
jennyharrisonauthor@gmail.com

www.ingramcontent.com/pod-product-compliance
Lightning Source LLC
Chambersburg PA
CBHW071249250626
47163CB00002B/393